DEEP SIX

A NOVEL OF LIFE, DEATH, DECEPTION AND BETRAYAL

DEEP SIX

A NOVEL OF LIFE, DEATH, DECEPTION AND BETRAYAL

BY

DONNA M. DEAN

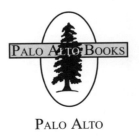

PALO ALTO BOOKS

PALO ALTO

2001

This book is Copyright © 2001 by Donna M. Dean
Published by Palo Alto Books
P.O. Box 341, Palo Alto, CA 94302
Tel. 800-711-8985
www.glencannon.com

Art Director: S.L. Hecht

First Edition, first printing.

Library of Congress Cataloging-in-Publication Data

Dean, Donna M., 1942-
    Deep six : a novel of life, death, deception, and betrayal / by Donna
      M. Dean -- 1st ed.
      p. cm.
  ISBN 1-889901-19-9 (softcover : alk. paper)
  1. Indian women--Fiction. 2. Racially mixed people--Fiction. 3. African
American women--Fiction. 4. Marin City (Calif.)--Fiction. I. Title.

PS3604.E36 D4 2001
813'.54--dc21

                                     2001029014

This is a work of fiction. While some names of people and places are real, they are used in a fictional sense. Marin City is very real; I spent most of my childhood there. The rest of Marin County, California, reputedly the richest county in the state, is still trying desperately to pretend that city does not exist.

Chief Petty Officer William Francis Manns was real, but he never engaged in any of the activities portrayed here. I use his name solely as a memorial and tribute to a man whom I consider the perfect Chief, and the most inspiring person with whom I ever had the privilege of working in the United States Navy. I hope he's somewhere in the Darkening Lands, reading this, and laughing.

As for the events, and the characters, none of this could possibly have happened. Could it?

ACKNOWLEDGMENTS

I wish to heartily thank my sister-friend, Janet Willard, for endlessly encouraging me to keep going with this, and my internet friend, Josette Dermody Wingo, for being my selfless helper in slogging through the drafts, and being eternally a cheering section, while gently dropping priceless suggestions, pointing out quirks in continuity, and, in general, being my Faerie Godmother; something I've always wanted, but never quite managed to catch.

Maureen Peer-Oliver and Jane Mather also read the manuscript, and offered invaluable aid and assistance, and Selene Weise shared her wisdom and experience selflessly.

I wish, too, to thank Walter Jaffee, editor of The Glencannon Press, for remembering this book, and Tondelayo and all who live within its pages, and for finally believing in all of it enough to keep trying to find a way.

Contents

Chapter 1

TONDELAYO

Sometimes I still think about Barbara Nadine and me as little kids, and it still makes me cry. Barbara Nadine Johnson and I go 'way back. 'Way, 'way back. She's always with me, even now. I see her sometimes, just out of the corner of my eye, disappearing around the corner in front of me, her stringy white trash hair blowing along behind her. Or I see her sitting at the edge of her rack in the barracks at O-dark-thirty in the morning, just before reveille.

It was all so long ago. It began when we were just little children. It would never have occurred to us that first day that one day I would be a Chief Warrant Officer, hold a Master's degree, and be working on a doctorate. It would never have occurred to us that anything but that particular moment, that particular day, that particular place, that particular situation mattered. I can still remember how it was one Saturday early in

1

July, still smell the hot, dry dirt squished between our bare toes like talc, and feel the occasional drop of water blowing on my skin and evaporating as the sprinkler whirled around in our tiny little yard. This scrawny, chicken-legged little white girl had edged closer and closer to where Ruby Anne and I were playing in the water, until she'd passed the invisible line onto our territory and violated our private space.

She wasn't much to look at, just another poor white trash kid, snotty nose caked with dirt and stringy tow headed braids looking like her mama hadn't combed her out in awhile. She had on droopy cut-down overhauls with the straps tied behind her scrawny neck to keep them up. You could tell she wasn't even wearing any underpants. My mama would have whaled my backside going out like that. Ruby Anne's mama would have whupped her behind, too.

"Hey, girl! Whatchu doin' here? This here's our sprinkler! You git now, afore we bust yo' ass!" I dropped my voice a little on that last, hopin' Mama couldn't hear me.

Silence. Dirty little feet edging a little closer.

"You hear me, girl? You don' speak English or somethin'? G'wan, git!" Ruby Anne and I closed up the gap until we were almost nose to nose. We could see those little green flecks in her light blue eyes, see the freckles through the dirt on her face.

"Ain't doin' nothin'. You don't own this street."

"Yeah? You lookin' to get mashed, white girl? We gon' slap you right upside yo' haid."

"Ain't 'fraid a you. You two think you' so tough? Sheeeeut!"

That got us. "Ass" was one thing, "shit" another. We didn't say that even when we were sure our mamas couldn't hear us. Even Jack, my big brother, would have washed our mouths out with soap for that one. He'd laugh when we said some things, but other times he didn't show any such patience. And saying "shit" was one of those times, no lie.

"Yeah?"

"Yeah!"

There was nothing for it but to establish our territorial rights. I don't remember which of the three of us hit first. But it didn't last long. Those scrawny little fists were fast. They were bony and sharp, too. Wiping the blood off my nose, I told Ruby Anne maybe we ought to let her play with us; you know, let her join our club. We could use fists like that in our club. So the three of us played in that sprinkler until our skin looked like prunes, and our mamas called us in to supper. I watched that poor white trash girl out there, still runnin' back and forth through the water; she was a whole lot cleaner by then. I guess her mama never did call her to go home for supper. Finally along about dark, I saw her wander off down the street to where that new family of white trash'd moved in. Figured she must belong to them. But from then on, it was the three of us; me, Ruby Anne and that little white trash girl, instead of just me and Ruby Anne, until we were women fully grown.

Her name was Barbara Nadine Johnson, and she was one of a large family that was to live a couple of doors down for years and years. The family was always seeming to produce more tow-headed, snotty-nosed babies, and Barbara Nadine's daddy drank. He was a mean drunk, too, and Mama and Papa encouraged Barbara Nadine to be at our house whenever she felt like it. I wasn't permitted to spend as much time at her house as I was Ruby Anne's, so I didn't know them well. I remember her mama spent a lot of time in bed, and always looked tired. She didn't pay much attention to Barbara Nadine or any of the others, so I don't think she even noticed her daughter began to disappear from home for whole days and nights, staying with me or Ruby Anne. There were older kids, including two big brothers that Barbara Nadine avoided like poison oak when she could. She never said anything, but whenever she'd been home for awhile, she'd show up with a lot of bruises and scratches, and didn't have a whole lot to say for herself. Mama and Papa would look sideways at each other and go off into their bedroom to talk, and Barbara Nadine would get extra treats and attention, which didn't seem fair at the time.

Still, Ruby Anne and I never really minded, because there was just something about the way she was so quiet that we knew something was really, really wrong. But nobody told us anything. We knowed the Johnsons were really poor, but so was Ruby Anne's mama, her daddy having been a travelin' man and gone before Ruby Anne was born, but Ruby Anne never got any bruises on her, and her mama'd smack us both, if she thought we needed it. Didn't really hurt, just "quieted us down," like they said when mama and papa reached their limits. But Barbara Nadine — I don't know. Once she showed up after being gone a week or more, and she had a broken shoulder. Had a store-bought sling and all. We were all impressed, I'm telling you. She said she fell off her bed. I didn't believe that, as I knew her bed was a peed-on old mattress just stuck on the floor and used by several of the other kids. Nasty, but not too far to fall, as the mattress was all crunched down. But Ruby Anne and I didn't say anything. I gave her my Slinky, though, and Mama pretended not to notice. She just bought me another one for my next birthday.

Yeah, but we had us some good times though, Barbara Nadine, Ruby Anne, me and a whole bunch of those other Marin City kids. I don't know why, people are always talking about Marin City kids like we were all hoodlums, or something. When we got out of Richardson Bay grade school and started high school at Tamalpais, in Mill Valley, we were pretty much left to ourselves. Not that we gave a damn. We'd all known each other most of our lives, and we were pretty much used to it. For one thing, most of us were "coloreds;" Negroes, (that was the term then) with a few Mexicans, Indians, and poor white trash thrown in for good measure. I was one a the Indians, with a little Negro mixed in from the Cajun and Burnt-Sugar Cherokee both. First thing we did with those white kids that showed up from time to time was to beat the shit out of them to see if they were going to fit in. If they did, nobody gave them any trouble after that. We were all poor, hardly anybody had a real daddy, like I did, and lots of men was just there. They'd get themselves these sharp cars, all these pretty colors, Fords, Lincolns, even Caddies, and put those little antennas on the back, driving 'round and 'round Marin City, drinking out of paper bags, and shootin' the shit with the other men until they either had no more money for gas or the Repo Man'd come for the cars. We kids mainly just stayed out their way.

There were the older boys, too, some of them gang boys. My big brother, Jack, was a one percenter biker from the time he was 14, and he was a *big* boy! He could be mean, and he wasn't scared of anything. He and I were tight, and he put out the word "...wadn't nobody gonna' mess wit' his sister, nor none'a the other little kids, either..." So we followed our own pursuits in safety, and played up in the hills above Marin City. It was all empty up there, with little valleys filled with trees, and grassy hills we could play slide-down on cardboard, or war, or spacemen, or whatever we wanted. No grownups ever went up there, and we'd be up there all day. We were supposed to be home by dark, and if we weren't, there'd be hell to pay. We were scared, anyway. Come evening, the fog'd start rolling in from over to the ocean, and it'd be thick and gray all of a sudden, like another world.

If we were anywhere *near* the old cemetery, we'd like to bust our britches running home. Man, that was a creepy place, all overgrown with bay and eucalyptus, roots everywhere to grab you and trip you, and ghosts screaming and squeaking in those old trees. There was a road going down the hill on the other side, to where they kept the bodies, I guess, and there were these huge old cypress trees looming over on either side of the road. We never got up enough nerve to go down it very far, because we were afraid we'd come upon those dead people, waiting to be put up in the graves.

There was a very old part, along the front of the hill, and just off the big curve, where the graves were all worn out and collapsed. You could see the holes where the skeletons (we thought!) were, and the old wood from the coffins. We didn't actually see any, but we knew they were there, where they could get out and walk around if they took a notion to, and we weren't about to be caught up there come dark. We used to go into the oldest section where they were though, the grave covers all broken up and covered with roots of bay trees like snakes. It smelt so good, but it was really weird and scary. The light was all greeny, even when it was sunny, and in places it was almost dark. On foggy days, it was worse, with water dripping down, making it sound like little footsteps were after us. We used to dare each other to go in there then. It was fun, but like it was fun to go to Playland and ride the Octopus. Made our stomachs kind of sick, and our legs shake.

Yes, I remember so much about how it was back then, when we were kids. Back then, we didn't know that it was different in other places. We had no real idea that the rest of the world thought of us as some sort of alien life forms, threatening, ugly, and a festering sore in what was rapidly becoming gentrified enough to eventually constitute the wealthiest county in the entire state of California. Marin County was to become the fabled icon of self indulgent excess; the very personification of the word, "Yuppiedom." Oddly, Marin City was to persist too; blatantly continuing to exist right in plain view along the freeway going north to San Francisco, and south to Lotus Land.

Oh, they tore down the old World War II wooden "chicken coops" I grew up in by 1965, erecting ugly blocks of high-rise low-income housing. The chicken coops had stood since the early days of the war, built hurriedly to house the burgeoning population of MarinShip workers imported mostly from the south. They were rectangular, flat-roofed structures, consisting merely of board exteriors and sheet-rocked interiors, so easily maintained that when the occasional car parked on a hill above one of the houses lost its brakes and careened down to smash into it, a tow truck merely came from Maintenance and pulled the wounded house back up onto its wooden pins. The walls and sheet rock were replaced, and life went on. The houses were duplexes, except for the small apartments clustered in the middle of the bowl, and all were equipped with kerosene cooking stoves, oil heaters in the living rooms, and old-fashioned iceboxes. We got chits for kerosene and ice.

I don't think the ugly, crammed lifestyle imposed starting in 1965 by the new concrete wastelands were an improvement.

Neighboring quiet little Mill Valley, home of the still extant Tamalpais High School, has undergone extreme changes, too. Our dear old Alma Mater, affectionately known as "Tam High," and in my day, known as the roughest high school in the entire state of California (Watts hadn't happened yet) was to undergo a most peculiar metamorphosis, as Mill Valley became the heartland of the artsy-craftsy intelligentsia, and the student body became an increasingly obvious dichotomy of the haves and the have-nots. Sausalito, on the other side of Waldo Grade became so expensively chic that today I am forced to avoid it lest I imperil my beloved lower-class roots. When we were kids, though, it was a sleepy little fishing village, with old wharves we fished off for perch, and ramshackle houseboats lining the shore in bohemian ignorance and disdain for the finer points of plumbing and sewage treatment.

Perhaps the greatest gift I will ever receive, however, is the unbelievable fortuitousness of the preservation of our beloved fairytale land of the hills above Marin City. Now a National Recreation Area, the Marin Headlands still stand unsullied and beautiful above the rest of the world, and our secret places are still there. There's a trail out to the beach now, and the last time I hiked it there was actually a young cougar playing off to the side, oblivious to the oohs and ahhs of the hikers. Oh, yes, it teems with Yuppies riding their damn mountain bikes along the fire roads, and hikers trekking along in thousands of dollars worth of L. L. Bean backpacks and drinking $3.00 water out of plastic with just the right labels, but it's still there. I sometimes wonder if those people ever realize what ghosts of us children run unheedingly amongst them darting into the copses and ravines playing our games, with bologna sandwiches on Wonder Bread, and jars of Koolaid to wash it down.

I doubt it.

Those people and their bikes and backpacks are gone at night, though. Then, the fog's in, and She Coyote still hunts the warm, rich scent of mouse blood. Barbara Nadine's spirit is there sometimes, too. I feel it. Even though her family refused to let her body lie where she had wanted, instead putting her into the militarily precise prison of an exactly laid out grave in Golden Gate National Cemetery in San Bruno, I know they couldn't keep her soul from going where it needed to. I made sure of that. But that was later.

Anyway. As we grew up in Marin City, in the late 1940s and 1950s, it was our home, our town. And we didn't know it was different.

I was a woman grown before I was master of my tongue, able to communicate on the higher, more couth level expected of one of my education and station in life. At the time of my youth, we thought everybody talked and sounded just like we did. (However, I do remember being somewhat taken aback to discover that my mother and father, too, were able to talk what the schools said was proper white English when absolutely necessary.) At home, Mama spoke a dialect strongly reminiscent of Gullah, with a heavy dose of Indian inflection thrown in with the Oklahoma drawl. The end result was a soft, buttery molasses I loved to hear, flowing gently in and out and around my ears and soul. Papa spoke a kind of English heavily influenced by the bayous and swamps of Louisiana, and frequently became almost entirely lost in a French patois when he was excited. Strangely, though, when he chose to sing the blues, his voice became the purest black rasp of river bottom Delta short of John Lee Hooker I've ever heard. To us kids, the soft tones of

Black and Southern, with the occasional Mexican aspiration were the norm.

In the Navy, too, I heard Southern all around me, although it tended to be white Southern. I automatically acquired the profane and colorful language of the "salty sailor", as well as the ability to turn it on and off as appropriate, and gradually learned how to speak "standard" (Whose?) English, mostly through books.

Books were my life from my earliest days, and I fear the language of my fantasies and day dreams carried the overwhelmingly plummy tones and cadences picked up from P. G. Wodehouse and Dorothy Sayers' Lord Peter Whimsey. My vocabulary was enriched at an early age by the "fetid, ghastly, moldy" descriptive ecstasies of H. P. Lovecraft, which made me rather a formidable conversationalist at times. At any rate, I was to become adept at many different languages and dialects, and to switch from one to another as appropriate without thought. So did we all have to adapt our protective coloration as we grew up and entered the wider world; a wider world which neither made us welcome, nor found us acceptable as we were.

But, as children, all this was still in the future, unknown to us. We were just who we happened to be; Marin City kids, and Marin City was just home. We didn't really know why outsiders seemed to feel we were all likely to be covered with cooties and carry switchblades, we just somehow knew it and stuck to ourselves and to one another on the occasions in which we found ourselves exposed to "others." Later, of course, many of us did carry switchblades, but who wouldn't?

Yes, it's been a long road, and a lot of years. Barbara Nadine and I have been through a lot of changes. It's quite a story.

HARD TIMES

"Aww, Mama, I don' wanna go down there and ax for some bones for the dog. The butcher man know we don' gotta dog, and he know it be fo' us, 'cause we ain't got food."

"Now, Tondelayo Cecile, you just get yourself down to that store, and ask that butcher for some bones! If you don't want to say they fo' the dog, just ask him for some soup bones. He give you some nice meat bones, maybe. No, go on, git! Here a fifty cent piece, you can buy a can a okra, and one a tomatoes, then he know you got money for food. He won't think you askin' for no free food for the family.

"An' jus' lissen here, Girl, ain' no disgrace to be po'. They lottsa po' folk here in Marin City since they close down that shipyard. Lots of 'em. Yo' papa ain' the only one a the mens ain' got no job, you know. An' you ain't too good to go on down to that there store and get us some bones to make soup. You and Barbara Nadine can each buy you a penny candy at the candy store. G'wan, now. I'm too tired to keep on arguin' wif you. Oooweee, that white lady done run my feets off to-day. 'Helen, would you do this? Helen, would you mind getting me that? Helen, I need you to just pop on over to the deli and pick up some pâté. Oh, and could you pick up the dry cleaning on the way? Make me a glass of your special mint ice tea before you go, would you? I have such a headache in this heat!'" Mama's voice took on the mincing, perfectly enunciated whine of the spoiled princess for whom she kept house.

I know she sighed as she watched the slumped angry back of her daughter dragging molasses feet slowly along, as Barbara Nadine harangued me. Barbara Nadine was not only thoroughly familiar with the routine of asking the butcher at the little store for "bones for the dog," she was accustomed to bringing in the wrinkled dollar bills and torn fives to the jailhouse to bail her drunken father out; something I never, ever would have to do. Given her druthers, she'd pick the grocery store every time. Besides, she knew the butcher was quite aware of how hungry many of his former paying customers were since the shipyard closed, and he often wrapped up meat turned just brown at the edges for free, or cut extra large pieces of the nickel-a-pound liver and lights he sold.

The little grocery was family owned, and had been there since Marin City was built. The family was kind and concerned about its little community. The produce section had piles of good, bright green turnip greens, blue-green collards, mustard greens, sacks of black-eyed peas and chick peas, and pinto beans for the Mexicans. They stocked what we ate, and it was cheap, and always fresh. The big stores in Sausalito often tried to sell wilted, old stuff and bad meat to us, marking it down cheaper than the other stuff they sold, but our own store never did that. Even with the "recession." Recession, hah! In Marin City, it was a full-blown Depression!

"Remember when the freezer broke, and the sto' let all us kids have all the free ice cream we could eat?" Barbara Nadine actually started to drool, and had to lick the corners of her mouth.

"Yeah. That be a great time, huh?" I began to feel a little more positive. After all, it wasn't as if I hadn't known the clerks and the butcher all my life, almost. And we found ourselves just two of quite a few kids asking for "bones for the dog." By the time we got home, chewing mightily on the wax bottles of our root beer candies, I was feeling pretty cheerful. We had a nice, bulky package for Mama, too. Then, we heard Papa's voice drifting out through the open window.

"Lordy, I purely hate to see my little girl out beggin' for food." Papa sounded so sad, I caught my breath. "You know, it surely would help if Barbara Nadine's daddy would give us even some a that welfare money he get for her. That man, he jus' drink it all up, and them kids a his jus' as skinny as plucked chickens. Why, I——"

"Jacques Armand Antoine Dubois! You just hush yo' mouth! I ain't listenin' to no cryin' about welfare money! It was us made the decision to bring Barbara Nadine home, and she our girl jus' like the other two our chil'run. We ain' takin' no welfare like some no 'count trash! We gettin' by jus' fine!" Papa shut up. When Mama rolled out the full syllables of his Cajun name, he knew he was perilously close to being in deep, deep shit.

"Now, honey, you know I don' mean that. I worked hard all my life, tha's all, and I hate to see my chil'run doin' without.

An' I hates havin' my wife pick up after some rich bitch white woman like she some kinda' slave, too. Anyways, I don' know how that little grocery sto' stays open. Half the folks ain' got no money to pay they bills, and he jus' keep runnin' 'em tabs if'n they got kids. Shit, they cain't be much better off'n we are. But I sho' do hate to see my beautiful wife ruinin' her nails cleanin' some white folks' toilets, my son out diggin' ditches for the P.G. and E., and me settin' aroun' the Union Hall like some bum."

"You're not sitting around like a bum, Jackie. You're out there every day with the rest of the mens, seein' if there's day work, waitin' for the trucks down there at the parkin' lot. You'll get steady work, I jus' know it. One day they be hirin' on at Mare Island Shipyard. Things lookin' hot over there in Korea. We gonna' have another war."

At that, Barbara Nadine and I stared at one another. A war! Jack was getting to draft age. He was so big and tall now—— a real man just beginning to live up to all that promise. He worked steady doing manual labor for the power company, keeping his head low and never sassing the boss man, and volunteering for all the extra hours he could. He also helped a friend of his with an embryo motorcycle repair business. He and my special friend, Napa Bob, were beginning to make a reputation with the other bikers with their skills, and they hoped to build up a real going concern. Now the draft could get them? We were two scared chil'ren, no shit. We banged open the screen door and noisily made our entry. Mama and Papa were really pleased with the results of our gleaning, and we ate well that night.

Later, bathed and tucked into our bunk beds, Barbara Nadine and I pondered the implications of what we had heard. Mr. Johnson was getting welfare money for Barbara Nadine? She'd been living with us forever, almost. How come? We fell asleep before we could come up with some kind of reasonable explanation. Neither one of us was really sure exactly what welfare money was, or how you got it, anyway. Mama and Papa had made it abundantly clear that the whole subject fell into the "death before dishonor" category, and that whatever it was, the Dubois family, Barbara Nadine included, would never have any personal experience with it, even over Mama and Papa's dead bodies. Now, there was a sobering thought! Secretly, though, I kind of hoped Mr. Johnson might get a chance to prove out this dead body thing. I hated him, and so did Barbara Nadine. So did Mama, Papa, and Jack, I think. Nobody ever said anything to us after that night Barbara Nadine came to live with us, but I never forgot what she had told me, nor the looks on Mama and Papa's faces when they slammed out of the door on their way over to the Johnson's, either. Once, I tried to talk to Jack about it, but he just told me to never mind, and shut up about it, or else. He didn't usually treat me like that, so it made a deep impression on me. I never mentioned it again, and shortly after Barbara Nadine and I got to share my room with new bunk beds, I sort of forgot she hadn't always been there. We never did get any welfare money, either.

Life went on its bumpy way in Marin City, and we kids continued to admire the slowly cruising cars, bright green and pink and black Fords, many with dagoed and lowered chassis. TV antennas sprouted from many of the roofs of the apartments huddled in the middle on the flats, surrounded by the bigger duplex houses that were simply long, wooden rectangles, exactly like chicken coops built all around the sides of the bowl. If one were to observe Marin City from some vantage point along the highway, one would be tempted to believe prosperity lurked just out of sight. Brand new cars cruising endlessly around and around the encircling streets, radios blaring out R & B, and sharply dressed men stopping and exchanging greetings constantly as they spotted friends and acquaintances equally at leisure. The colors of the cars were brilliant, even garish, and no spot of dust or bird dropping was permitted to sully their shining surfaces, hand waxed with Blue Coral at least weekly. White wall tires and TV antennas attested to a show of impressive affluence. From the outside looking in, Marin City's residents had money to burn, and plenty of time to burn it in.

The phrase was, "A dollar down, and a dollar a month for the rest of your life, or until they catch you, whichever comes first." Loan sharks and easy credit at astronomical rates made it possible to buy one of these gleaming new "pacifiers," and a man could look like a man to his friends and neighbors, even if just for awhile. Repo Men were far less visible, and far faster, working mainly at night. The TV antennas were often connected only briefly to actual television sets, which were prone to a peculiarly ephemeral presence within any given home. Oh, things could look good, but it was more shadow than substance, especially now, with the shipyard closed. The blacks and southern whites lured from the desperation and red clay of Georgia, North Carolina, South Carolina, Mississippi, Alabama, the Ozarks, by the promise of good paying jobs at MarinShip during the 1940s were left, abandoned and without hope when World War II ended and the yard closed down. They were stranded, an embarrassing clutch of dragon's eggs, hatching brown and black and Okie-white offspring, feared and hated in their sheltering lair of hills.

The rest of Marin County, overwhelmingly white, upwardly mobile, and relentlessly middle class, preferred to pretend we weren't even here, and prayers wafted upward nightly that we'd damn well stay in what was thought of as a nasty, dangerous, fetid hole, never venturing out to endanger the good and righteous folk outside. Marin City didn't even have the cachet of poverty-stricken Indian reservations where wide-eyed tourists could cruise through, marveling at the sloth and idleness of the shiftless Natives. Everyone was too afraid to even set foot in Marin City, let alone tour it.

Barbara Nadine and I just thought it was home, though, and we joined the rest of the residents in just living out our lives the best we could. We knew we were perfectly safe in daylight, and night, too, for the most part. Of course, we avoided groups of drinking men, and didn't lurk around in the shadows among the apartments, but what parent worthy of the title allowed their kids out 'til all hours anyway?

It was a good time to be a kid, in spite of everything. We had all the freedom we could use, and the entire Marin Headlands for our playground. We even had a play field with slides, and swings, merry-go-rounds, monkey rings, monkey bars, and tether ball besides ball fields right there in the flats. There was a really scary Tarzan rope swing just up the hill to the left, in deep woods and hanging over a good-sized ravine, to say nothing of a wonderful cliff to climb up and down, thrilling our foolish little hearts no end. If our respective parents had known about the cliff, I suspect, or that we habitually risked life and limb playing up and down it, I'm sure some bottoms would have been warmed. I look at it now, and I wonder at our youthful confidence in our own immortality. It's a very steep, fairly high cliff, strewn with scree and unstable shales. I never heard of any kid being seriously hurt on it, though. I do remember the rope breaking mid-swing with me once while I was playing at the Tarzan swing, and I remember Barbara Nadine running for Jack as I lay gasping for breath on the bottom, but I lived through it, Jack just yelled at us a little, and he didn't tell Mama. Within the next few days there was a new rope on the swing.

And now, it's all different.

My name is Tondelayo Cecile Dubois, and I am a Chief-Fuckin' Warrant Officer in the U-fuckin'-nited States Navy. I have the ghosts of hash marks from my fuckin' wrist to my fuckin' shoulder, and I can trash any sonnuvabitch on land or on sea who says otherwise. I'm one day older than water, and I'd been around the world when Christ was still an Ensign. I am one phantom with whom you do not want to fuck.

Well, anyway, that's how I let the world see me now. It makes it easier in this man's Navy, especially when some snot-nosed, wet-behind-the ears Ensign thinks he's hot shit and knows it all, or some boot thinks he too much man to take orders from a woman. Huh! Sheeeut, gimme a week and those boys'll wet they drawers ever' time I give 'em a look. Yeah, I'm one tough baby, and I don' take no shit off nobody, with or without gold on they sleeve.

Barbara Nadine? She been dead some years. Murdered.

Chapter 2

KIDS

*T*he She Coyote was waiting, just within the fringe of trees, invisible with the sun dappling her coat of gold, brown, gray, black, white. No one could ever really remember what color she was after they'd seen her, and very, very few had ever seen her. No one at all had even glimpsed her for a long, long time.

Once, the red ones who'd come and gone along the coast had seen her, though infrequently. She was unusually large, and often alone, though she was seen occasionally with a pack, obviously the leader, and sometimes with pups playing around her. On winter evenings, in the slow times in winter camp, stories were spun around her like gossamer wisps of spider silk, never quite catching and holding her. At times, she'd find piles of smoked rabbit or beaver meat, or even a fish or two, which she appreciated for the difference in her diet, and she was aware they were honoring her as best they could.

Now, her stories were dead with the red people, and she had been seen less and less. The Russians had hunted her, seeking that glorious

17

coat, but she was smoke; there and gone beyond recall. The Portu-
guese fishermen were busy with their boats, and the few sheep and
cow herders told no tales beyond the usual complaints of losing the
occasional lamb or calf to the coyotes and cougars that prowled those
desolate hills.

But it was time. She knew little of why she had to come closer to
humans; it had been a very long time. She knew only that one of her
own was present. A child, a pup, but hers, and she was compelled to
wait. So, she waited, not even her pricked ears moving. She heard
them.

After awhile, she contented herself with following, unseen. Lis-
tening, and watching. Years later, Tondelayo remembered seeing a
shadow, fleeting through the edges of her mind, touching briefly, but
so lightly she was never sure it wasn't just some dream fragment, left
eddying in a backwash of her brain, inexplicable, yet familiar.

"Hey! Wait up! Donna! Hey, you guys!"

"Oh, shoot! Here come Ruby Anne. C'mon, les' hide in
the trees." The four little figures scurried furtively into the line
of cypress trees on the bank, trying to blend in unobtrusively
behind the trunks.

"Hey, Tondelayo. Whachu' doin'? Kin I go?" Ruby Anne's
bright eyes beamed up at the girls, poorly hidden above her.
"C'mon, lemme go." A grubby paw groped in a gaping overall
pocket, then emerged triumphantly laden. "I got a Milky Way,
you guys." Four mouths watered. Four wills wavered.

"Oh, well, OK." The Madden twins looked at one another,
and agreed. Barbara Nadine and I had no choice but to go
along. Donna and Patsy were the ones who knew how to find
the old cemetery, not us, and if we wanted to see it, we'd have
to go along with the decision made by the twins. Besides, the
Madden twins were twelve, teenagers, and no ten-year old kids
were going to question their decisions. Ruby Anne's candy bar
had just bought her passage.

"Where we goin'? What're you'all doin' here, anyhow?"
"Here" indicated a small house deeply set into the hill, with an

overgrown garden, and a high bank lined with tall cypress trees along the sides. The house was vacant, with a vague sense of unease about it.

"Don't you'all know where we be? This house where that man found hanging!" This awesome news was delivered with appropriate hushed respect by Patsy Madden, the blond twin.

Donna nodded vigorously. "Yeah! His ghost hang aroun' here at night. Joanne seen it. Well, c'mon if we goin'. Gotta get there and back before it git dark." The dark-haired twin set off purposefully, heading up the hill and into the woods.

The crashing and branch-crackling of our passage was not necessary to cover the silent padding of the companion that followed us effortlessly. I couldn't have said just what it was that went with us, but I could feel something, as I so often did, up there in the hills, and I knew it was no threat. I even felt a warm, sort of comforting feeling I couldn't begin to put into coherent thoughts. It was just there, like always.

Where we goin'?" Ruby Anne puffed hurriedly after Barbara Nadine's rapidly disappearing back.

"Donna and Patsy's gonna take us to the old cemetery. They's graves up there, open ones, with skelingtons, and ever'thin.'" Barbara Nadine swelled with importance as she imparted this news.

"Oh, shoot. You lyin', Girl. Oooweee! You all ain' gonna go up there! They's dead..." She noticed no one had stopped but her, and she had to run to catch up again.

"Nuh, uh. I ain't. Ain't no lie, Girl. The twins been all over up here, and they foun' it one day. Tondelayo and me ain't never been up here befo'. We ain't never gone past the water tower."

"Me, neither. My mama say to stay up on the side of the hill where she can see me. It's too far, anyhow. I don' believe you." Ruby Anne's lips clamped together and she stopped, sturdy legs planted firmly on the ground.

"Wait! I'm comin'!" We other four had paid no attention to her protestations, and were continuing to make a path through the woods, following a small ravine carved by runoffs in rainy seasons past. She said nothing further, as we labored in a generally upward direction, frequently being forced to detour around clumps of poison oak and stretches of undergrowth too dense to penetrate easily.

Finally, we came to the edge of the woods, and were able to make better time through the grasslands and sparse clumps of brush growing up to the ridge where the water tower stood. It loomed above us, casting a shadow far down the slope as we stopped to rest. A dirt road ran from west to east along the top of the ridge, ending at the tower, but it was obvious no vehicle had been up there in some time. The road existed merely as a fire break and for fire-fighting access in the dry hills, and was normally deserted.

Far below us to the south we could see all of Marin City set in its bowl, with the glint of the San Francisco Bay off to the west. The northern slope stretched down across the track, with the same sort of isolated brush clumps we had just traversed. Ravines and draws made folds in the hills, hiding secret belts of dense trees and woods, and we could see a large wooded area reaching up toward us from the east. Beyond, the Tennessee Valley wound its empty way through the rolling series of hills until it reached the ocean's edge, out of sight, and to the north. The Marin Headlands were still beautiful, wild pieces of land not yet raped and almost murdered by man.

Our little group sat at the side of the road, and gazed over the stunning view while we shared our tuna biscuit sandwiches and lemonade. Fortunately, Mama had anticipated a possible state of near-starvation, and had packed adequately for five. Donna and Patsy's mother had provided peanut butter and banana sandwiches, oranges, and a big bag of popcorn, so we felt ourselves quite well provisioned. Ruby Anne pulled another crushed and melted Milky Way out of her seemingly bottomless overall pocket, and everything was generously offered around.

"No, thank you, peanut butter makes me sick." Barbara Nadine had brought nothing as usual, but Mama had antici-

pated that, and packed tuna biscuits for her, too. Ruby Anne
looked surprised at the idea that someone wouldn't eat peanut
butter, although she thought bananas, lettuce and mayonnaise
with it on the same sandwich were kind of strange, but she
knew I never drank milk because I was an Indian, and figured it
must be something like that. We concentrated on eating, oblivious to the small lives going on all around us.

*A mouse daringly crept close, and triumphantly bore off a dropped
biscuit fragment, well rewarded for its temerity. A black beetle deter-
minedly continued on its self-important way, indifferent to the invad-
ers. Bright eyes of a coyote hunting the grasses behind them, surveyed
the scene, scented the She Coyote reclining in the shadow of a nearby
thicket, and left quietly but hurriedly. No interest there, anyway. Just
an assortment of little girls. The Madden twins; one dark, betraying
Indian blood which remained hidden in her fair, pale sister. Ruby
Anne Hamilton, small of stature, but determination evident in every
line of her compact body, gap-toothed grin in a dark brown face,
topped by nappy hair done in numerous braids tied with string. Barbara Nadine Johnson, tall and thin, looked peaked somehow. She had
white hair so fine it looked like Christmas angel hair carelessly pulled
into ragged pigtails, and a curiously clear skin of fine porcelain touched
with the faintest blush of pink on the cheeks and an enchanting sprinkle
of freckles just across the small, straight nose and high cheekbones.
Better fed and freed of whatever devils beset her, she would have
shown promise of becoming a woman of uncommon and delicate
beauty. Even now, underfed and unnurtured, she possessed an elfin
and elusive promise that flashed in her startling green-blue eyes as she
giggled at one of Ruby Anne's jokes. A study in contrast, her sister-
friend Tondelayo Dubois was a sturdy, brown child whose Cajun
father and Burnt Sugar Cherokee mother had contributed African
genes on both sides. She would grow up to be a powerful woman of
intriguing, even striking looks.*

A hawk screamed, then swooped far to the north, toward the
ocean. The girls looked, but saw nothing. Donna stood up, brushing
off the seat of her jeans, and pointed toward the woods to the east.

"Down there. Now we got to be careful. Go down to the woods as quiet as you can, and use the bushes for cover. People can see us from Tennessee Valley Road if we ain't careful." She set off, dodging from clump to clump, and warily scouting each forward dash. Her sister did the same, lithe as a deer, and swift. Barbara Nadine, Ruby Anne and I did our best to imitate the twins, snaking and dodging from cover to cover until we reached the thin edge of the woods. Suddenly, an open expanse dotted with headstones and groomed plots appeared. We gaped at the place, noting several sites heaped with fresh flowers.

"Jeeze! Lookie there! They's been funerals!" The stifling sweet smell of stock assaulted our noses as the breeze shifted. It was utterly still in the somnolence of the afternoon, and even bird calls were seldom and far away. Dragonflies darted over the stagnant water sitting in up-ended vases, and bees visited the flowers around the plots. We walked from level to level, enchanted with this new world.

"Well, I don't see no open graves." A Barbara Nadine grown petulant eyed Patsy Madden. "You said they's open graves, and skelingtons. Girl, they ain't nothin' of the sort." She snorted.

"Are, too!" Patsy's indignant retort defended her honor as a guide with the vehemence of truth. "Over there, in the woods." She and Donna turned toward the long line of gloomy cypresses winding along the road leading down the hill. Climbing down the rocks stabilizing the banks cut in for the road, we entered the woods which crept out at the sharp curve, threatening to swallow the old pavement. Suddenly, it was darker, and quieter. The sharp pungency of bay and eucalyptus lay heavily here, barely modified by the dusty sunlight filtering in streaks through the canopy of intertwined branches. Roots tangled and tripped, reaching under and into ancient concrete grave pads. Long toppled and broken gravestones peered blindly from recumbent positions, pieces scattered and missing. Lichen had eaten away at most of the names and dates, but here and there a faded "Rosa" or "Silva" bore mute testimony to the fates of long-ago Portuguese fishermen who had made their homes in the area at one time. Here, erosion had continued over years, shifting earth particles and runlets joining the eager bay rootlets snaking toward sunlight and freedom. Yawning caves stretched back under the blankets of concrete, and pieces of rotting wood belied dusty promises of eternity once spoken by sonorous casket salesmen. No one came here; no one tended the graves. It was probably forgotten, and its inhabitants as well.

"Ooooweee! It's creepy here!"

"What's that?" A deer crashed away, its unseen haunches springing over branches and breaking twigs in startled haste.

The She Coyote flattened her ears at the sound, but did not otherwise move.

"Les' get outta here, Man!" The panic spread, fanned by the gathering darkness, and we bolted, stumbling and tripping, through the threatening gloom. No one had admitted the growing sense of foreboding and fear that the lonely isolation had engendered. The dark, silent wood seemed so far from the everyday world that we had begun to think we had inadvertently wandered into another realm. The wan, watery light that struggled weakly through the trees seemed depleted and evanescent. The crashing of the startled deer had served as a catalyst, releasing all the pent-up and unacknowledged fright. We ran headlong toward light and open space. When we finally regained the relative sanctuary of the old road, we were all liberally scratched and bleeding, and Ruby Anne had a broken overall strap dangling down her back, grabbing branch still stuck in its buckle. We were not heartened to discover it had grown nearly dark, so long had we been poking around and marveling in delicious terror. Now we were all going to be in deep, deep trouble. The trip up the hill and over was considerably faster and more direct than the initial descent had been.

As we sped out of the woods, lights were flicking on all over Marin City. It was almost fully dark, and our small forms flitted around the dark bulk of the houses as though we ourselves were ghosts. The homey smell of cooking ham hocks and lima beans assailed our hungry nostrils as Ruby Anne opened her door, spilling warm light and kerosene fumes into the night.

"See ya!" And she was gone. The Madden twins split off toward their house, leaving me and Barbara Nadine to make our own way to our street. We found Mama frying chicken, and just about to send Jack out to look for us.

The She Coyote had followed, staying in the shadows cast by the bulk of the houses, but she was nervous and jumpy at being so close to the humans and their dogs. A dog barked in the distance, and she bristled and lifted her lips from her teeth silently. A powerful need overcame her desire to flee back up into the hills and safety, and she finally flowed noiselessly into the deeper shadow of the dense, aromatic growth of pelargonium along the wall of the Dubois house. The windows were all open, and she could easily hear and smell all that went on inside.

"Where in the world have you girls been? Tondelayo Cecile Dubois, you know you're supposed to be home before dark. Your papa's gonna have somethin' to say to you, young lady."

"Yes'um. We sorry. Truly, mam'n. We was jus' playin'. We was playin' with the Madden twins up in the hills, and it got late 'thout us noticin'. Mama, can Barbara Nadine stay to supper?" A change in subject seemed in order at this point.

"No! You jus' git yo'sef in and wash yo' hands and set the table! Barbara Nadine, ain't yo' mama goin' be worriet 'bout chu?"

"No'um. She don' care. Daddy's drinkin' agin', and she jus' says to stay outta' his way. I be goin' along, now. Thank you kindly, mam'n." A disconsolate little girl turned toward the door, scrawny shoulders hunched.

"Oh, now. Wait a minute. Oh, all right, Barbara Nadine. You go on in and wash your hands, and help Tondelayo set the table." Resigned sigh. Then she spotted blood. "Mercy! What's all them scratches? Umph!" Resolve to be tough evaporated, Mama dabbed at the bloody lines criss-crossing the our faces and arms, apparently relieved to see the wounds were superficial.

"Tondelayo, bring me the iodine."

"Awwwww, Mama..."

"Now, Tondelayo Cecile!" Deciding retreat was the better part of valor, this errant child dragged her feet into the bathroom and reached into the medicine cabinet. Fortunately, fried chicken was known to have a salubrious effect upon most wounds, and when Mama blew on the iodined cuts, it lessened the sting, although the high-pitched yelp I let out must have made anyone or anything nearby flinch. Barbara Nadine bore her medicine without flinching. This was nothing compared to what her daddy could inflict when he was drunk, and mean. There wadn't no fried chicken afterwards, either. Sent to bed without supper, more like. And what happened after she went to bed was nothing she cared to think about, either, I learned later.

Papa arrived home just as we finished setting the table. He grabbed Mama and gave her a big hug and kiss, bending her over backwards in a theatrical move worthy of Duncan Reynaldo at his suavest.

"Well! My, my. Aren't we energetic tonight!" Mama straightened her apron, laughing suggestively at her husband's beaming face. Papa leered jokingly at her as he swept me and Barbara Nadine into his arms. Startled at first, Barbara Nadine stiffened, her eyes widened.

Outside, the She Coyote caught the sudden drenching smell of fear, and rose suddenly to her feet, fur bristling.

But almost immediately, Barbara Nadine's body relaxed, and she melted into Jackie's warm chest and wrapped her thin arms around his waist.

"And what do we have here? Have I got another kid here?" He tweaked a braid, and smiled down.

"Mama said she could stay for supper. C'mon. We set the table by ourselves." I proudly dragged my father over the kitchen table, and Mama leaned out of the living room window to summon Jack, tinkering with his Harley Davidson outside in the parking area.

The family sat down to eat. Mama and Papa led the round of thanks offered to the spirits of the food they were about to eat, with each member contributing his or her own thanks. Barbara Nadine joined in, thoroughly accustomed to the routine by now. She considered herself a member of the family, as did all of us, and her thanks were heartfelt. In the Dubois household she felt safe and warm, and even loved. She even dared to sneak the chicken liver off Papa's plate when he wasn't looking, and nearly choked with laughter when he roared with mock ferociousness about "chicken-livered chicken liver thieves" when he saw the gap in his food. Hungry from our adventures, we managed to stow an awesome amount of mashed potatoes and milk gravy away, and we attacked the pole beans and cole slaw with gusto.

Later, the She Coyote heard as Helen and Jackie talked. Tondelayo was in bed, and Jack had dropped Barbara Nadine off at her house as he rode his bike out of town for a meeting of his motorcycle club, the Copperheads.

"What's that chile's mama thinkin' of? Letting a ten-year old girl run wild like that! Why, she over here more than she home. And she's such a puny little thing. Honey, what's goin' on with them Johnsons, anyway? Jackie furrowed his brow with irritation, and lit another cigarette. He was crazy about Barbara Nadine, and it made him angry when she had to be trundled off to the Johnson house.

"Yeah. They po' white trash, no lie. I seen her, Pearlie Mae, in the grocery sto' the other day. She din't have nothin' but beer, sody crackers, and dried soup packages in her cart. Lots of beer. I don't think them kids 'a hers get any kinda' reg'lar cooking at home. Those young'uns with they dirty diapers always full, and always draggin' off aroun' that nasty, dirty yard — and them wild older ones! Phew! I

don' know how Barbara Nadine turned out so good. She's al'us tryin' to wash hersef when she's here, says she likes the pretty smelling soap we got in the bathroom. Shoot! Ain' nothin' but Cashmere Bouquet; cheapest thang in the sto'. I jus' naturally wash those scraggly braids of hers when I wash Tondelayo's hair. She jus' sits between my knees, quiet as ary mouse when I comb out all those snarls. Never lets out a whimper. She says she loves it so when I brush her nice clean hair that it's worth it to have me comb it out first. I bought her a bottle of cream rinse, and you'da thought I bought her the moon! I guess it a good thang I learnt how to do white hair workin' for my ladies. Sometime, they ax me to do they kids' hair, or even theirs. Funny, thin, fly-away stuff Barbara Nadine has, too."

"I see ole' Harry Lee down there, hangin' aroun' with the other drunk white boys aroun' the parkin' lot at the bus station. He a piece of work, no shit."

"Yeah." Helen looked sad, and heaved a sigh.

"Well, you jus' go on, makin' that chile welcome, and let her be. Tondelayo's good for her, and she good for our little spoiled brat. I wish we could do somethin' more, but I don' know what." Jackie looked pensive.

"Jackie, I was thinkin'. We got to get Tondelayo a new bed anyhow; that ole' youth bed's gonna' be too small soon. Why'nt we look at bunk beds? Then Tawny could have someone to sleep over, did she want to."

"That's a good idea, Sugar. In fac', me, your loving husband, Jacques Dubois, am one of de greates' natchural born carpenters in de lan'. Yes. There some wood under the house, and I could build some bunk beds, with a ladder, and a top to make tents with when they playin' inside on rainy days. I could even put up shelves for toys, or whatever. And put a trundle bed, or drawers underneath..." Jackie was lost in the grandeur of the plans for a major construction project.

"Whoa! Easy, Boy! Les' start out simple, with jus' the bunk beds. You can always do the rest after that, if you got a mind. I saw some mattresses in the Thrift Shop that look new, and don' cost hardly nothin'." Helen was not overly impressed with the grandiose plans that might never come to fruition. Beds first, gee-gaws later.

"Hah! You don' trust your Jackie! Unfaithful wench, you! Jackie lunged at his wife, and thrusting his hands up under her skirt, pinched her lightly on the behind.

"Oh, you nasty man!" Helen chased him down the hall and into their bedroom, where she pushed him onto the bed and landed on top of him, tickling him on both sides. He whooped, and struggled to free himself. Helen became all hands and mouth. After awhile, it was quiet.

Just down the street, Barbara Nadine pulled the thin quilt over her shoulders, and turned on her side, trying to avoid the spreading wet under her younger brother's bottom. Finally, she got up and put a dry diaper on him, shushing his wails of discomfort, and quietly eased the bedroom door open to peer down the hallway. No sound. Good. Daddy must not be home yet. She could see the shadow of her mother, bent over the sink in the kitchen, listening to the nasal whines of country music pouring out of the little plastic radio on the shelf. The box of Cheerios which had served for dinner still sat on the table, next to the fruit jar of thin, blue milk mixed out of a box. Noiselessly, the little girl crept into the bathroom and deposited the reeking diaper in the already full diaper pail. When she returned, she lay down on the tattered rag rug next to the mattress, pulling her winter coat over herself. She got up once to pull on two pairs of socks, both with holes in the heels, then finally fell into a troubled sleep. She did not hear her father's lurching passage down the hall just as a sullen grey dawn was breaking. Mercifully, he was too drunk to bother looking into his sleeping children's room to look for his daughter.

Marin City slept in the early dawn as the She Coyote stretched and trotted into the hills, nose seeking out early-stirring breakfast.

Chapter 3

SCHOOL DAYS, SCHOOL DAYS

There I was, sitting on the throne in the stall in the Girl's bathroom at Drake. A bunch of us had come over from Tam for the big basketball game, and we knew we were not popular with the rich white kids that went to Drake. A few of the kids who had been kicked out of Tam for too many infractions were enrolled in the other area high schools; Sir Francis Drake, in San Anselmo, our arch rival, San Rafael, and Dominican, the Catholic school, while they served out their sentences of expulsion from Tamalpais. All the other schools feared us, the student body being heavily populated by Marin City's denizens, but we were so civilized that the race riot was a scheduled annual ritual observed, by and large, by both sides. On the chosen date, Tamalpais became "all" Negro, with the entire student body backing the dear old Alma Mater, and Drake became "all" white, regardless of actual skin tone. (With the exception of the loyal Tam exiles, of course.) There was a lot of playing the role, and strutting and exaggeration of tough expressions at games and other events where the schools mixed, but by and large, it was mostly talk. Still, we tended to travel in packs, and to avoid territories mutually agreed upon as belonging to one school or another. Of course, Marin City kids tended to stick pretty close to home, not having either bread nor wheels to get around the way the white kids in the surrounding towns did.

Still, I was alone in my stall, peacefully contemplating nature when I heard them come in. I knew who they were; Bobbie had previously attended Tamalpais, since she lived in Mill Valley, and she was a real snot. I hated her for herself, not just for her cashmere sweater sets, and her poodle skirts, and her shoes that matched her outfits. We'd exchanged words once, I believe, over a section of wall I considered my own during lunch hour. I prevailed, and she moved. Quickly.

"Oh, Pamela! I'm so glad my mother is going to let me transfer to Drake! I simply could not bear another day at Tam! I want to go out for cheerleader, so we can be on the squad together. Do you think I can get on?"

"If I say I want you on, you'll get on, Bobbie. After all, cousins have to stick together, don't they? How did you talk your parents into it, anyway?" Artificially correct voices issued from the two girls at the counter in front of the wall-to-wall mirror, and I recognized Bobbie Corbett's nasal tones. The other one must be her cousin, Pamela Goldberg, social arbiter and role model of the sophomore class at Sir Francis Drake High School. I could see the bottoms of their genuine plaid kilts imported from Scotland under the bottom of the door to my sheltering cave, and their soft golden bucks topped by pristine white knee socks. Bobbie had always worn dresses that fairly screamed Bobbie Brooks and Lantz, or expensive skirts and sweaters, and I just knew shoes lined the floor of her walk-in closet three pairs deep, while the shelves groaned under the weight of every imaginable color of sweater set. Cashmere was no stranger to her closet, and her coat was real camel hair.

"And your hair! How ever...?" I couldn't see her hair, of course, but I could imagine. I decided not to reveal my presence, and to listen to them. In reality, I was curious as to what the white bitches talked about. I wondered if they were like us at all.

"Like it? I spent the summer in New York with Daddy, and he took me to have it bleached and styled at this really, really boss hair salon on Fifth Avenue. Mother had a fit, of course, but then she decided she liked it after I told her Daddy wanted me to get my ears pierced so I could wear these cute little diamonds, but I said 'no'. I didn't want to look like some gypsy or something." Platinum tresses gleamed silver-white in the overhead light as Bobbie shook her head gracefully at her envious cousin. "And I got to transfer after I told her those colored boys at Tam were bothering me to go out with them all the time. She really flipped over that! And here I am, going to Drake!" Gales of laughter. That almost got me up and outta there, ready to stomp ass and take names. Wasn't no way our boys would be hustlin' those bitches! They had better sense. Better taste, too.

"What! Oh, no! Did they really? Did they try to touch you? You wouldn't, would you?"

"No, of course not, they wouldn't dare. I just told Mother that so she'd let me go to school here. They better not touch me! Mother'd call the police!"

"It must be terrible to have to go to Tamalpais with all those Negroes. And those Marin City kids are so awful! But, did you see that girl sitting on the Tam side? A white girl was sitting with some colored, and one of them had his arm around her. She kept talking to this dark-looking girl next to her. They look so rough! Even the girls had on leather jackets. She was the only white girl, though. I wonder what she was doing with them."

Bobbie grimaced, and lowered her voice confidentially as she leaned closer to Pamela. "Yes. That's Barbara Nadine Johnson and Tondelayo Dubois. They're sisters, or so they say."

"Sisters!"

"Well, not really. But Barbara Nadine lives with Tondelayo's family. They live in Marin City, of course. What can you expect?" I could just see Bobbie allowing her thickly plastered red lips to form a slight sneer, seriously threatening to crack her lipstick. I heard her pulling out her compact so she could paint another coat, and I pictured her maliciously enjoying her power in making her cousin wait for once. Bobbie tended heavily toward the "sniveler" role, and I was sure Pamela called the shots most of the time.

"They live together, and ride motorcycles! Tondelayo's big brother is one of those motorcycle hoods! The girls go out with older guys, though." She leaned even closer. "They carry switchblades! The girls! And they have these taps all over their shoes. They sound like horses walking down the sidewalk. They're really awful."

"Does she go with coloreds? Ooooh, how could she! Can you imagine? Can you see them kissing?"

"I don't know. I think they both date coloreds and whites. They don't associate with my crowd, of course, so I don't know what all they do. I can imagine, though. They're all so awful. There's a gang of them that hang out together, and they're really tough. This kid called Barbara Nadine a nigger-lover once, and Tondelayo actually knocked out her front tooth! I think Tondelayo's one of those "high yellows", or whatever they are. Anyway, she and Barbara Nadine are always together, and after she hit Marsha, another girl hit her back. Then there was this big fight, and they all got kicked out of school for the semester. I guess they had to go to San Rafael for awhile. There's a girl named Ruby Anne, a really dark Negro, that's always with them, too, and sometimes I've seen her wearing Barbara Nadine's sweater!"

"That's terrible! You're jazzing me."

"It's true. They have the most awful clothes, and sometimes they wear the same skirt all week. I think they all only have a couple outfits among them. I guess they just don't care. Well, forget them! What do you think we ought to wear for the tryouts? I've got these really cute bermudas..."

The hated voices faded away, and the bathroom door whooshed shut behind them. I continued to sit there for awhile, shaking with anger, yet somehow feeling sick with shame. Shame for being something I couldn't quite put my finger on, shame for being somehow found wanting. We were all like that; we'd learned as we got older that there was something deeply, deeply wrong about us, and that we weren't quite as good as kids from other places. We never fully understood what it was all about: we simply absorbed it through our pores. We understood it when adults, white adults, obviously tried to avoid sitting next to a colored person on the bus, we understood it when we were invisible at drive-ins outside of Marin City, and we understood it when adults grew nervous and tried to cross the street to avoid passing us when there were more than two of us walking or standing anywhere. And we began to know it was a kind of power. We began to know we had fear on our side, if nothing else, and we began to learn to manipulate it without even realizing it. We never really talked about it amongst ourselves, but we learned from the older kids.

Still, I felt sick, as well as enraged. I would pay dear little Miss Pamela and Miss Bobbie back some day, I vowed.

When I went back to the kids I was with, I didn't say anything. But I did take out my switchblade and start to clean my nails with it. Jerome slapped my arm and made me put it away, and we finished out the game without further incident. Soon enough we'd be back home, in Marin City, where we all knew each other, and we felt comfortable.

"Hey, Bitch!"

"Hey, yo'sef, Bitch. Wha's happenin'?"

"Man, it is so cool. I mean, cool! You know who-all be at the Fillmore this weekend? It be some kinda boss, no shit! Fats Domino, the Coasters, B. B. King, and the Man, hisself, Bo Diddley goin' be there Friday and Sattidy. I be goin' to that, Man!"

"No shit! Damn! Bo Diddley! Oooohwee! I jus' love them Coasters, too. And Fats! No lie? I be there too, Man. I jus' got to go see that show. Bo Diddley, he the Man, no lie. Hey, Girl. Whatchu' talkin'? Yo' Momma don' let you an' Barbara Nadine go into the City, no way."

"Ah, Ruby Anne, you know we be goin'. Somehow. Bo Diddley!" I wasn't nearly as confident as I sounded though; Barbara Nadine and I had more than one knock-down dragout fight with Mama and Papa about who, how, what, and when we were allowed to go out. There were rules, strict ones, which seemed more than a little unreasonable at times. Even Jack had sided with our folks from the beginning, saying no way were we ever going to give the big eye to any of the Copperheads. Whenever we were hanging out with them, either he or Napa Bob, usually both, guarded us like some damn vestal virgins. The bikers knew better than to even think about messing with us, too. And there was no driving to San Francisco at night with boys, either. It wasn't going to be easy.

I shifted my books to the other hip, and popped my gum thoughtfully. It was lunch time at Tamalpais High School, and I was waiting for Barbara Nadine to come out of English class. "Lessee, if'n you was to go wit' Chick, and me wit' Lionel, and then Barbara Nadine would go wit' William.....no, that ain't gone' work. Ummmmmm..." I chewed my gum absently, then blew a big, pink bubble which threatened to collapse all over my face. I sucked its tatters back to the safety of my mouth at the last instant. "Well, I guess I could ask Napa to take all of us." Secretly, though, I doubted the wisdom of this plan. Napa let me ride with him, and he liked Barbara Nadine and Ruby Anne, too, but he was not likely to be thrilled with taking us. More likely, he and the other Copperheads would go and show the colors, and that meant we weren't invited. We were only allowed to ride with the full gang on very rare, very special occasions. Jack and Napa Bob had said a long time ago the Boys were too rough to let us be around them much. They said it was hard on the Boys, and there'd be trouble if they overdid it. We didn't exactly agree; some of those Copperheads were really cool, but we knew the Copperheads weren't your average

Sunday school choir boys, either. So, by and large, we hadn't argued with Jack and Napa. In return, they'd taught all three of us to ride the big bikes ourselves, and we were all quite proudly proficient riders on the big hogs. Mama and Papa were not pleased, and Jack and Papa got into it pretty bad for awhile, but finally Papa agreed we could do it if it was only on back roads and no traffic. Other times, we rode behind, like the biker girls.

"Nuh uh, Girl. Ain't no way my mama's goin' let me go wit' him. He bad, he too bad. My Mama say she sho' he kilt somebody a'reddy, an' she skin my lil' black ass do I be wit' him. Even wit' chu." Ruby Anne shook her head and unwrapped another pink square of bubblegum to soothe her anxiety at the thought of getting caught in the company of Napa Bob, and going to The City at that. Her mother would slap her up side the head, no shit. We both felt glum. We just had to go!

"Hey, Bitches!" Barbara Nadine shimmied out of class, popping her fingers and bopping on down the stairs. She was laughing, until she spotted our long faces.

"Hey, Barbara Nadine. You be done?"

"Yeah. Les' go get some potato chips and Cokes, an' go set on the steps." We three girls started off to the little store on the corner. "How come you guys lookin' so down? Been kicked outta' school again, Ruby Anne?"

"No, I ain't, Smart Ass! Sheeeut. Kicked out. Sheeeut!" Ruby Anne managed to assume an air of injured innocence. "Hey, Barbara Nadine. Us gotta' figure out how we gon' go to The City this weekend to see the show at the Fillmore. It goin' be wailin' there Friday and Sattidy. Bo Diddley, B. B. King, the Coasters, Fats Domino, we gotta' go! You got any ideas?"

"Well, you know Papa ain' goin' let us go wit' no boys. Tondelayo, d'you think Napa Bob would take us? Oh, no, Ruby Anne, yo' mama won' 'low that, will she?" Ruby Anne had the grace to look ashamed, but she nodded her head reluctantly. "She don' like Napa Bob. Say he too bad."

"Yeah, well, he be bad. No lie. But he don' never hurt any us. He be a brother to us. Mama and Papa say they don' worry 'bout us when we wit' him. He goin' back to the base tomorra anyway. His leave be up." Our shoulders slumped. No one wanted to say it, but we all knew that Jack would have taken us. Jack, the big brother and steadfast friend. But Jack had died in Korea last year. He was buried with full honors in the Golden Gate National Cemetery, with a full honor guard of bikers. Napa Bob had ridden at the head of the procession. Hells Angels, Mo Fo's, Rattlers, and his own Copperheads escorted him to his resting place, Harleys draped with red roses, and proud colors flaunted on the backs of the men who came to pay him the final tribute. The sailors in the honor guard from his ship had briefly contemplated a small rumble with the bikers, posturing and looking as tough as they could, but prudence won out as the sailors realized they were outnumbered by some fifteen to one. (And everybody was outnumbered by the cops, who swarmed like bees to honey wherever outlaw bikers gathered; and this was a BIG gathering.)

Mama looked at Papa. Papa looked at me and Barbara Nadine, our faces importunate and desperate. I know he was thinking sadly about how fast his little girls were growing up, and he sighed at the intrusive thought of his son, lost forever now. He and Mama knew exactly how badly we longed to go to the Fillmore to see our idols, and they didn't want to be unreasonable. But the way they must have seen it, we were only sixteen, and as parents, they were not about to let us go trekking off to San Francisco with boys. We knew the rules: no dating alone, no drinking, no smoking dope, no fooling around, no cars unless the drivers were older and then, only as far as Mill Valley or Sausalito, parents meet and approve of all would-be dates, curfew strictly enforced. Maybe day trips to San Anselmo or the beach would be allowed, if we were home before 10:00 at night. We were "good girls," and we were going to stay that way. Jack had always ensured that before. Before his death, the neighborhood boys knew full well who Jack was, and had no intentions of messing with his sisters. But now — Papa sighed again, and raised his eyebrow at Mama.

"Jackie, ain't Bo Diddley one of your main men?" Mama's dimple flashed at the corner of her mouth, but she managed to hold her solemn look. "We know them boys, of course. They been trying to tear the house apart wailin' to KWBR for years." The peace and quiet of the Dubois house was frequently ripped apart by gyrating teenagers and the coolest R & B hits from the radio.

"Yeah, yeah, he is. Why? These girls don' wanna go wit' their ole man, do they?"

Mama laughed at the sudden look of alarm on my face. Barbara Nadine just swallowed quickly.

"No, I don' think so, you ancient thing. But, maybe you could drive them, and go sit someplace else, then they could meet their friends there. You be let in the Fillmore, you think?"

"Watch it, woman!" Jackie aimed a squinty-eyed glare at her. "I ain't that old, you know. You oughtta be careful, me, I have strong women fallin' down on the groun' and bitin' sticks, I be at the Fillmore by mysef. I be a reglar fox, you know! Me, I put on my uptown threads, and look out, Daddio's on the prowl." He preened himself ostentatiously, running a vain hand over his mass of tight, black curls while he rendered a passable rendition of Bo Diddley's "I'm a Man." The earring in his left ear flashed suddenly, as he tossed his head. He was a fox, all right, and the girls did pant after him; Mama was well aware of that every time they were out together. Even at the grocery store, girls gave him the big eye. They didn't think she saw them, but she did. Oh, yes. She did. She smiled smugly to herself, though. She had what it took to keep his attention right there at home. No lie.

"Me, I gotta' have my lady wit' me, I go off to the Fillmore. Ain't no way I got the energy to fight off all them wimmin' givin' me the big eye and tryin' to make time. No way. Helen, you got to go, too. Protect me." Papa turned exaggeratedly innocent eyes upon his beloved.

Mama considered it. Maybe she'd go. She and Papa hadn't been on a date for a very, very long time. "I might have to go along just to keep you straight, you Cajun devil, you." She twitched her hips suggestively, making Papa grin so widely his gold side teeth glittered in the light. She then countered his song with a slightly modified verse from "Bring It To Jerome." We averted our eyes in horrified modesty. At their age! But as the idea simmered in our heads, we began to see how it could work. After all, the wheels one used to get there and back could be kept discretely separate from the actual attendance at the show.

"Would you, Papa? We could take Ruby Anne, and meet the guys there. C'mon, Papa, please?" I widened my big, brown eyes even further, as I pleaded. My mama hadn't raised no fool, and I knew when to accept a compromise. After all, if our parents dropped us off two blocks away, and their seats were far, far away, we could pretend they weren't actually there. And if Papa drove, we could be sure we'd get to eat on the way home. The boys we hung out with weren't always flush enough to make sure we didn't starve to death on dates.

"If you do it, Papa, I'll make you some pecan pie." Barbara Nadine knew that would do it. She won every time she trotted out that particular bribe, so she used it only in the most urgent situations. Her heart leaped as she saw acquiescence beginning to form in Papa's face. Happy and excited, she started to hug him, but awkwardly changed to a quick pat on the shoulder, then flew off to the kitchen. Watching her go, Mama sighed, and glanced quickly at Papa, unspoken words hanging in the air. The girl desperately wanted to hug her Jackie and Helen, now "Mama" and "Papa," wanted to have them be as easy and loving with her as they were with me, but she simply could not do it. Barbara Nadine was quick to shy away at any suggestion of touch or close physical encounters, and we all respected her need for personal space. Mama had tucked her in, and put damp washcloths over her forehead when she was sick, but she maintained a far greater distance than she did with me. Barbara Nadine wanted it that way. With Papa, she expressed her affection with banter and smiles, allowing herself only the briefest contact at rare intervals. I know Papa sensed a deep fear in her, and although he loved her deeply, he did not try to push the invisible boundaries. If he allowed himself to think about why Barbara Nadine was like that, he became enraged. He tried not to think about it very much. He just gave her as much love as she could accept, and let her know he was always there if she wanted him or needed him. He and Mama had long ago begun to think of their "three kids".

Now "two kids." He wasn't about to risk losing another one.

Friday afternoon after school and all day Saturday the Dubois house was a beehive of activity. Ruby Anne had learned to sew in home economics, and she was making outfits for herself and us. Between the three of us, we had enough babysitting and beaded earring money to purchase materials we found on sale at the little department store between the grocery and the candy store. Mama wisely stayed out of it, but she had promised us we could wear the long, dangly earrings we coveted for the first time. Our ears were pierced, of course, but we were restricted to smaller earrings and gold hoops. I was rushing in and out of Mama and Papa's room where the ancient treadle machine was whirring its heart out, consulting with the frantically sewing dressmaker on bead color combinations. Barbara Nadine was fetching and carrying, and setting curlers into hair that kept moving out of target range. It was a madhouse, and Mama said she was seriously considering the wisdom of firmly putting three over-excited teenagers down for a nap. Papa, the clever man, spent the day outside, head buried in the bowels of the loyal old Buick. He told Mama he "wanted to be sure the carriage was ready to carry the ladies of the Court to the ball."

After a hurried dinner during which all three of us had to be repeatedly threatened with staying home if we didn't eat, we disappeared into our bedroom. One at a time, someone darted out, slammed the door of the bathroom, and ran gallons of hot water through the shower. The steam billowed out in smother-

ing waves. Mama and Papa quietly went next door to understanding neighbors to bathe. Muffled giggling and screaming
punctuated a steady stream of high-pitched chatter and bickering.

Then, the door opened, and the young women walked out.
We knew the change was breathtaking, and we felt suddenly
very grown up and very solemn. Mama and Papa could only
blink, their hearts aching with what must have been an uncon-
scious sense of loss. I don't think it had actually sunk in to
them that we really were growing up so — almost adults. Ruby
Anne had suddenly shot up over the past year, and assumed a
willowy grace that was entirely unexpected. In her closely
fitted old gold velvet sheath dress she was simply stunning.
Unadorned except for black and gold beaded earrings, her deep
brown skin glowed like satin. Her unruly hair had been sub-
dued into a french twist, and her feet showed themselves to be
elegantly long and slender in the brown suede flats. She had
small-boned, delicately thin wrists and hands, which moved
with an unstudied grace and beauty. Her back, proudly upright
and straight, flowed up to a long, beautiful neck, now exposed
by her new hairdo. Somehow, when nobody was looking, she'd
shape-shifted from a compact urchin into a tall, beautiful slip
of femininity. Few women of thirty could have hoped for the
natural beauty and sensual promise she exuded. Ruby Anne
reflected the regal strength and carriage of ancient African royal
lineage as she flowed noiselessly across the living room.

Barbara Nadine followed, her pale blondness and fair skin
somehow turned to pearlescence in her muted silvery-gray dress
of some soft, faintly shimmery fabric. She appeared to be covered by some magical weave of spider's silk, softly whispering
words of enchantment as she moved. Her thin frame was softened and rounded by the long sleeves and full skirt, tightly
cinched at the narrow waist by an iridescent sequined belt. The
waves of shining, gossamer hair cascading down her back were
simply held off her face in front by a thin band of the same
fabric, then left to float freely behind her. She wore earrings of

crystal and silver, with her slender neck and wrists repeating the jeweled emphasis by a single strand encircling them. She looked like a faerie wraith, other worldly and heartbreakingly insubstantial. Her silver flats barely anchored her in the everyday world of Marin City.

I was last, walking slowly and carefully, aware of the impact of the dress I wore. It was a dark copper satin slip dress with narrow spaghetti straps, which served only to keep the dress from flowing down my body like a river, and away. A stole of black stripes on deep copper taffeta covered my arms and shoulders. Sturdier and more substantial than either of the other two girls, I felt grounded and very real. The copper dress brought out the red-gold undertones of my skin and highlighted the symmetry of my form. As I look back at photographs taken that night, I see the woman emerging from the child, caught in the camera's eye like a moth in the wax of a melting candle. Like my friends, I was tall, and my bones paid homage to my African and Cherokee ancestry. My curls were gathered behind my head, leaving my ears exposed, and I wore earrings fashioned into ears of golden and multi-colored corn, sheathed in pale green husks. A beaded pendant adorned my neck, with the outline of a magnificently antlered stag barely visible behind trunks and branches of trees. The pendant was beaded entirely in shades of browns and blacks, so that the stag flashed in and out of conscious sight. In the picture, captured forever in time, I bear no resemblance to the rowdy, tough high schooler my parents knew. Rather, I see a woman-child who has awakened echoes of ancient and timeless earth energies, powerful and barely sleeping until the time to walk once more. Mama was stunned. She told me later she remembered misty things her grandmothers had spoken of, in the dark, fire-lit nights of her own childhood left behind so long ago.

For a long moment, no one spoke. Then Papa heaved a sigh, and gave a long, low whistle. "Oh, yeah! I be the Man tonight!" His comment broke the tension, and everyone laughed.

"Hey, Daddio! You be one righteous dude! And yo' Mama! Ow, wow. You guys're really boss!"

Papa wore a zoot suit of black with a white pinstripe, full pleated trousers narrowing suddenly into pegged pants, jacket falling from impossibly wide shoulders almost to his knees. A gold watch chain hung below the jacket, swinging importantly against his leg. A black satin shirt, and the narrowest of white ties completed the ensemble, and he wore black and white wing tips with thick soles on his feet. Most surprisingly of all, he wore a sharp-looking broad-brimmed fedora over his slicked-back and brilliantined curls, and what appeared to be a diamond earring borrowed from Mama (well, almost-diamond!) had taken the place of his customary small gold hoop. Mama was a match for all the sartorial splendor in a blood-red velvet sheath, her still-perfect figure amply displayed in its loving embrace. She stood atop 4-inch spike heels of strappy pumps, and a slit skirt teasingly showed long, long lengths of gorgeous leg as she walked. The skirt curved ever so slightly around and under her glorious rump, and her hips swayed enticingly toward and away from Papa as she sashayed to the door. Her long, glossy black hair was pulled to the top of her head, then fell in a ponytail of heavy silk below her shoulders. Mama owned no diamonds, but the glitter and flash of rhinestones did yeoman service to her golden skin. I think Papa was stricken by an intense need to stay home and take care of business, but his four women gave him no options.

In a solemn moment that was to mark the transition from girls to young women, Mama smudged us all with sage, sweetgrass and cedar, and we stood there, awed with our new status in our family. We had, of course, had the proper ceremonies when we reached our first moon times, but that was different. This time, we knew we were about to see a new freedom and permission to exercise our own judgment in what we did. Then, it was off to see the legends of R & B we went, one of the last times Mama and Papa would try to keep us little girls.

I've seen a lot of concerts since then, even going to the Newport Jazz festival a couple times, but that night shimmers in my memory like no other. The men who would become legends transcending time even in the white world, even though then the white stations wouldn't play their music, put on a show that had us rockin' and rollin' in the aisles. Fats Domino glistened with sweat and grinned his sweet, sweet smile, his fingers pounding so all the diamonds turned to fire in the spotlights, and Bo Diddley made me ache when he convinced me he was a man. Oh, yeah. We laughed at the Coasters singing *Poison Ivy* and *Charlie Brown*, and were mesmerized by B.B. King wailin' those deep down and dirty blues. Oh, it was a night to remember!

Chapter 4

BARBARA
NADINE'S STORY

Sex. Making love. Having intercourse. Fucking. Doing it.
Humping. How many ways there are to say it, and how
wide is the range of meaning. For a little three-letter
word like "sex" there is a world of pain, and joy, and indiffer-
ence. For us kids, at seven or eight, "it" was something to which
we devoted quite a little thought. We had few accurate facts, at
first, just vague portents of things to come. Our bodies weren't
much to look at, although we knew we would experience changes
in due time. Our opinions of this somewhat murky future were
pretty mixed, if not outright rebellious. Somehow, we knew
we'd be "too old" for a lot of things we were accustomed to
doing and the ways in which we were accustomed to doing
them. Curiosity was great, too, at least with most of us. Barbara
Nadine never had anything to say about the subject, fascinating as it might have been to the rest of us.

I had a slightly younger cousin, Terry Waitingsnake, who lived with her family in the City. At that time, a lot of Cherokee had been "relocated" from Indian Country in Oklahoma, along with various other Indians from tribes all over the country to the major cities, where they were dumped. There they languished, jobless for the most part, ignorant of city ways and city things, and in bitter poverty and longing for the tribal homelands, extended families, and familiar ways. The Waitingsnakes were among them. The Waitingsnakes lived on another branch of the family tree, Auntie Mary being Mama's sister. Anyway, they had several kids, but Terry was closest in age to me, and so we were often together for family gatherings. Terry was a "terror," a "hellion," or a "lively child," depending on Mama's and Auntie Mary's reactions to her behavior at any given time. And Terry had some very unique, original, and bizarre information to impart regarding the mechanics and theory of procreation one weekend while our family was attending a pow wow with the Waitingsnakes when I was about eight. I was amazed. I simply could not envision such things amongst humans at all, let alone my parents. They were one day older than water, anyway, and certainly far, far beyond the gymnastics Terry had described to me.

Now, my knowledge was a bit vague about such things, but Mama had always taught me to be modest in the Indian way, and I knew to never let Papa or Jack see me in less than a bathrobe and nightie, and I knew babies grew in their mother's stomachs. I had seen kittens born, a revolting process with which I wanted no further truck, and had been told human babies entered the world in much the same fashion. This news did not thrill me either, as I simply couldn't imagine my mother licking me like that, but I knew better than to argue, so I just filed the information away for later elucidation. After my session with Terry, though, I thought I had better ask Mama. Because if what Terry had said was true, I was going to have to seriously rethink whether I wanted to continue the process of growing up or not.

Now, that got a reaction! I was mortified when Mama laughed so hard she peed her pants when I told her what Terry had told me. She hooted and hollered, and said she could hardly wait to tell Auntie Mary what her daughter was transmitting as gospel. Then she got kind of sad, and asked me why I was so interested in such things, since I was just a baby. When I bridled at this, and started to stalk off in a huff, she grabbed me and hugged me, and said she was sorry, that she just wasn't ready to lose her little girl yet. I told her I wasn't going anywhere, and I was still her little girl, but I sure wasn't a baby! After some more of that typical grownup footshufflin' and off-the-subject meandering, we got down to business. Mama didn't believe in telling more stories and lies to children, but she didn't believe in overdoing it, either. I got a basic outline, an assurance that, yes, she and Papa did make love (no bad words here) from time to time, because they loved each other, and it was something married people were free to do, and that one day I'd fall in love, marry someone, and do it, too. This, I doubted. The whole thing sounded pretty peculiar to me, in truth. Then, I got the standard cautionary lecture about strange men, boys, and dark corners, and was sent off to play with a cookie and a strong feeling that Terry's version sounded a lot more interesting.

Of course, Barbara Nadine and Ruby Anne were filled in immediately with the straight skinny, and we had fodder for discussion for weeks. Ruby Anne and I did, that is. Barbara Nadine was characteristically silent and uninterested in the topic. When we asked her outright if she thought her folks "did it," she got a pinched, angry look on her face and said, "Like damn rabbits. Where do you think all them snot-nosed brats come from?" Then she turned her back and went off to play by herself, building a ranch in the dirt. Barbara Nadine loved to build miniature ranches in the dirt, building fences, and planting orchards of twigs, and making tiny bricks of mud she dried in the sun. She used to make little houses out of the bricks, and there was always a little one off to the side, that she said belonged to the daughter, who was allowed to have her very own house with white furniture, and a white rug made of sheepskin so her feet were never cold, and a white bed all hung with white ruffles like in the fairy tale books. There were never any doors or windows facing the main house, only on the far side. Usually, Ruby Anne and I were allowed to help build the ranches, but not this time. Barbara Nadine wouldn't even talk to us, and grimly set about building one of the most elaborate ranches she'd ever done. It had orchards, and a lake, and even a little rock garden outside the Princess's small house. It took her all day, not even stopping for lunch. She worked on it, on her knees in the dirt, bucket of water beside her, long after we lost interest and wandered off to the Tarzan swing. When we came home for supper, she was gone, but her ranch lay in ruins, stomped and smashed into smithereens. We could see the deep gouges the heels of her tennis shoes made, and we realized Barbara Nadine had destroyed her creation herself.

Shocked into silence, and somehow frightened by the intensity of the rage that had destroyed that little world, we glanced at one another and mutually agreed in total silence that this would never, ever be mentioned. We hurried more than we normally did to the warm, welcoming kitchens of our respective homes and our mothers cooking dinner. As we skirted Barbara Nadine's house on the opposite side of the street, we could see her daddy sitting drinking beer in front of the flickering TV, and all the kids fighting over a box of crackers and canned soup in the kitchen. Mrs. Johnson would hit one, then another, on the head with a ladle as they grabbed and fought. Barbara Nadine was just sitting there, not even trying to protect her chipped tea cup of soup. One of the others grabbed it and drank it, and she just sat there. For some reason, I felt like crying when I got home, and had to ask to be excused before I finished my spaghetti. Mama came in to my room and asked if I felt sick, and I told her, "yes, some." She felt my forehead, put me to bed, and made me some milk toast.

I can still remember the day Barbara Nadine told us. It was one of those gray, foggy days of winter, and we were up in the hills playing hide-and-seek among the clumps of bushes that loomed up and disappeared as the fog swirled around in ragged curtains. It was exhilaratingly spooky, and we were breathless from running and laughing as we frantically tried to be will-o'-the-wisps in the unpredictable fog. One minute we would be invisible, cloaked in secrecy and silent, cottony wetness, the next, exposed to the view of "It" in awful clarity. Shrieking, we tried to reach "home," but as often as not, were tagged and "It" for awhile.

Our stomachs told us it was lunch time, and we headed for our "throne." This was a large, squarish rock of some size, sitting in isolated splendor overlooking the valley leading down to the Waldo Grade. It had a perfect indentation on top for a properly regal seat, and the Queen Of the Day could sit there surveying her kingdom with its scurrying cars far below on a clear day. Today, it sat, remote and glistening with diamond droplets, with the sharp scent of the ice plants and hen and chickens that grew in its many pockets so piquant it was almost palpable. Below, the entire world was hidden by the cottony blanket of fog, and it was easy to pretend that we inhabited our own alien, distant world, far, far away from home, and parents, and the everyday. Here, it was closed, and secret, and serene, our kingdom, our world, known only to ourselves and the small animals that rustled occasionally in the tall, dead stalks of grass. Once, I thought I got a fleeting glimpse of a large, dark shape and the gleam of a golden-green eye, but it was gone before I could really register it, and I decided it was a trick of the fog. I was not in the least frightened, or even uneasy, somehow knowing whatever it might have been it was friendly and merely curious, and I felt no need or desire to even mention it to the other two girls.

While we did feel a sense of heightened awareness of our surroundings and the sounds, smells, sights, and feel of things up there, especially when it was foggy, we never felt fear or uneasiness. In fact, I felt particularly safe and secure, although I could never have explained it. I had a vague sense of being watched over and protected that hovered just below the level of consciousness, and was never hesitant about being up so far into the isolated hills. Mama and Papa were fully aware of our habitual playing areas, and did not seem to worry about us. Now, I wonder at how things have changed, and how children would never be permitted to spend entire days up in the hills, but then, there seemed no cause for concern. Other kids occasionally played in the woods surrounding the Tarzan swing, and a few ventured further into the hills, but by and large, it was our private kingdom. We never saw a grown-up up there, and the older boys never went up there either. It was entirely our personal, private, safe world as far as we were concerned.

So, that winter day seemed no different from any other day, and we set out for the throne for lunch with minimal bickering over whose turn it was to be queen.

"Nuh unh, Barbara Nadine, it ain' neither yo' turn! I be queen! You was queen last Satiddy. It be me!" Ruby Anne turned to me for support.

"Yeah, it be Ruby Anne's turn, Barbara Nadine. She right. I'us queen Sunday, and now it be hers."

"Oh, yeah. OK." Barbara Nadine shrugged, and trudged on up the slope toward the throne.

Ruby Anne stared after her, taken aback by the lack of a good, rousing argument before she surrendered. She had known all along that Barbara Nadine was perfectly aware that it was not her turn, and had picked up on the cue to engage in honorable battle before the matter was rightfully settled. After all, Barbara Nadine had flung down the gauntlet by announcing she was on her way to assume the throne. Ruby Anne had picked it up, and stood ready to engage, but then Barbara Nadine had caved in without another salvo, and the whole thing seemed anticlimactic somehow. As the middle of six kids, Ruby Anne enjoyed a good donnybrook just for the exercise. As a rule, she could count on at least five minutes of assaults and counter charges over who was to assume the throne for the day, and here she was, left feeling cut off at the knees. Something had to be wrong.

"Uh, Barbara Nadine, do you want to, you can have my turn. It's OK. You wanna' be Queen?" An incredible gesture of good will, and indicative of just how worried she was.

"Nuh unh. Tha's OK." Oh, oh. It was looking worse and worse.

"I got bologna for lunch, and you kin have some. You hongry? I got a jar a' real milk, too. Mama got paid yestiddy." The biggest offer of all. Real milk was in short supply in Ruby Anne's house, as it was in a lot of Marin City homes. The powdered stuff was cheaper, and kept longer, whether there was ice in the icebox or not.

"OK. I don' care." The three of us arrived at the throne, and Ruby Anne and I ceremoniously handed Barbara Nadine up to her seat. There she sat, arms wrapped around her middle, head bowed, elbows sticking out through the holes of the worn old man's flannel shirt she wore for a jacket.

"Hey, Barbara Nadine, 'kin I wear yo' shirt? You kin wear my jacket." We often traded clothes, and she looked so thin and cold. I had a quilted corduroy jacket with a hood, and the thought of giving it up, all nice and warmed up inside as it was gave me a momentary qualm. But I was feeling charitable, even though I couldn't say it, let alone spell it, and I really did want Barbara Nadine to liven up. It made my stomach feel tight to see her like this.

It was when she took off the shirt that Ruby Anne and I saw her arms and gasped. Barbara Nadine had removed the shirt without thinking, seeming to be off somewhere else, or she would never have let us see. Her arms were black and blue and purple, on top of old yellow bruises, with new and half-healed cuts running up and down in parallel streaks. Pus was welling out of some of them, and we could see they continued around her body inside the gaping holes of her undershirt. Realizing that she had let us see, she convulsively grabbed for the shirt, and tried to cover up again, but it was too late. She looked at our stunned faces, and started to snarl, "Wha'chu lookin' at?" but her face crumbled before she finished the words.

Tears she fought to keep from erupting started falling anyway, and she began to cry so hard we were afraid she was going to choke. Both of us were unsure what to do, and finally, we just hugged her until she got through the worst of it.

Then, she started to talk.

Her voice, flat and progressively more hill country, chronicled things we had never heard before, had never even imagined, and were not ready to hear. Ruby Anne's daddy had been a travelin' man, and she had never even seen him, though "uncles" of varying temperament had lived briefly with them for short periods. Her mama worked two or three jobs, while the "uncles" stayed home and watched the kids, and when they left, her mama got welfare to feed the mouths that kept appearing for awhile, but nobody ever did the things to her that Barbara Nadine was talking about.

Certainly, Mama and Papa were strict with me, and Jack could be a tad too like them for my taste at times, but I was never slapped in the face, or hurt like that. The most I got was a light swat on the fanny, and the worst thing that could happen to me no matter how bad I was was to be sent to my room and not allowed to read or play with my toys. Since I loved reading, and had a whole bookcase of books, this was a fate worse than death.

Barbara Nadine's daddy had been doing things to her since she was a small baby, things like Mama had told me about that went on between man and wife, yes, but also things I had never heard of.

"He makes me put his thang in my mouf, and go up and down on it, and lick it. He grabs my hair and pulls it out, and sounds like a pig, then he shoots nasty horrible stuff in my mouf, and makes me swallow it. He laughs when I throw up, and it gets all hard and ugly again. It goes soft in my mouth, and gets little. After it's hard again, he sticks it in me, and says things like, 'You like to be ass-fucked this time, kid?' or he sticks it in me down there and squeezes my arms or hits me while he shoves in and out of me. Then he started cutting me with a knife to see if he could make me cry, but I won' do that no more. If'n I cry, it jus' make him real happy, and sometime he jus' do it agin. I ain' gonna let that bastid see me cry. I ain' no baby." Barbara Nadine looked defiant even with her red-rimmed eyes and snot running down her face.

"Did you tell yo' mama? He didn't oughtta' be doin' them things to you." Ruby Anne finally managed to say.

"Huh! He wait until she at the sto', or asleep. My big brothers al'us on me, too. When he gone, drinkin', or in jail. He caught 'em onct, and jus' watched and laughed. He say they growin' up to be real mens. Then he beat the shit outta them, and tol' em I his lil' girl. They jus' wait 'til he gone, though, or they catch me outside and drag me under the house. They say they kill me if'n I tell. Daddy tol' me he kill me and Maw did I tell her. I think she know, though, but she don' never say nothin' to him 'bout nothin. He beat her up real bad all the time, and she ain' about to go upside him about me. My big sister, Jessie Louise, what run away? She come back onct', to talk to Maw 'bout me comin' to live wit' her, but Maw 'tol her she wa'nt gonna let me go live with no 'ho like she was. They had a big screamin' fight, and Jessie Louise run out the house and hasn't never come back. Maw jus' look at me and say I got to stay aroun' and he'p her wit' the fambly responsibilities."

She buttoned my jacket over those poor, bleeding arms, and said, "C'mon. Le's eat. I'm hongry. I even got us some candy. Took it outta' Daddy's pocket when he passed out." She proudly held out a handful of mints like the ones kept at the cash registers of bars. It was seldom she had anything to contribute to our picnics, and we just shared around. It was a big deal when she was able to hold up her side, and we were duly impressed.

As we ate, I made up my mind.

"OK. Thas' it! Thas' jus' IT! We gon' go on down to my house, and we gon' tell my Mama and Papa. You kin live wit' us. I got them bunk beds Papa made for us, and you kin' jus' live wit' us. Mama and Papa ain't gone let them do that to you; they loves you. I heard 'em say so. Ain' nothin' like that at our house! When Mama and Papa fight, don' nobody hit nobody else. Oh, they yells sometime, or they send me to my room and don' let me read or do nothin' but they shorely don' do stuff like that! Once Mama was real mad at Papa, and she made beans for supper that was half cooked, and din' have no salt, nor ham, nor nothin' in 'em, and made him eat it like it was reg'lar supper, but he don' never hit her. Jus' think! You kin be my sister!"

As we all thought about it, the idea seemed better and better. Ruby Anne briefly considered the possibility of contesting me for the rights to house Barbara Nadine, but she already had five brothers and sisters crammed into the two bedrooms of the house they lived in, and her mama slept on a day bed in the living room. She soon yielded to me. We sat up there around the throne until nearly dark, plotting how to convince Mama and Papa to go along with our scheme. I knew they would do something when they found out, but I wasn't at all sure they were ready to acquire another child on a full time basis. It wasn't always easy to feed me and Jack as it was, although nothing was ever said to me. I just knew it from the general talk around the house. The shipyard had closed down some time ago, and Papa didn't always have work. Still, I had faith that they'd see how little Barbara Nadine ate, and she could wear my clothes, and she was over at our house all the time anyway, so it wouldn't be such a big change, anyway, and...

We suddenly realized the afternoon had stolen away, and the short winter evening had given way to dark. We picked up our sandwich wrappers and milk jars, and set off running down the familiar road. Bursting out of the woods, we ran through the houses in well-known shortcuts for home. Lights were on in kitchens, looking warm and welcoming as we raced through between the houses, keeping in lights cast from windows. We could smell the glorious food smells of collards here, fried chicken there, something unknown but deliciously spicy coming from over there. As we burst breathless into my house, we could smell the lima beans and ham hocks simmering on the kerosene stove, and our mouths were watering.

"You girls! Late again! What'm I gonna do with you all?" Mama banged her wooden spoon down in the sink and turned to look at us.

"Ruby Anne! Barbara Nadine! Y'all jus' run along home now, hear?" She was aggravated enough not to notice our agitation right away. When my two friends made no move to obey, but stood solidly on either side of me, she frowned and looked closer at our solemn faces.

"Please, Mama, we gotta' talk to you. We gotta' tell you somethin'."

"What? What's wrong with you girls? Did something happen? Did something happen up there? Tell me! Are you kids OK?" She started counting arms and legs and looking for blood.

"No, no, Mama, it isn't that. We jus' need to talk to you. "Bout Barbara Nadine." The child in question started to sidle toward the front door at this, muttering words to the effect of "Never mind. It's OK. I be OK." Mama corralled her before she got to the door, marched us all into the living room and sat us in a row on the sofa.

"You jus' sit there. I'll call yo' mama, Ruby Anne, and tell her you gonna' eat wit' us." Ruby Anne brightened at this, until I kicked her ankle. Then she remembered why we were there, and sat with her hands folded while Mama made the call.

Then we told her.

Afterward, Mama just sat there, tears rolling down her face. Then she drew Barbara Nadine into her lap, and gently cradled her while she took my jacket off her, revealing the awful evidence. "OK. OK. There ain't gonna be no more, Baby. It's OK now, Baby. You'll see. You gonna be safe, now, Baby. Oh, my pore Baby!" She rocked Barbara Nadine in her arms, and Barbara Nadine began to cry again. Ruby Anne and I were sent to wash up and set the table.

Papa and Jack came in, and Mama told us to go to my room and get Barbara Nadine another shirt, then to set down and eat. She ladled out steaming bowls of beans and ham and put corn bread on a platter. Papa had seen Barbara Nadine's arms, and opened his mouth to exclaim, but Mama shushed him with a glance and they went into their room. Jack was allowed to go with them, since he was seventeen and almost a man. He was taller than Papa, and solid muscle. He already had a motorcycle bought with money he made from working after school, and he rode with the Copperheads, over in Oakland.

We ate with relative silence, wondering what they were saying, but not daring to approach the closed door. While we were all antsy, wondering how things would turn out, we were also near starvation, and ate copious quantities of the savory beans and cornbread. We weren't as enthusiastic about the mustard greens, but with white vinegar on them, and pieces of fatback hidden here and there in the folds, they were a lot better than we let on.

After awhile they came out, and sat down to eat. Papa was gray with rage, and his hands shook as he spooned food into his mouth, but he kissed all three of us on top of our heads before he sat down. Jack buttered a piece of cornbread extra thick and gave it to Barbara Nadine, but he just passed the platter to me and Ruby Anne when we asked for seconds. No one said anything.

Finally, the meal was over, and Mama sent Ruby Anne home. She took Barbara Nadine into the bathroom and cleaned up the sores on her arms, then dressed her up in one of my flannel nighties like she was a baby. She told us we could read in my room for awhile, then had to go to bed, and that she, Papa, and Jack were going to go out for awhile and tell the Johnsons Barbara Nadine was going to be living with us. At that, we gleefully smiled at each other, and ran to my, no, our, room. Mama asked Miz Whitney from next door to kindly step over and stay with us for awhile, and they left.

I don't know exactly what was said or done that night, but they weren't gone long. Both Mama and Papa came in to tuck us in, and kissed us good night, and even Jack stuck his head in the door and said, "Night, you little boogers. I suppose you gonna' be double trouble, huh?" before closing the door almost all the way.

Very late that night, I woke up to the sound of a sort of scratching-knocking at the front door. I could hear Mama and Papa grumbling and mumbling in bed, then Papa got up and kind of staggered to the door. I heard him cock the shotgun he kept 'way up over the door where we couldn't reach it.

"What? Who dere?" He didn't sound too welcoming.

A soft, scared voice I couldn't make out. I shook Barbara Nadine awake to listen. This had to be interesting.

It be Barbara Nadine's mama! When Papa found out who it was, he let her in and went to get Mama. We had to shut the door quickly, because she looked to make sure we were asleep. We just made it back to bed. As soon as she shut the door, we were up and out again, easing the door open.

"Mr. Dubois, I know you don' wanna' talk to me, and you got ever' right not to let me in yo' house. But, if I could jus' talk to Mrs. Dubois a minute?"

"Umph. You wanna' talk to her, Helen? I'll make you all some tea."

"Thank you, Jackie. C'mon in, Mrs. Johnson, and set. You look frozen. We have some tea in jus' a minute. What you like to tell me?" Mama sounded calm and easy, but not happy, if that could be. I think she was ready to stomp ass and take names, but wanting to be fair before she did it.

"Well, uh, well, Mrs. Dubois, it like this. I know you think I ain' no kinda mama, nor Harry Lee no kinda' daddy. And you right. You right. I know what Harry Lee done gonna' get him straight to hell and damnation. It ain' I didn't try, but I jus' couldn't keep him off them girls. He done made my Jesse Louise run off and start 'ho'in in the City, and wan't nothin' I could do to get her back. Then, he after Barbara Nadine, and it jus' break my heart. But I can't make him stop."

"Have you ever tried to leave him, or have him arrested?"

"Oh, Lawdy! He'd kill me! I cain't put him in no jail! What'ud the kids and me do then? And I can't leave him. Where'ud we go, me 'n' all them kids? Harry Lee ain't a bad man, really, he ain't. It jus' he get liquored up, and he don' have good sense. It jus' that ole' booze that make him mean. Why, he couldn' get along, 'thout me lookin' after him. '"Sides, when the preacher said 'until death do us part,' I reckon that's the way it gotta' be.

"But what I come to say is I'm right glad and thankful you done took Barbara Nadine in. She my baby girl, and I love her fierce. It be better for her here with you'uns, and I thank God she have a chance. My Daddy done me like Harry Lee's doin' her, and I wisht I coulda' got away somehow, but I didn't. Not 'til Harry Lee married me when I'us fourteen. If I have to lose her, it's best to good folk like you, 'stead of the City like Jesse Louise, shamin' us all by bein' a 'ho."

"Why, Mrs. Johnson, I know you love your baby girl, and me 'n' Jackie do, too. I know it hard for you to give her up, but I promise you, we gonna' raise her up right, and you'll be right proud 'a her. Maybe you can visit her when Harry Lee not home or somethin'.

"Would you like more tea?"

"No, no. Thank you kindly. I best get back befo' Harry Lee wake up and find me gone. He do wake up some time. Mrs. Dubois ..."

"I know, I know. It be OK, Mrs. Johnson." Both womens were crying, and I could hear Barbara Nadine snivelin' beside me. Suddenly, she darted out of the room and hugged her Mama, real tight. Then she ran back and slammed our door.

And that was how Barbara Nadine came to live with us. After awhile, it seemed like she had always been there.

I loved having a sister, and we settled into our new lives with gusto. We started scouring the whole of Marin City look-ing for snuff can lids so Mama could make us matching jingle dresses for pow wows, and we started to learn the fancy dancing. Terry Waitingsnake was already winning prizes, and was rapidly evolving into the champion women's fancy dancer she would become. She had her own shawl, and Mama and Auntie Mary even beaded her a buckskin dress. Barbara Nadine and I liked the jingle dancing better, and our dresses were made of felt trade cloth and trimmed with cowry shells and the triangular jingle bells made of the bent snuff lids. Ruby Anne could only dance in the "All Tribes" round dances, of course, but she had a dress and all anyway. She went with us to the pow wows most of the time, just to watch us. We all started to learn beading, and made our first moccasins and leggings before we were twelve.

Once, when Barbara Nadine and I were fighting over some stupid little thing, I called her "white trash." Immediately after it left my mouth, I was horrified, and Mama washed my mouth out with Fels Naptha soap, then made me apologize in writing. After, she sat us both down and told us Barbara Nadine was Cherokee and Cajun now, just like me, and that she was entitled to dance all the Cherokee or All-Tribes dances, because she was adopted into the tribe by living with us as a daughter. She wasn't the only blond head at the dances, either, just as I wasn't the only African-Indian-White. Everybody just accepted us just like we were.

It's too bad this wasn't true outside of Marin City.

Chapter 5

NAPA

I don't remember quite when I began to see Napa Bob different. He had always been around, more than the others, because he was Jack's best friend. When I was little, he was sort of an extension of Jack, just another big brother. He and Jack were both Copperheads when they got to be fourteen, and often the whole bunch of them would ride into Marin City in formation, and mill around awhile playing the role, and amazing the locals. Mama and Papa always made any of them welcome, and there'd often be several just sitting around talking' bikes with Papa, or drinkin' pop or whatever. Mama didn't allow no drinkin', or nothin' in the house. Most of 'em were a lot older, of course, and the younger ones were more or less "in training," running errands and such. It was a reg'lar motorcycle gang, "one percenters," called that after some American Motorcycle Association guy made a statement that most bikers were law-abiding, good citizens, members of the AMA, and the rest, the hoodlums and the rough "outlaw" bikers like the Copperheads, the Mo-Fos, (them's really "Mother-Fuckers," but they like to see they name in the papers an' all, and wouldn't none a the papers print it that way, so they took up callin' theyselfs the "Mo-Fos. 'Course, the cops woulda' arrested 'em for wearing colors with "Mother-Fuckers" on 'em, too, so usin' the short name took care of a couple things at onct.) and the Hells Angels, were less than one percent of bike riders. Well, of course, the boys took that up, and a lot of them proudly wore a "1%" emblem on their colors to emphasize how tough they were. And they were, of course, some more than others. The Copperheads mostly played the role though, riding around in formation and lookin' good.

Jack and Napa Bob used to ride us around, and Napa became my special friend. He would take me to Playland, and let me ride anything I wanted. He always had money, because he worked in a bike shop as a mechanic. He lived by hissef on an old houseboat down by Sausalito, even though he was only a kid, and if he was home when Barbara Nadine, Ruby Anne and me walked by going to or from the old wharf in Sausalito where we used to go to fish for perch, he'd have us come in and give us pop he kept just for us. He had a cool place, with lots of stray cats he fed; he really liked cats. He named them all, and took 'em to the vet for doctoring, and to be fixed so they wouldn't have no more babies. He didn't mess much with anybody but Jack and us, and he liked Mama and Papa, even gave Mama flowers, store-bought flowers!, on Mother's Day and Christmas, but otherwise he din't have much to say to "citizens," which was what the bikers called the non-bikers.

I suppose us kids was citizens, but we was girls, and little. There weren't no girls had their own bikes, just "biker girls" who hung around, and "Old ladies," who were married to the guys. I don't think they liked us much, but nobody messed with Jack or Napa, even the older guys. They were afraid.

When we got to be teenagers, we figured out that Napa Bob was considered real cool, and real, real bad. A mean motorcycle an' a bad go-getter. He was so tough nobody would fight him. He moved like a cat, and always could get a knife out and open before you could blink. Him and Jack never talked about what they did with the Copperheads, but I heard Papa yellin' at 'em from time to time. Jack al'us told him that they weren't doin' nothin' bad, and things'd cool down after a bit.

Napa got his name from havin' to go on down and stay at Napa State Hospital from time to time. Wad'nt really nothin' wrong wit' him, but he got a little crazy sometimes, and would sit in his houseboat in the dark, smokin' and not eatin' or nothing.' Then Jack would go get him, and take him in for a "vacation," they called it. He al'us lef' food and water for the cats, though; enough to last 'em when he felt it comin' on. He never hurt nobody, least of all us, so Mama and Papa never minded us hangin' around him. Sometimes him and Jack'd take us to the beach, and we'd have a high ole' time, playin' in the water. I noticed as I got older, though, him and Jack quit roughhousin' with me 'n' Barbara Nadine quite as much. But they still took us, and splashed us and chased us, an' stuff.

It was one of those times, at Muir Beach, that I noticed him. Really noticed him, for the first time. I was about fifteen, and Napa Bob musta' been about twenty, I guess, and it was just Napa Bob and me. Barbara Nadine had gone to visit the Waitingsnakes with Mama, and Ruby Anne was off somewhere. She was in love with some ole' bus driver then, and used to hang around the Greyhound bus station, waiting to have him drive in. She knew his schedule, and would just hang around all day, waiting for him to come in. He knew her, and would sometimes buy her a coke if he had a layover for a few minutes, and she'd go on and on about it for weeks after. It was sorrowful, no shit. He was an old man, f'crissakes, and pro'ly had about a hundert kids. But she thought he was so cool! Jack was in the Navy, stationed at Treasure Island, and I guess he din't have off. Napa Bob was in the Army, and he'd come and go, but he was around for awhile.

"Hey, Napa, you know, you don't never say nothin' 'bout where you go or what you do in the Army. You changed since you been in. What's happenin', Daddio?"

"Tawny, you never mind. It ain't nothin' you wanta' hear. You hungry? I'll go get us somethin' to eat."

It was always like that. Change the damn subject. He never said nothin' 'bout the Army, jus' disappear for months at a time, then show up again. Not like Jack, who was on a ship outta' Treasure Island, and came home a lot. Bof'um on leave from the Copperheads, but Jack a Road Captain. Talk was, Napa Bob'ud be a War Captain when he come outta' the Army.

"Yeah. I could eat somethin'. Want me to come?"

"Nah. I be right back."

I watched his body flow sinuously over to his bike and over the smooth leather of the saddle. His lean legs with their silken, hairless skin molded themselves over the swell of the machine like a snake fitting itself over a warm belly. His powerful thighs tightened and gripped as he kicked the starter over. He was only wearing low-slung Levi cutoffs and biker boots pulled on over his wet skin, and his blue black skin gleamed with water. The sight made me feel strange, with a hot ache between my legs. It surprised me, and I thought about him while he was gone.

By then, I'd read a lot, and realized his family must have been direct from Africa after the slaving days, as he apparently had no white blood at all. He was a beautiful blue black, with high cheekbones and a hooked nose. Once he said something about his family coming from Damascus, but I didn't understand it at the time. In school, and the way folks talked, "we" were all just "coloreds," or "niggers," or, politely, "Negroes," lumped together like we were all the same, no matter what the reality was. My family was really Cajun-Burnt Sugar Cherokee, but to everybody else outside of Marin City or Indian country, we were just "niggers." But we saw differences amongst ourselves, and, we, too, mostly believed the whiter, the better. And no white slave owner had ever darkened his great-grandmother's door! He was tall, with broad shoulders, and smooth muscles everywhere. His belly was flat, and caved in to his hipbones, with a tiny, thin line of baby soft hair barely visible running down his belly into the unknown wonders of his jeans. I read a lot of what Mama called "trashy romance novels" then, and had an idea that what lay beyond the rolled-over borders of his jeans waist band was equally fascinating.

But I also knew Mama'd kill me. Or Jack. Kill Napa Bob, too. And I knew Napa Bob wouldn't ever take advantage of me, either. I think, though, that he'd noticed that I'd grown up, and once in awhile, I caught him looking at me with a strange look on his face. But with his shades, it was hard to tell.

When he got back with the hamburgers, fries, and cokes, I tried again.

"Napa, how come you didn't join the Navy like Jack? He be real disappointed, I think. You guys was al'us talkin' 'bout how you'd join up together and all."

"Yeah, I know. I tried, Tawny, but the Navy wouldn't take me because of me goin' to Napa. The Army did, though." He snorted, then said, "Fuckin' Army take anybody. Jus' cannon fodder."

"Cannon fodder?"

"Yeah. Jus' meat to be killed for some white man's oil company, or bananas, or somethin'. Ain't never over somethin' for us niggers, you can bet."

"Whatchu' sayin'? That sending men to war ain't to save democracy, or somethin'?"

"Sheeeeut. Fuck this, Tondelayo. Lay off. Jus' don' pay no nevermind about that bullshit they teach you in school about wars, and why we fight them. You unnerstan' mo' when yo' older."

"Napa Bob, I ain't no baby! I'm fifteen, I read the papers, I listen to the radio, and I'm a woman!"

At that, he turned and looked at me, leisurely and thoroughly. I felt the hot, tingling ache again.

"Well, you gettin' there, baby. You gettin' there. You gonna' be a real worry to me'n Jack, ain't you? Maybe it time we put out the word to them boys al'us hangin' 'round yo' house." His voice took on a teasing tone.

"Huh! Don't you worry, Big Man, I kin take care'a mysef! Don' need no babysitter runnin' mens away."

"Mens. Sheeeeeut!" He scooped up a handful of sand and threw it on my legs, then got up in one fluid motion and ran into the water. I watched his tight, round ass and smiled, feeling something new, yet very, very nice. I raced after him, and we both got caught by a big wave that threw us to the sand, laughing and sputtering. We were rolled over and into each other, a tangle of arms and legs and bodies, and I felt an electric thrill run through me when he momentarily was over me. I think I hoped he'd touch my breast or something, but he didn't. Shit.

Two years later, there was a definite change in us all. Barbara Nadine and I were seventeen, and going out with boys. Barbara Nadine never wanted to go out with anybody alone, so we always double-dated. Papa and Mama liked that better, too. We had a midnight curfew, and had to bring anyone we went out with over to meet Mama and Papa first, but we were allowed to go out in cars and so on. Napa Bob and Jack were men, fully grown, and Korea was a nightmare never far from our thoughts. Napa was gone even more, and when he was home, he was real quiet and still. He hardly seemed to move, and his face showed nothing. He was War Captain with the Copperheads and spent most of his time with them when he was around, but he still came over sometimes. Then, he'd smile and tease us some, but it was different. He wore shades all the time. Even his brothers in the Copperheads feared him, and later, one of them told me they were uneasy because he was a man who could kill so easily, so casually, with no apparent feelings at all. At the time, of course, none of us had any idea he ever killed anybody, nor that the Copperheads were beginning to do some business that was quite a lot more serious than they used to do. He was still on leave, sort of, but still War

Captain because he was home for a few months at a time when he was home. Jack wasn't President anymore, because his ship was at sea most of the time now, but the other Presidents kept Napa on as War Captain even though there were others who lusted after the opportunity to fill his position. Jack used to talk with us about it sometimes; now I think he wanted us to see a little better what bikers really were, and not just think of them all as brothers. He said these guys loved the excitement, the exhilaration of blood and total life and death power. Some of them sought out opportunities to inflict pain, even to torture and kill animals, because they felt such a clawing need to release their desires. But it was Napa Bob the Presidents wanted as War Captain, and he never even seemed interested in what he was doing. He just took care of business when it was necessary.

When he was with our family, though, he was different. Oh, he was still a lot quieter, and still, like a cat, but he would laugh and tease the folks and us girls like always. He sent us stuff, sometimes, when he was away; stuff from the Far East. Some of it was from Japan, fans and incense, and little incense burners, but some of it was from other places, with writing on it we didn't recognize. He was away for our Sweet Sixteen birthday party, but he sent each of us beautiful gold chains with a pearl and matching rings and earrings. Man, were all the other girls at school jealous!

It was a raw, wet November day, and Barbara Nadine and I were in school. The Principal came to our classroom doors; I was in English, bored to tears, while we labored through "Macbeth," stumblingly read aloud by the self-conscious victims picked by Miss Jones, and Barbara Nadine was in Chemistry, fooling around with some kind of stuff that turned into pink foam, she said. Our teachers spoke with the Principal, then called us out into the hall. My heart stopped, and I knew. I just knew. So did Barbara Nadine, she told me later. We were taken to our shared locker to get our things, and we just looked at each other, got our books out and went with the Principal. He drove us home himself. When we got to the house, we saw the black Navy car parked next to Papa's, who was supposed to be working, and the preacher came driving up just as we did. Neighbor ladies were going in and out, and everybody treated us like some kind of fairy princesses as we walked up the walk and along the porch. The Principal even had his hands on our shoulders. Inside, Mama was sitting next to Papa, kind of leaning against him, and she looked like she was stoned. Papa was holding her, and tears were streaming down his face, even though he wasn't crying. Two Navy officers in their dress uniforms were there; one with a cross on his collar sitting on Mama's other side and patting her hand. Mama looked like she didn't even know he was there. The doctor was just packing up his bag, and he said to nobody in particular, "maybe I'd best wait a minute here."

Mama blearily looked up and saw us, and big tears slid down her face. She tried to say something, but couldn't get the words out. Papa held out his other arm, and gathered us in, kissing us on top of our heads, and choking out, "Your brother's dead. Our Jack's done been killed in the war. His ship went down and there were no survivors. Oh, Lawdy, Lawdy, our baby boy's dead, girls!" He began to cry in earnest, then, and so did Barbara Nadine and I. Oh, my God. It couldn't be real. Not Jack. Not Jack.

I don't remember too much after that. I don't want to. The Navy officers went away, and fixed it with the Army so Napa Bob could come home on Compassionate Leave for the funeral. They came back a couple times, and did all the stuff to help put things together for the funeral, and the burial in the National Cemetery in San Bruno. Napa was always there, it seemed, helping out wherever he was needed. On the day of the funeral, the Copperheads, The Hell's Angels, the Mo Fos and all the other one percenter clubs formed a cortege that was miles long. The Copperhead's bikes were draped with blankets of red roses, and all the clubs sent huge floral pieces. Jack was a past President and a hero to all the clubs, dying in battle like a man. He'd been liked by everyone, even in the other clubs, and the turnout for the funeral has never been equaled for another biker. The Navy did the funeral, with a twenty-one gun salute, and a the flag draped over the coffin was folded up smartly and presented to Mama just so. It was really impressive, and it made us feel like the Navy thought a lot of Jack, too, even though he wasn't even an officer, just another sailor. The cemetery was so clean, and the lines of headstones so absolutely even and white; it was nothing like our old cemetery up over the hill. The rows and rows of headstones marking the last resting places of the dead made you think, though. So many dead from all the wars, and all lined up like that, so neat and exact. I wondered if their spirits ever realized they weren't in the military anymore, or if one or two of them managed to shift just ever so slightly out of line. But mostly, I held Mama's and Barbara Nadine's hands, and cried.

The neighbor ladies kept bringing food over, and we ended up having to throw a lot of it out, because we couldn't eat it all. The pastor dropped by, and even the Catholic priest came by, Papa being a Cajun and all. He was what you'd call a "lapsed Catholic." Mama was no Christian either, of course, being raised in the Old Ways, but she was polite and did her best to show a nice face to them when they called. She burned cedar, sweetgrass and sage, and offered sacred tobacco every day for a long time, though.

The family just tried to go on from day to day, and to deal with the knowledge that our Jack was never coming back. Every place I looked, I saw reminders of him. The kimonos he'd sent us girls, and the pearls Mama wore so proud with her black dress at the funeral. His boots and colors were buried with him, like he would have wanted, but the rest of his clothes were still there. Mama finally gave them to Napa Bob to give to anyone in the Copperheads who wanted or needed them. Napa was a lot taller and thinner than Jack, so he couldn't wear them. He did keep his German helmet with the spike on it though, and wore it from then on.

It turned out that Jack had made a will through the Legal Officer on his ship, and he left me his Hog. He and Napa Bob had taught us both how to ride a long time ago, and once in awhile, they'd let us ride them alone up in the hills, but I never thought I'd ever own my very own Harley Davidson, let alone his precious chopper, gleaming with chrome and black lacquer until it must've been six inches deep. Man, if that didn't cause all kinda' hell and ruckus at home! Papa was "damned if his 'lil baby girl was gonna' ride bikes wit' hoods and become one' a them biker 'hos'." Mama didn't like it either; many's the fight we'd had about me and Barbara Nadine turnin' into hoods; but she said if Papa had thought it was "OK for his son, then, by God, it was OK for his daughter." Besides which, I weren't raised to be no 'ho, any more'n Jack had been raised to be a hood, and jus' havin' my own bike wouldn't turn me away from my raisin'. There was a whole lotta' shakin' goin' on; yellin' and Papa sleepin' on the couch, and cryin' about Jack. We all got pretty wound up, but finally, we all realized it wasn't no Harley we was all upset so about, it was our Jack, dead. After that, we all jus' accepted the Hog as mine.

Barbara Nadine got his gold watch, and he had a lot of government insurance in the name of Mama and Papa. But none of it made up for his being gone.

It was right around then, I think, that Mama and Papa started really talking about leaving Marin City and "going home." Both Barbara Nadine and I, of course, wanted to stay and finish school right there, and Mama and Papa agreed that was impor-tant, so they wouldn't do anything until we graduated, but they did try and sort out where "home" would be. Papa wanted to go back to Loosiana, and his family, and Mama wanted to go back to the rez in Oklahoma and her family. They used to fight and argue something fierce. But either way, with Jack dead, and sleeping in San Bruno, they were troubled in their hearts about leaving him wherever they went. As for Barbara Nadine and me, we were ascared about growin' up and having to become whatever we were going to be. To think of doing it without

Mama and Papa, to say nothing of Jack, made it even harder to face getting up in the morning.

Nobody knew what to say to us when we went back to school, and the teachers were really nice to us for a change. There was an assembly once, and the school band played taps after the Principal gave a sad little speech, and read off a list of names of the dead who had graduated from Tamalpais, or gone there. That made us cry, but there were a lot of people crying, even some boys. There were a lot of names from Marin City.

After awhile, Napa Bob's leave was up, and he had to go. That was terrible. We all cried and cried, and held on to him like we were afraid he was going to leave and not come back either, just like Jack. He hugged and kissed Mama and Papa, and me and Barbara Nadine, and told us he'd be back for sure; he was too damn mean to die.

I rode Jack's Hog, now mine, back to the Golden Gate with him, and we went off to the little beach at Fort Barry for a while, just to delay his going. I started to cry again, and that was when he held me, and kissed me. It started out just one of those kisses like he'd been giving Mama and us, then it wasn't like that any more. He started pressing my lips harder, and his separated just when mine did. We were both breathing hard, and when I felt his tongue enter my mouth, I got so weak-kneed I almost fell. He put both hands under my butt and pressed me up against him, and I could feel him grown big and hard and urgent. The kiss went on and on, and we were entirely lost in it. My hips were grinding into him, without my willing it, and I could feel the most wonderful, burning, aching heat that frantically needed to be dealt with. I don't know what would have happened if we hadn't suddenly been slapped hard with a wave on the incoming tide and had to run for it. When we got back up the steep path to where our bikes were parked, he just got on his, and kicked the starter over.

"Bye, Tondelayo. Just remember, I'm always comin' back." He peeled out, headed for the bridge and was gone.

Chapter 6

THE DECISION

Suddenly, it was graduation, and Barbara Nadine and I were going to be officially grown up. It didn't feel like it in a lot of ways. Several of the girls from our class were getting married right after graduation, and some had already gotten pregnant and had babies, so it was fairly certain that we were getting there, anyway, even if we felt a little scared and excited, all at the same time.

We knew what we wanted, too. Not for us the big bellies and eternal tiredness of our friends who were in such a hurry to marry or have babies. Both of us had managed to remain virgins, being scared to death of becoming pregnant and ruining everything. Nossir. Not that we didn't mess around a little, of course, but "technical virgins" we were, and that's the way we'd stay. We wanted to end up differently than so many of the girls in Marin City, and we were determined to make real lives for ourselves. Mama, Papa, and Napa Bob had a lot to do with the way we thought, too. They wanted something better for us than poverty and hopeless, dead end jobs. All we had to look forward to was maid or blues singer (extremely unlikely, since I can't sing) for me, and maid, file clerk, or store clerk for Barbara Nadine. Nuh uh, honey chile', not us.

After Napa Bob got out of the Army, we had us a talk. He said he loved me as much as he could ever love anybody, but that he would never marry or live like an ordinary person. He couldn't. He didn't explain, but, somehow, I knew what he meant. He was like a wild leopard, solitary and living in the night, and he still wore his shades all the time.

Napa was even handsomer as a man, and biker girls tried to press their breasts and hips against him when they walked by and they were sure their old men weren't watching. But he never paid any attention, and he never stayed with any woman. Once in awhile he just fucked one of them, still wearing his shades. He took them off at our house, but his eyes were just black pits, and they scared me. Mama and Papa still welcomed him, and tried to treat him like the son he'd always been, but he didn't come by much. Once in awhile, he'd come for us, and we'd go to the beach, or up in the hills, one of us on my Hog, and the other riding with one of us. When I rode with him, I'd press myself hard against his back, and sometimes slide my hands up his chest and down his belly. He'd let me do it a little, then he'd move my hand. He told me he wasn't going to ruin me, and that he wasn't going to treat me like some biker girl. He said he knew someday I'd find the right man, and things would be good for us, but we both knew it couldn't be like that with us. And I knew he was right, damn it to hell. But he swore neither Barbara Nadine nor I would ever be harmed by anyone as long as he could prevent it.

So, anyway, the whole family sat around the breakfast table one day just before graduation, and talked about futures. Barbara Nadine and I both wanted to go to college. We knew that. What we didn't know was how, or what we wanted to do if we got there. Needless to say, money was a problem. Marin City wasn't noted for being able to send its kids to college, although good old Ruby Anne had actually won a scholarship to go to modeling school, in New York, no less. No one was looking when she had suddenly become extremely tall and willowy, and very, very beautiful. Neither one of us was likely to have the same fate befall us, and, oh, shit, we were going to miss her! Her going off to New York was the end of something we'd never really believed could end.

Mama and Papa said no chil'run of theirs were going to be maids, even though his own wife had had to do it, and there was no shame in good, honest work. So, Barbara Nadine and I felt it was time to tell them what we'd decided to do. We were going to enlist in the Navy, earn money from the G.I. Bill, take what courses we could on active duty, and get our degrees that way.

For a moment, there was total silence, except for Mama's sharp intake of breath. Papa looked stricken. Napa Bob slowly pushed his shades up on his forehead and looked at us. Both of us started talking at once, explaining all the benefits of this plan, and trying to come up with more and more reasons why this was the perfect solution. We both knew Jack's death lay heavy all around us at that moment, and we'd have to do some fast convincing to make them see this wasn't the same thing.

"Well, women don't have to go aboard ships, do they?" Bless Napa Bob.

"No. They mostly do office work, or work on radios or electronics, stuff like that. There's a whole lot of jobs..."

"You girls been talkin' to the recruiter, haven't you?" Papa held up his hand for silence. "I know. I know. There was women in the service during the Big War, you know. Did a fine job, too."

"Would you have to go to war?" Mama's voice shook a little, but she made a mighty effort to sound reasonable and calm. Signs were around that something was happening over in the Far East again, and Napa Bob had said he might be called up for active service again. The government said nothing was going on, but you'd have to be blind not to notice all the ships coming in and out of port, and all the troops passing through Alameda and TI. We were going to have a war, all right, no matter what the government said.

"No, no. Women can't serve in combat, fly planes, go on ships, none of that. Just nurses, and they're all officers." (Truthfully, though, we both thought it'd be pretty exciting to go to war; both of us thought submarines would be cool; sneaking around under water like that, striking where least expected. But, no way. Still, being in the Navy, and wearing the uniform was cool enough, we thought. The Navy had the coolest uniforms, and besides, Jack would never have let us do anything else. His opinions of the other services tended toward the obscene. Except for the Army, of course, and Napa Bob.)

And so it was decided.

Off to boot camp we went, of which the less said, the better. It turned out that Negroes, Indians, Japanese, Chinese or any kinds of girl but whites were rarer than hens teeth in the Navy. There were more in the Army, but then, there were more women in the Army. From the beginning, I could see how things were going to be. But I could stomp ass and take names with the best of 'em, and after awhile, everybody got used to looking at me. At first, a lot of curiosity was evident, and some of the southern girls bitched about me sleeping in the same barracks and eating in the same chow hall, but they soon learned to keep their mouths shut. We were in Bainbridge, Maryland, the real South, and I had a lot of real shocks, especially when we got liberty and went off base, but mostly, Barbara Nadine and I stayed on base with the few friends we made, and didn't go "on the beach." (The Navy talks differently; sometime back in the dawn of time, some of them had crawled out of the sea onto dry land, and had never managed to make the adjustment. So, everything was called the same as the parts and places of a ship. After awhile you got used to it, and forgot there had ever been another way to refer to things.) On base they had all sorts of things to do anyway, and we enjoyed ourselves. There was a movie theater, and a rec hall, and all sorts of classes in crafts, and bikes to rent, and other stuff. We didn't really want to go off base and deal with all the hassles. The streets were full of wise-ass, snot-nosed male recruits, pimples, shaved heads, and big mouths, anyway, and who needed that shit? God knows, not one of them could have lasted five minutes up against the smallest biker we knew.

By the end of the ten weeks, both Barbara Nadine and I were, by God, sailors. Squared away, and standing tall. When orders were finally posted, we were elated to discover we were going to be stationed near home. I would be going to Hospital Corpsman School in Great Lakes, then on to Oak Knoll Naval Hospital in Alameda, and Barbara Nadine was going to Yeoman School then to the Commandant, Twelfth Naval District, Treasure Island. Just across the Bay from home! But far enough away to still feel independent and grown-up. But before our schools, LEAVE!! Mama and Papa had so wanted to come to graduation to see us graduate, but of course, they couldn't afford it. So, they hadn't seen us in all that time, although we sent them our big color pictures of us in uniform, proudly holding our prized bucket hats on our laps with our pristinely white-gloved hands, collars perfectly starched, ties immaculate in the epitome of square knots, ends neatly stowed beneath our collar points. Everybody's was the same, with the same flag behind them, but to us, they were the very symbols of pride and individual achievement. We knew what they meant to Mama and Papa, and we were equally sure they were passed around all over Marin City and Indian country in San Francisco, Oakland, San Jose, and every place else relatives or friends were likely to be found.

Stepping off the bus in that familiar circle with the little wooden shack of a bus station we felt like conquering heroes. Even though we'd been riding Greyhounds so long we thought we were paralyzed, we managed to step high as we got off the bus. The driver had waited patiently for us at the last stop in San Rafael as we ran into the station and combed, primped, and put on fresh shirts and pumps. Off with the Granny Boots and fore and aft caps, on with real glory! He was really nice, and even got off and handed us down, saluting us smartly when we were on the ground. I guess he'd been in the Navy once, or something. Anyway, he was so nice to us, even though he was white! It hadn't been that way all the time, believe me. On the trip home, some of the states even had signs for whites and "coloreds" over the water fountains and bathrooms, and we refused to use them. Luckily, there was a little bathroom on the bus, and the drivers were all at least polite. No shit, some of the stuff we saw and endured came as a big, big shock. Barbara Nadine had it bad too, because we were together. I thought California was bad, but, man, did I have a lot to learn! Well, anyway, we were finally home!

Looked like half the population of Marin City was there, everybody clapping and hollering, and making us show 'em our single little stripes. I gotta' admit, though, we were pretty proud of those stripes, too. And pretty soon, we'd get two of 'em, and striker emblems, too, when we went to our schools.

We got to the house, and Mama and Papa had a big party for us. Papa'd got a lot of shrimp somewhere, and we had filé gumbo, and dirty rice, and boiled shrimp, and black-eyed peas, and okra, and collards, and milk gravy and——well, it wasn't no Navy chow, I'll tell you that.

Of course, the next day it was up and into the hills. We were up there all day, just going to our favorite places. They looked and smelled just the same. Grown up or not, we sure were glad to be up there again. Now we really knew we were home.

It was almost dark when we finally started back down the hill to go home, and we were just crossing the ravine where the Tarzan swing still hung when I saw her. She suddenly was there, where nothing but trees fading into the shadows had been a split second before. She faced me full on, looking me square in the eyes, just standing there. She was the biggest coyote I'd ever seen, and I remembered seeing her up there in the hills a couple of other times. I knew it was the same one, and had wondered about it, but I also felt deep in my spirit that she was the one who had been around me, following me, all my life. It was all right. I felt a deep, blood connection, and a sort of glad bonding in my soul. I heard Barbara Nadine take in a quick breath, then there were no sounds, no trees, no swing. Just me and her. She seemed to shimmer as she turned, and was gone as silently as she had appeared. Neither Barbara Nadine nor I said anything, just started to walk on back down to the house. Both of us jumped about a mile when a great big old owl swooped down right in front of us, its huge wings almost brushing Barbara Nadine's face. After that, we quit walking, and could have been described as running, if young lady sailors do things like that. The bright yellow lights from the houses never looked so welcoming before, and opening our own door and walking into the warmth and smells of Mama's cooking created a moment that I can still call up in the most minute detail.

Barbara Nadine said she heard that owl calling her name outside the window that night, but I didn't hear anything. Too much cornbread, I think.

By the time we finished our schools and reported to our duty stations, it was obvious we were at war, regardless of whatever bullshit the Feds were putting down. At the hospital, I saw a continuous stream of casualties coming in, and the stream got heavier by the day. The guys were in terrible shape, too, something I wasn't equipped to deal with. It took awhile to adjust. I was glad I wasn't a nurse. I also began to realize that going to war wasn't as glorious and exciting as I'd originally thought, submarine or no submarine. Later, I got to literally hate John Wayne for all his stupid movies and the way he convinced us all with such a horrendous lie about what war was really like. I hated him already for what he said about Indians (somebody asked him once if he didn't feel bad killing off all those Indians in his movies, and he replied to the effect that we were all a bunch of dirty, lazy savages that weren't using the land anyway, and killing us off was a heroic present to the rightful owners, or something), but now, I would like to have personally escorted him to Vietnam for a tour. Because that's where it was, the war; Vietnam. And Laos.   And Cambodia. And all those funny little countries nobody ever heard of before.

Napa Bob got called back, and off he went again. He didn't say good-bye this time. He just sent me a picture of him in some jungle, hung all over with bandoleers of ammo, guns, assault weapons, knives, no shirt (Ohhhhhhh, baby!) and shades.

Barbara Nadine was assigned to the Admin. office at COM12 at first, but she soon got moved right onto the Admiral's Staff. The Admiral's Writer, a most powerful Master Chief Petty Officer, Chief Manns, noticed how good her work was, and how squared away she was, and just snatched her up. I guess the Admin. Officer raised holy hell about it, but what the Admiral's Staff wants, the Admiral's Staff gets. Her job involved screening and separating all the incoming message traffic for the Admiral, so she had to get a high level security check. That got kind of complicated for awhile, and we had to explain that she wasn't really my sister, nor had my parents ever adopted her, or even been awarded guardianship, but she was over eighteen and could choose her own home, so her home of record became officially ours. We had a little party at home when that was settled; somehow it made it official. We were sisters!

Anyway, with me seeing the casualty lists every day, and Barbara Nadine reading all the message traffic, we didn't need to check the news. The government continued to lie, the hippies started demonstrating against the war the government said wasn't happening, and the coffins kept piling up in Alameda. It was a weird feeling, knowing what we knew, and being part of it, even if it was on the edges, and seeing the President and all those other politicians bullshitting and denying everything on TV. Then the TV started showing what wasn't happening, every day, in living color.

Barbara Nadine and I agreed we were actually quite glad we couldn't go to war. What we were doing was too close for comfort as it was.

Meantime, life went on, and we went to work, lived our lives in the barracks, and went home when we could. It never occurred to us that we shouldn't. If it weren't for the war, we'd have been having the times of our lives. Both of us took night classes toward our degrees, and we both got straight 4.0's on our evaluations, inspections, and tests. We were smart, were doing worthwhile and challenging jobs, and having a great time. We'd see our old girlfriends and people we'd gone to high school with, babies hanging on them, or digging ditches for the PG and E; those guys that missed being drafted somehow, and feel so lucky we'd made the decision we had.

For liberty, if we didn't go home, we'd go into the City, sometimes, and hang out at some of the bars where we wouldn't get hassled for my color. Sometimes, we'd go to one of the movies, just for a change, even though it cost a whole lot more than going to the movies on base. There were men, of course, but nothing serious or special. Barbara Nadine still wouldn't go out unless it was doubling with me, even though a lot of the white boys thought she was a fox. She didn't get a lot of shit, though, because being on the Admiral's personal staff kind of protected her. Her Chief, Master Chief Manns, was like God, and wadn't nobody gonna' mess wit' him! She was his assistant, now, and we both had our Petty Officer chevrons.

Man, that was one big thrill! Non-commissioned officers, man! Big time! Making rate was fast because of the war, and we both made it first time when we were eligible. My boss, Miss Monroe at the hospital must have been one of only a couple black nurses in the Navy, and she'd come back from 'Nam. Nobody gave her any shit, either, and she saw to it that I got temporarily moved around most of the hospital so I could learn as much as possible. She said if I was gonna' make it, I'd have to be two or three times as good, and I was damn well gonna' be, even if it killed me. She was from Oakland, and knew all about Marin City Kids, and what that meant. Meanwhile, she was teaching me couth, and all that shit, too, so I could "pass" as I went through the ranks. Of course, I already knew how to speak "properly," meaning "white," but it took some practice to do it when it was appropriate, and to revert back to "real Navy" for everyday purposes. Man, the Navy talk was a whole lot more colorful than we had been in Marin City. I soon learned that no job, no event, no accomplishment could be done in the Navy without the magic word, "fuck" utilized at least every other word in all its many permutations. It required an agility of tongue to get it right the first time, every time. I also had to learn how to look worshipful of my seniors, innocent of any thoughts of opposition, while figuring out how to do or get things done right. It was quite a tap dance, believe me. It took a week just to learn the "enlisted stare," which divulged nothing, while speaking volumes. And, of course, my compulsive reading continued unabated, which increased my knowledge base in so many ways.

Man, between Master Chief Manns and Lieutenant Monroe, Barbara Nadine and I were groomed to be princesses. It was they who convinced us to start taking college courses on base at night or on weekends, working toward commissions.

What with work, and school, and home, and so on, we didn't have a lot of spare time just for hanging around. That was good, because, it could be fatal it people noticed two women hanging around together a lot, regardless of the reason. Being "salt and pepper," Barbara Nadine and I were even more obvious than two white girls would have been. The Navy brass was convinced that all military women were either whores or dykes, and were death on women who were friends. So, there weren't a lot of friendships between or among women, period. The Women's Representatives were supposed to enhance friendship and solidarity amongst us, though, by taking us all on camping trips, and forming bowling leagues, and such. I never could figure that out. We weren't allowed to play baseball, though. Too "butch".

There were frequent witch hunts looking for lesbians, where whole groups of women were called in by the Security creeps and questioned over and over again. Shit, if even half the women were queer that they suspected, we never would have had time to go to work! But the mere whisper of Naval Investigative Service Office, or NISO, was enough to scare us all to death. F'crissakes, the truth was, most of us were virgins, and a lot of the girls didn't even know how dykes managed to "do it," or what it meant. Barbara Nadine and I did know one couple, and they were among the nicest, kindest, and hardest working girls in the barracks. Some of those other girls were a dead loss, man.

Anyway, there'd be a witch hunt, we'd all be hauled in and questioned and questioned, and questioned, and made to sign all sorts of shit that was supposed to be what we had said, and never was, and the agents would torment us, and threaten us, and try to scare us into giving them names of girls we thought were queer, or would say someone had said we were, and all that shit, but Barbara Nadine and I just played it cool. Hanging around with the Copperheads and Napa Bob had made it a little harder to scare us, I suppose. What was really terrible, though, was the time some poor little ole' girl for some itty bitty town in Alabama cut her throat in the bathroom after those NISO bastards had been after her for weeks. Shit, she didn't even know what it meant! But she was so scared after they said they'd tell her parents, and that she'd get a bad conduct discharge she just came back from questioning one day, walked through the day room with this funny, blank look on her face, and went into the bathroom. She didn't come out for such a long time, one of the other girls went in to see if something was wrong, and about screamed the barracks down. Man, blood everywhere! And here this poor little thing lay, blood slid down the basin, with her head off at this weird angle. She looked so small on that tile floor, and like such a baby. I don't think she was much past eighteen. I think her mama and daddy would have preferred her being homosexual to what they got back.

Yeah, not everything was copasetic in the Navy, that was for sure. There was a lot of shit, including nasty stuff like rapes and beatings, and abuse by seniors, but we were lucky.

Oh, of course there were the non-stop yells and jeers of the men when they saw women sailors, and there was the never-ending bitch about us women taking up all the shore billets forcing men to go to sea and all that, but it didn't bother us much. In the first place, if they didn't want to go to sea, why'd they join the Navy? Then, there were only a few thousand of us, anyway, so we couldn't possibly be taking up all the shore billets. But men like to bitch, and bitching is a way of life in the service anyway. Or, "gritching," I should say. A combination of bitching and griping. Master Chief Manns used to say if you couldn't hear a low, grumbling sound of constant gritching, you'd best go see what was comin' down, because it probably meant real trouble. That ole' Chief, he was one day older than water, and had been a Chief since Christ was an Ensign, and there wadn't nothin' that man didn't know. Nothing. He kept the Admiral afloat, no lie. Admiral admitted it, too!

Of course, by the time Barbara Nadine and I made Second, we could have requested to move out of the barracks and live on the beach. But rent was so expensive, and we had us a real room now, being PO2's and all, that we decided not to. Marin City wasn't the same, since they'd torn down all the old houses, and put up big, ugly cement high rises. The streets were even rerouted, and all the friendly little neighborhood places bull-dozed down to make concrete ghettos. Mama and Papa hated it, and kept talking about going back to Louisiana or Okla-homa to Mama's family's allotment land. Marin County was building up something terrible, and it made me sick to see what was happening all over. Some asshole was even going to build this city right over the beach on the headlands for rich people, and I felt like I was being raped when I heard about it. Fortu-nately, he was stopped, but Marin County was not the place I loved as a child. Marin City was still there, and Mama and

Papa, but going home wasn't the same. So, we just stayed in the barracks, and considered it home. We saved a lot of money that way, and were even able to give Mama and Papa some nice presents. We wanted to give them money to help out, but they wouldn't hear of it. So, we bought a refrigerator, and a stove, and a big color TV, and stuff like that for Christmas and birthdays. One year, we even bought Mama some little diamond earrings they had on sale at the Exchange! Oh, the look on her face!

Chapter 7

YELLOW BIRD

"Shee-ut, I'm tired of this damn rain, rain, rain." (Chorus of grunts of assent from all around.) "Gotta' get us some fuckin' wheels, Tondelayo."

Slouching around in the day room we're dispiritedly watching the steam form drops on the windows until one or two would add enough weight to overcome the inertia and run down to the sill in a sullen mini-rivulet. Other WAVES wandered in and out, curlers and bathrobes appearing to be the uniform of the day. The desultory slap of cards and the occasional whine of dismay at a misspent checkers move were virtually the only interruptions to the sound of rain.

"Yeah. I was thinking that myself. I was thinking maybe I oughta' give the Hog to Napa. He's spent so fucking much time taking care of it, and chroming it, and chopping it, and so on, I know he'd really love it like his own chile'. Maybe it'd cheer him up. He's so ... I dunno, blank or somethin' since he got back from 'Nam. We're due for orders in awhile, and I'm pretty sure the Detailer pukes won't let us stay here again. We could end up stationed clear across country or overseas. We need to get us four wheels apiece."

"Yeah. It's changin' so, anyways. And Mama 'n' Papa's talkin' 'bout leaving here now we're all grown. Marin City's not the same since they tore our houses down, and I think Mama wants to go back to Indian Country. She say she feel Jack cryin' some-time, wantin' to go back home. He born in Oklahoma, you know, and he don' like how things not the same here no mo'. I think Papa's beginnin' to think about Indian country, too. No work in Loosiana, jus' 'gators and snakes and big bugs. He don' like Marin City no mo, neither."

"Not the same, no shit! All those weirdos outside the gate alla'time, demonstratin', and tokin' in the Park in the City. Damn! Them hippie assholes are somethin' else! What the hell they know about war. Oughta' draft the whole damn bunch of 'em."

"I hope to shit in your flat hat, they are. Asshole rich kids, pretendin' to be pore. They oughtta' try it for real, see how fast they run back to Daddy. Shee-ut, Daddy sendin' money whilst they beg on the streets anyhow. Aw well, fuck 'em. Anyhow. That's a great idea about the Hog! Jack woulda' liked that. We've had our fun on it. Don't look too cool for Second Classes to be bikers, either, I guess. To say nothin' about rain, and cold, and shit from the cops alla' time. I don't like what's happenin' to the bikers. That Sonny Barger is some kinda' businessman, and where the Hell's Angels go, the other clubs follow. Shit, how long's it been since we's down at the Copperheads?"

"Long time. Napa don't want us hangin' around wit' them, and I gotta say, he right."

"What kinda' car you want? I want me a fuckin' long, black Cadillac." Barbara Nadine had a big, shit-eating grin splitting her face as she moved over to the sofa where I was flipping idly through an old copy of *Ebony*. This encouraged Jolene and Marsha to quit pretending to play cards and to move over to us to discuss this boss new topic, and the rest of the girls in the dayroom decided helping make this big decision beat the hell out of whatever they were doing, too. Soon, we had quite a group.

"Ooh ooh wee, Barbara Nadine. That's cool! You really gonna' get a Caddy, no shit?" Jolene was a little fluffy thang from Texas, about as smart as a box of rocks, and inclined to lust after big cars and old men. It was a new idea to her that Cadillacs could be procured by women in the same way men got them. Her heavily mascaraed lashes assumed their widest position as she leaned toward the source of all this new intellectual stimulation.

"Oh, Jolene, don't be stupid. She's probably going to get a Jag. Man, I can just see you, cruising around in a Jag convertible, your hair blowing in the wind!" Nancy, an Ohio girl, was an incurable romantic, forever dreaming of sunsets at the beach and handsome beach boys strumming ukuleles around her as she quaffed something revolting with a paper umbrella sticking out of it. (She got orders for Adak, though. Last I heard, she didn't like it much.)

We all happily discussed makes, models, and merits of various cars for the rest of the afternoon. It was a surprise to discover we barely had time to dress and make it to the Mess Hall for evening chow, where we resumed our discussion on tailfins, Continental kits, and leather tuck'n'roll. The rain had thoughtfully ceased some time prior, and the air smelled clean and freshly salted as we hurried over to eat.

Next day at work, I opened the discussion to include my buddies and co-workers at the hospital.

"Man, you gotta' get plenty of horses! Chick like you needs lots of horses under the hood! Say, you know Chuck over in the Pharmacy? He's got a GTO for sale, it's almost cherry. Got flames painted comin' out the hood, man, and dual pipes, glaspaks, dagoed and lowered..." Lord, I thought Joe was gonna' come, jus' talkin' about it. I dunno, though. GTO's don't turn me on like they do the boys. But, I agree to check it out.

"Wilson, over in Admin. has a Spider he brought back from England, he's talking about selling it now his wife's got herself pregnant."

"Yeah, but it ain't street legal, is it?"

The debate was the numero uno topic for days, as fantasies and vicarious dreams played out all over the dispensary. It was the same at Headquarters, only the suggestions tended to have less to do with torque and horsepower and more to do with reliability and dependability. Most of Barbara Nadine's coworkers were settled, married men with families, and they had a paternal interest in ensuring we foolish little girls didn't get seduced by shiny paint and white sidewalls. Girls, of course, could be depended upon to be completely innocent of carnal knowledge of mechanical things. They thought Barbara Nadine and I would be easy prey for such seduction, and they felt it was their duty to ensure we got the most for our hard earned money.

"Well, you can't go wrong with a Buick. I've always stuck to Buicks, and they've never let me down."

"I had one once. Biggest mistake I ever made. It spent more time in the shop than it did on the road. Burned oil like it was going out of style. Give me a Ford, any day."

Meanwhile, we made do with the Hog, and spent evenings and weekends cruising around, looking. Barbara Nadine stuck to the ideal Cadillac thing, but I was waiting for lightning to strike. The GTO, as it happened, wasn't as cherry as it was made out to be. The crumpled flames on its sides bore mute testimony to the losing side of an unequal conflict with an unyielding hard surface. The Spider was so small it was invisible to the hordes of trucks continually menacing it on the freeways. Chevys, Fords, Buicks, even the odd Lincoln, massively aging, but still breathing pimp's elegance. None of them me.

Life went on. The war, inevitably, was harshly present in the Commandant's office and at the hospital. I was assigned to a ward where I assisted the nurses in caring for surgical casualties, and their wounds were terrible beyond thought. It became a relief, an essential escape, for us to leave the barracks and head off on the Harley for San Francisco, Oakland, Marin, Santa Rosa. We spent whole weekends riding up and down the coast, and into the interior of Marin and Sonoma counties, exploring back roads winding in the valleys and hills, going out to Bodega Bay and seeing the gathering of the seagulls as ominous reminders of Alfred Hitchcock's "The Birds".

Then, lightning struck. Me'n'Barbara Nadine was out cruisin' around Marin on a beautiful, early spring Saturday. It was warm and sunny, and we was feelin' all right, Baby, in the groove. We was jus' making it on down the road in San Rafael when I seen her. Nearly killed us both, I hit the corner so fast. Barbara Nadine and me was layin' that ole' bike down on the road there for awhile before I could straighten us up and stop.

"Damn, Tawny, what the fuck?" Then she saw her, too. "Oh, migod. Ohmigod, ohmigod, ohmigod." We both stared transfixed at the used car lot on the corner. There she was, gleaming soft lemon yellow, pure and clean as spring.

We both started singing at the same time.

> "I saw her standin' on the corner, a yellow ribbon in her hair.
> "I tried to talk, but I jus' stuttered,
> "I tried to walk, but I was lame
> "I couldn't keep mysef from shouting,
> "Lookie there, lookie there, lookie there, lookie there!
> "Young Blood, Young Blood,
> "I can't get her outta' my mind!"*

Oh, yeah, man. Look so fine! She make my heart sing, and I knew she was gonna' be mine. Couldn't be no other way. We got off the Hog and sortta' dream-walked over to her. A cherry 1956 yellow Thunderbird, not a scratch marring her soft glowing sides. Oh, Lord, it's love.

"Hello there, young ladies. Yes, isn't she just a beaut? Just got her in today. Won't last long, that little jewel." The salesman

---

* "Young Blood" by The Coasters.

had come out of his trailer just as our impromptu chorus was ending. He put his hand caressingly on the gleaming yellow fender and ran it along the side and over the saucy Continental kit in a way I felt in my gut as taking obscene liberties. Hands off her, mutha! Slap you up the side 'yo haid! "I can see you know class when you see it. Don't see too many of these around anymore. We got a great deal on this, too. The owner died of old age, and he had it from the beginning. Real low mileage. Hardly ever drove it, must kept it in the garage and took it out to have it washed and waxed. He was 96, you know. Some sweet auto-mo-bile, isn't it?

"Umm." I tried to sound unconvinced, noncommittal, although I knew he knew. "It's kinda' old, though. Been around a long time." I tried not to let my tenderness show as I drank it in. Not a nick, not a scratch. Creamy leather seats and mahogany dash, brilliant chrome. It smelled like ambrosia, with a distinct new car smell. Not, of course, that I didn't know about spray cans of new car smell, and blacking of tires, and all that. But the brake pedal and gas pedal showed virtually no wear, the ash tray had never been sullied by a single ash, and the seats didn't show the impression of anybody's ass. Oh oh, Baby, you the one!

"Some things get better with age. Like women and fine wine," the salesman responded with a wink. "These little babies are classics. The new T-Birds aren't even in the same ballpark as the '55's, '56's and '57's. They get bigger and clunkier every year. And this one, why, she's practically like new. Say, how'd you like to take her out for a little spin?" I could tell he was willing to overlook our black leather and powerful Hog, considering the amount of financial security and independence they surely represented. (He hadn't missed the base sticker, either, and used car salesmen and cheap jewelry stores dearly loved sailors.) I hated the smirk on his shiny, greasy face as he handed me the keys with yet another wink. Showing me how broadminded he was. Willing to let a nigger girl drive his car, the Big Man. Shee-ut.

"You OK with this?" Barbara Nadine smiled and nodded.

"Yeah. I'll stay with the bike. You go on. Don't run down any cops, though!" She laughed as I gingerly backed the little buggy out of its space and drove away, slowly and sedately. For about two blocks. Then, gradually, my foot got heavier, and I fairly zoomed onto the freeway, the little Bird leaping joyously at my command.

"Got both tops, too." The salesman seemed to have his eyes mentally squeezed shut, with his grin falsely plastered against his teeth as we zipped along just slightly over the maximum speed limit. Finally, unable to contain himself any longer, he said, "Maybe you'd best slow down. Lots of CHP cars around this time of day." So, I obligingly let up on the gas, and took the next exit off the freeway. We made our way back to the dealership at a more reasonable pace, as I concentrated on shifting and listening to the faultless purr of the powerful engine.

"You know, Honey, if anything goes wrong, all you have to do is call me," he said, standing a whole lot closer than I liked. I casually swung around like I was going to say something to Barbara Nadine, and my motorcycle boot just happened to nick his shin. Hard. He moved back quickly, and continued, "I'll help you out, not that anything will go wrong," he hastily amended. "You can let me have your telephone number, too, so I can call and make sure she's running right for you." Clever, clever, you honky pig, I thought.

"Uh huh. Well, I'd like my father and boyfriend to come and have a look. What's your bottom price?" I may be smitten, but I'm not stupid. He named a figure significantly lower than the one on the windshield, but not low enough for Navy pay. I knew from that, though, that he was ready to do business. I studiously ignored the request for my telephone number, but gifted him with one of my more enchanting smiles just to keep him cooperative. Nothing like a stiff-dicked white man trying to show how liberal he is to do business with. I can bring them here this evening, if you're open?" I utilized my most formal version of the King's English to show how sincere and serious I was.

"Well, there's another party looking at her —," he replied with false thoughtfulness. "But, you know, I really would love to see you have her. You two are made for each other. Tell you what, you give me a hundred down and I'll hold her for you until tomorrow. You and your father come back and see what you think (What happened to my "boyfriend"?), but I tell you, she's made for you!" He was already assuming it was a done deal. And if it wasn't, well, he'd be a hundred bucks ahead, cash on the barrelhead, and nobody the wiser. I knew wasn't nobody else looking at her, she'd have told me somehow. She was saving herself for me. He had little doubt in his mind, though; he knew I was besotted.

"A hundred. Well —," I bit my lip. "I don't carry that kind of money with me. Uh, Barbara Nadine, how much cash are you carrying? I can write a check for $25.00, but I only have about $20.00 in cash."

"I can only come up with five bucks. That'd give us $50.00." Barbara Nadine didn't look up so the salesman wouldn't see the smile she was trying to hide. She was as fully aware as I was that we had both accumulated substantial sums in our respective bank accounts. Our shipping over bonuses and leftovers from our frugal living had been dedicated to providing ourselves with suitably elegant wheels. We'd been saving for over a year. Barbara Nadine had long ago quit providing her shithead parents with the major part of her paycheck. She'd found out they were still claiming her as a dependent for the Welfare, even though she'd been living with us since she was little, and was now in the Navy. That had really pissed her off. We'd both been sending Mama and Papa a regular allotment, but I had found out they weren't spending it, they were just keeping it for us. Daddy had told Barbara Nadine, "No, Sweetheart. That's your money to do with whatever you want. You jus' as much our baby as Tondelayo, and chil'run don' owe they folks a livin'."

So, it wouldn't hurt either of us to come up with a hundred bucks, but I noticed that nothing had been said about us getting anything back if we didn't buy the car. I'd cut my losses, if there should happen to be any. I would also demand a receipt.

"Well, we can only cover $50.00. This was unexpected. If that's not enough —." I let my voice trail off, and turned slightly, preparing to go off and leave my heart's desire forever. It was a virtuoso performance that almost wrung my own heart. Barbara Nadine swung her leg into the saddle, raising the kickstand as she did so. She straddled the machine, turning it on and revving up the engine to a smooth roar as it idled, ready to hit the road. Before I got my helmet on, he submitted.

"Well, OK. Since you girls weren't really prepared to find this little gem, I can understand the problem. You just give me the $50.00, and I'll cover the rest myself, square it with the boss. I'll need your telephone number, though, in case I don't hear from you." Uh huh. I quickly scribbled down the number for Napa State Hospital after we gave him our accumulated funds.

"We'd like a receipt, please." I widened my eyes and Barbara Nadine gave him a slightly shark-like smile. Grudgingly, he wrote out a promise to hold one yellow 1956 Thunderbird, California license plate DBR 1056 until the next day, with option to buy for Tondelayo Cecile Dubois, HM2, USN, upon satisfactory completion of a mechanical inspection by a mechanic of her choice. When he saw the USN, he looked stunned. He'd figured the bike belonged to my boyfriend. I could see the train of thought flashing through his nasty little mind. A woman sailor? That meant a regular paycheck, and cheap booze at the clubs. And a nigger, too. (At least he thought so. Asshole white people didn't seem to know what Indians looked like without their feathers and beads.) Too cool, man. It turned him on. This was everybody's lucky day! He adjusted his tight polyester pants that were betraying his thoughts, and was carefully smoothing the ducktail he had painstakingly combed over his bald spot as we dug out and roared off. My heart was pounding like a jack hammer. I slapped Barbara Nadine on the back, and we both laughed like idiots as we headed for Marin City.

Napa Bob was a real hot-shot mechanic, and he and Papa would go over that little beauty with a fine-tooth comb. With

Papa's stocky, powerful presence augmented by the looming person of Napa Bob, who was threatening even with a big smile on his scarred face, that honky salesman might find doing business with this "girl" a bit more daunting than he thought. He needed taking down a peg, the pig.

Well, Papa said it sounded good, he liked the little T-Birds, too, and I called Napa and asked him if he'd come over and go along to check her out. He seemed more interested in this than in anything in a long time; almost animated, and readily agreed. I hadn't seen him for quite awhile. When he got there, off we went.

The salesman came bustling out of his trailer when we all drove in, the old Buick with Papa and Mama, Napa on his monster Hog, and Barbara Nadine and me on mine. He stopped his advance abruptly when he got a look at Napa, who was, as always, dressed completely in matte black leather, with only a razor-embellished chain over one shoulder to relieve the darkness so deep it sucked in all the light around him. Only the shades reflected the lights of the car lot. There wasn't any "Honey" this time, by God. All business. The Copperhead colors did not go unnoticed either.

It didn't take long. She was mine!

So, it was a joyful and exuberant party that followed my triumphant entry into Mama and Papa's parking area back at the house in Marin City. Thelma, our neighbor, came dashing out of her house, brandishing a champagne bottle and followed by all the other neighbors, who were oohing and aahing in envious admiration. "It's only water," Thelma whispered when I looked alarmed, "I got the bottle from Joyce. You can christen her by pouring some on the hood, and I'll wipe it right off." She showed me the soft, much-laundered birdseye diaper she had in her capacious apron pocket.

"I name thee Yellow Bird!" The careful drops were poured onto the lemon meringue surface just behind the proud Thunderbird hood ornament and hastily wiped off. Sage appeared as if by magic from Mama's ubiquitous apron pocket, and the car, proud new owner, and the interior were smudged and purified as is only proper. The celebrating neighbors were also smudged and purified as they came forward shyly, one by one. They might not know exactly what was going on, or why they suddenly wanted the gentle, cleansing smoke to embrace them, but they recognized and respected the power, wanting to partake of its graceful sharing of itself. The party moved into the house, and fried chicken, potato salad, and an astounding array of tasty viands began to appear as from nowhere. It became a block party that would be talked about for months. Everyone celebrated my good fortune, and I was wrapped in a blanket of good wishes and proud congratulations.

I think that while it was still mercifully far away, a lot of the neighbors knew full well what Vietnam portended, and that the inseparable pair of little girls everybody had known almost all their lives were women fully grown now, and in the military, like so many of their sons and fathers. The coming of Yellow Bird gave reason for partying and joy, if only for the moment.

Chapter 8

DEATH

Oh, shit. Ohshitohshitohshit. Everything was white, with a thick, choking blanket of fog obscuring everything; all sound, all color. Just shapes. Lt. Monroe, her mouth moving, leaning toward me. Lt. Madden, her hand outstretched, tears coursing down her face. Why is she crying? Why can't I hear anything? Then, utter stillness, blackness. Nothing.

I woke up with Lt. Monroe holding my head down over the wastebasket, and felt the surge of bitter vomit coming. I couldn't stop it. Her hand was cool on my forehead, like Mama's when I had been sick as a little girl. But it was shaking. And she was crying, too. Officers crying? What the fuck? There was screaming in my head, back there somewhere. I could barely hear it. What was I doing? Why was I vomiting in the WR's office, for crissakes? And in front of not only my Women's Representative, but Barbara Nadine's. My God, what kind of sailor was I? I didn't hear what they said. Don't want to. No. No no no no no no.

"I'm sorry, honey. Barbara Nadine is dead."

What the bloody fuck is she talking about? This is ridiculous.

"Tondelayo, Barbara Nadine was found dead in the duty room this morning. They found her when she didn't show up for work after standing duty last night. The Chaplain and a Casualty Assistant Calls Officer are going out to her parents to notify them. I know she lives — uh, lived — with you and your family, but the Johnsons are still her legal next of kin. Maybe, if you feel you can, you'd like to go along. The Chaplain will go to your family, too."

"Dead? How can she be dead? She was fine when I left for school three weeks ago. What happened?"

"We don't know yet. There'll be an autopsy. The room was still locked from the inside, there's no sign of anybody getting in, and nothing obvious. She was just dressing for work, I guess, and death was sudden. Her heart, maybe. We just don't know yet. But, Tondelayo, you need time to absorb all this. I'm putting you on basket leave right now, and you go on home. The Chaplain will drive you. I'll take you over to the barracks to gather up anything you need. I know you probably haven't had time to unpack from school." The words were brisk, official again. Easier to respond to. Time to think about it later. Now, deal with business.

"No, thank you, Miss Monroe. I'm OK. I can drive. I want to get home and tell Mama myself before the Chaplain gets to my house. We'll call Papa to come home from work." So much easier not to think. Just take one step at a time, taking care of business. Gotta' think what to do.

As I wheeled Yellow Bird out of the gate and onto the Oakland Bay Bridge, I tried to think how to handle things. The Johnsons, well, Harry Lee, anyhow, would probably make a scene, hoping to get something out of it. They didn't know Barbara Nadine had changed her GI insurance over to Mama and Papa, and had listed them as Next of Kin, legal or not. There was bound to be trouble, those white trash shits. They'd kept listing her as a dependent for Welfare long after she'd moved in with us after Papa found out her Daddy had interfered with her since she was a baby. I hoped the shock would kill them, but probably no such luck.

The radio was on KWBR and playing loudly, as usual, but I was only partially aware of it as I threaded my way over to Marin City. Then, the doleful wailing struck home.

> "*...that was the death of an angel,*
> "*don' know why, oh why*
> "*I wanna' be beside her,*
> "*but I'm 'fraid to die...*"[*]

Oh, shit. How many times had we soulfully sung that in restrooms and cars? How many times had we really let loose on the screaming and crying at the end? *Death of An Angel* was our favorite song. And now, it had come true. I was crying, really crying, as I swung into the parking lot in front of the house. The Chaplain and the CACO were still there. Apparently, they'd gone there first, which was pretty fucking damn decent. I gathered myself together, wiping my nose, and stepped out onto the familiar packed dirt. I walked along the walk lined with Mama's "garden;" pots filled with pungent rosemary, geraniums, oregano, and other scented herbs. We didn't have our own yard anymore, but Mama refused to give up her garden. Between the pots, a riot of purple violets carpeted the open spaces, and an apricot tree miraculously spared by the bulldozers when the old houses came down and the new "cages" went up stood in solitary splendor. When the old houses were there, every one of them had a single fruit tree in the yard. It made me sad. More losses.

No! Military bearing! I marched myself up to the door, willing myself not to cry. I was a sailor, dammit.

"Oh, Baby! You're here!." Mama opened the door as I stepped up to it, and we hugged desperately. Her eyes were red, and her

---

[*] "Death of an Angel." Don Woods and the Velairs.

cheeks wet, but she was in control of herself. Papa was right behind her, and swept us both into his embrace.

"I can't believe it! How could it happen?" Mama kept repeating it. Papa just held her, and smoothed her hair, talking to her in Creole and ignoring the tears silently streaming down his own face. The Chaplain offered to pray with us, but Mama managed to say that we would do our own religious rites. She was dignified and polite, but firm. Mentally, I inventoried our supply of cedar, sage, sweetgrass and Indian tobacco, in case we needed to send to our cousins for some immediately. I thought we had plenty. If not, I was sure the Waitingsnakes in San Francisco would. The Chaplain took it with good grace, and satisfied himself with looking compassionate and offering to do anything he could to help us through. He was really very nice

The CACO cleared his throat, and spoke.

"Well, Barbara Nadine did name you folks as beneficiaries for her SGLI, and she also left a will leaving all her possessions to Tondelayo. She was of age, so she could do that. I couldn't find a Power of Attorney, though, regarding her wishes for a funeral, nor to whom she delegated the decision-making authority. That may prove contentious, as her birth parents may wish to participate in that decision. The Navy, of course, will provide all possible assistance with filing necessary forms, funeral arrangements, and so on. I will be at your service in any way possible to help you all through this sad time." The CACO was very young, and nervous, which made him sound somewhat pompous, but he seemed eager to help. "The Chaplain and I should go notify her birth parents now. Tondelayo, would you feel like going with us? It may be of some comfort to them. Your mother and father have said they feel they should go over to offer condolences a little later, after the Johnsons have had time to absorb the shock.."

"Hell, no, I don't want to. She despised them, and they treated her like dirt. Just wanted what they could get out of her."

"Now, Baby, I think maybe you're being a little hard on Barbara Nadine's mama. You know she loved her, and she'll be hit hard. It isn't right you lump her in with Harry Lee." Always the sweet voice of reason, Mama. I didn't feel like being reasonable. I wanted to hate both Johnsons. I wanted to kill anybody who got in my way. I wanted to do whatever it took to make it not true. Rage and despairing grief fought with one another in my gut. But I knew what I had to do.

"Oh, OK. I know I should. I'll go. It may get down and dirty when they find out they aren't gonna' get anything. I don't want to miss the look on their faces." Grimly, I turned to follow the men out the door.

"Tawny, honey ..."

"Yeah, Mama, I know. Maybe somewhere in her little shriveled up heart her mama cared about her. I'll try." I went out and caught up with the Chaplain and the CACO. We got in the car, me in back, and drove over to the part of town the Johnsons infested now. Since the rebuilding, they no longer lived within spitting distance of us, and that had been a blessing to us. Barbara Nadine had tried to see her brothers and sisters from time to time, but it never seemed to go very well. But her mother had given her birth, raised her from a baby, and maybe she did have some sort of feeling for her. Who knows. Anyway, her daughter was dead. Barbara Nadine Johnson was dead. My sister, my friend, my soulmate was dead. And now, I was going to that boar's nest to tell her biological parents. Shit. This whole thing sucked. But it was just one more thing to get through without breaking.

It was, if possible, even worse than I'd expected. Harry Lee Johnson was home, and drunk, of course. Drunk, and mean. Pearlie Mae was resting, and came out of the back of the house when Harry Lee bellowed for her to come to answer the door when he saw us coming up the walk. The door hung open, with the broken screen hanging crookedly on its one remaining hinge. We could smell the stale smoke, booze and pee a long ways before we got to the door. Pearlie Mae looked faded and doughy, with a floury lump of a face with its moist, reddened beak of a nose poking out. Most of her teeth were missing. Stringy no-color hair hung greasily around her shoulders, and she was wearing broken down house slippers far too big for her so she scuffed like some kind of mental patient across the filthy floor. She looked at me dispiritedly, then at the uniformed officers behind me, and moved aside to let us in without saying anything. Then she backed into the kitchen, half in, half out, knowing this was bound to be a man's matter.

The stench of dirty diapers permeated the room, and empty beer cans and empty half pints of cheap whiskey littered the floor around the broken down recliner that constituted Harry Lee's throne. An ancient black and white console TV sat directly in front of the split plastic footrest protruding like a sullen underhung lip of the chair, so situated that anyone attempting to pass through the living room had to squeeze painfully around the front of the oil stove to get to the dingy hallway leading to the rest of the house. The uncarpeted floor was liberally splattered with spilled ash and burned spots where cigarettes had obviously been left to smolder out on their own when Harry Lee's dangling fingers had lost their numb grip. A baby screamed down the hall, and Pearlie Mae scuttled around the TV, pushing her gelatinous mass into the wall to avoid disturbing the snarl of extension cords and antenna lead.

Harry Lee blurrily looked at us, and some stray ray of thought penetrated his befogged brain that there were fully uniformed, official-looking officers standing in his living room.

"What?"

"Mr. and Mrs. Johnson, I am Chaplain DeMarco, and this is Lieutenant Junior Grade Wilson. It is our sad duty on behalf of the United States Navy to inform you that your daughter, Barbara Nadine Johnson, died this morning. We are here to assist you in any way possible."

"Oh, Lordy, Lordy. My pore' 'lil gal! She's done gone and 'lef me!" Harry Lee sniveled and tried to generate a tear. He failed. I was surprised he remembered who Barbara Nadine was.

"Oh, Mama! Our chile' is gone! The angels done take her to the Lord!" Harry Lee sniveling was a grotesque sight. Particularly since his little ferret eyes peeked out from under his hairy brows to gauge the effect of his grieving upon his audience. It was a relief when he judged his lamentations adequately expressed, and got down to business. Pearlie Mae's face had crumpled, and she was wiping snot on her sleeve, but she didn't say anything. I looked closer at her, and decided like she looked pretty much like death herself. Maybe she did care. At this point, I didn't care if she did. Barbara Nadine was dead, and it was everybody's fault, including her mama's.

"Now, who's gonna' pay for the buryin' and all? We's pore folk, and it seems like ..." He didn't even bother to ask what had happened.

"There is no problem, Mr. Johnson." The CACO's face remained bland and expressionless. Good for him! Junior he may be, but he could mask his feelings like a pro. "The Navy will, of course, provide assistance with all the arrangements, and if a military service and burial in a military cemetery is desired, we will make all the arrangements." The CACO shuddered almost imperceptibly as he moved closer to Harry Lee's chair, and he tried to look suitably compassionate while presenting an air of capable officialdom. "Now, Barbara Nadine did list the Dubois family as her Next of Kin, so ..."

"Insurance. Ain't they some kinda' gov'mint insurance?" Harry Lee interrupted him.

"Yes, there is. However, the policy beneficiaries are shown as the Dubois'. I have a copy here for you, as well as a copy of her will." The CACO handed a manila envelope to Harry Lee and hastily backed away.

"Shit. I cain't read. Ain't got my reading glasses. What's all this shit say?" Reading glasses, my ass. The sonuvabitch was illiterate.

"Well, Mr. Johnson, as I said, the insurance benefits will be paid to the Dubois family. The balance of her estate; her personal effects, her bank accounts, and so on, are all specifically willed to Tondelayo Dubois." A smirk almost made it across the CACO's face, but not quite. The Chaplain moved closer to me.

"What! Why them niggrahs ain't ..." Harry Lee stopped himself in a spray of indignant spittle, and a furtive look entered his eyes. He remember he was supposed to be a grieving daddy. Time enough to deal with this later. Surely no no-'count niggers could usurp a loving father's true rights to his own daughter's insurance money. "Well, what does that mean, anyhow? Does that mean they got to pay for the buryin' and all?"

"No, not necessarily, Mr. Johnson." The Chaplain intervened. "As I explained, if a military service and burial in a national cemetery is desired, it will be covered by the government. If other arrangements are preferred, then a certain amount of assistance will be made available. It isn't clear just to whom Barbara Nadine wished to leave the responsibility for decisions regarding her funeral, but perhaps you and the Dubois would want to mutually agree upon the details. She was your birth daughter, of course, and I'm sure she would have wanted both her families involved."

Bullshit. She fucking wouldn't have wanted any fucking thing of the kind. Some father and mother you were, you fuckers! Well, be nice, Tondelayo, be nice.

"We can all decide together, maybe. I think Barbara Nadine would like to be cremated, and her ashes be scattered up in the hills ..."

"No! No, by God. My chile' ain't gonna be burned up like no savage! An' I wanna' know what happened to her!" This last part was a desperate screech. Pearlie Mae's eruption surprised us all. I'd almost forgotten she was lurking there in the shadows, baby straddling her hip. She looked astounded at her own temerity, and glanced quickly at Harry Lee to see if he was going to tolerate such an unprecedented outburst. She edged back around the TV and resumed her place in the kitchen doorway. Two small children edged out in her wake, grimy hands clutching her faded apron.

"Now wait a minute here. Me'n' the wife's gotta' think about this. You say the Navy will put her in the military cemetery? Free?"

"Yes, and if you like, with full military ceremony; an honor guard and a 21-gun salute, and Taps at the end." The Chaplain dangled the carrot in front of Harry Lee, hoping to soothe him. It would not do for Harry Lee Johnson to lose what little control he did have, and he was obviously spoiling for a fight.

"There some kinda' death payment or somethin' if we go that way?" Old Harry wasn't going to miss a shot.

"I'm sorry, there are no funds other than those standard funds included in Barbara Nadine's SGLI policy."

"That cain't be. Who's tryin' to rob us? Usn's got rights! Here we done los' our pore lil angel chile', our own blood, and some uppity niggers got they fingers in the pie. We'll sue!" His face purple, Harry Lee suddenly seemed to realize his attitude might not be making a good impression on the officers, who simply stood and gazed implacably at him. He deflated, and muttering, sat back in his filthy chair.

"But I certainly do want to have your help in deciding the funeral arrangements," I interjected, to distract him. I was surprised that Pearlie Mae had defied her normally silent assigned role to speak out, and felt that maybe I ought to consider her wants if she felt so strongly about it. Maybe she even dimly felt some shame about her betrayal of her daughter, and wanted somehow to make amends. But I was tired, and slightly sick, and just wanted to go home. I'd think about it later.

Just then, Harry Lee belched, and spoke, "We wants us a military funeral. You heard the wife. We ain't gon' have our girl burned up like some savage, then jus' thow'ed away like trash." For the first time, he turned and looked directly at me, hatred contorting his face. "Yeah, I jus' bet you'd like to thow her away up there! You kids up there in them hills alla' time. Gawd only knows what you be doin'. I never shoulda' let them uppity folks o'yourn..." He shut up abruptly when I raised my eyebrow at him. He knew damn good and well why Barbara Nadine came to live with us, and why he permitted it. Fuckin' A, Bubba, he knew. With his low cunning, he realized he didn't particularly relish having it brought up right now. The statute of limitations was not a topic upon which he felt knowledgeable. I could see him switching gears in his alcohol-soaked remaining brain cell. *Just like this uppity nigger bitch to make something out of nothing, and get his sorry ass in the slammer.* He returned to his original lachrymose babbling.

"Our lil' gal done give her life in the service of her country." I suspected he could not rightly remember just what branch of the service she had been in right now, but no matter. "We wanna' see her done right by. One a' them horses with the boots turned backwards, and one'a them wagon things with the casket, ever'body marchin' slow and mournful..." Harry Lee had been deeply impressed by movies of funeral rites for fallen leaders. He watched a lot of late night movies on TV. The nobility of it all got to him, and he wiped a drool of snot off his nose with the back of his hand. Then, he picked up the church key tied to his chair arm and popped open the beer can Pearlie Mae had rushed into his grasp at some subliminal signal. *Man needed a bracer, he did, losin' his lil' girlie thataway. Wan't ever' day a man was a grieving father, lost his chile' to the fortunes of war.* For a moment Harry Lee contemplated the sorrow of life, and the evil serpent's tooth of ungrateful chil'run. Then he philosophically belched again, and held out his hand for another restorative brew he knew without thinking would be there within his reach. The interview was over.

After we hurried away from that awful place, the CACO and I agreed that he would come over tomorrow and we would make all the necessary arrangements. I entered my house, and seeing Mama and Papa talking quietly together over all the old photo albums, headed for the room Barbara Nadine and I had shared for so long. I climbed into some Levi's and a sweater, just leaving my uniform on the floor to be cleaned. I wouldn't wear it again, tainted as it was with the miasma of the Johnson lair. I wasn't sure I could make it all the way back out of the door and up the road into the hills, but I was going to try. My lungs felt dirty and suffocated with the dismal stink of where

I'd been, and I was shaking with weariness and something else as I flung a quick "I'll be back later" in my parents' direction. Rage. Yes. Blinding, sick rage. That was the "something else". It fueled me all the way up to the throne rock before I collapsed and allowed the tears to begin. Him! Him and his pious, dirty, drunken mouth. That fucker! Him going on about her like that; like he ever gave a shit about her except to use her like a grown woman from the time she was a baby. I rolled on my stomach and pounded my fists into the soft, forgiving grass. I was screaming, mouth wide open, throat tortured, but no sound came. Finally, when it seemed my lungs would burst, and blood vessels explode under the pressure, a high ragged keening burst forth. I had never heard myself make sounds like that, and I pray I never do again.

The She Coyote heard the sound as she trotted along a dry wash, and she stopped and gave voice in sympathy.

Darkness had fallen, and the fog had wrapped a soft blanket over the girl sleeping the utterly still sleep of exhaustion. If she awoke at all, it was to merely sense the comfort of a soft, warm back against hers, and to turn over to bury her face into the sweet, grass-smelling fur. She slept, warm, and somehow protected. She never felt the soft, quick tongue cleaning the tearstains from her face.

Chapter 9

GOOD-BYE

"Tawny! Tondelayo! Wake up, baby!" Mama shook my shoulder, and folded a thick, woolly blanket around me.

For a moment, I couldn't orient myself. "Mama! What — what time is it? What're you doin' here? And Papa?" As I realized where I was, I said, "Oh, I must've fallen asleep up here. Damn! This ground's harder than it used to be." I started to say I wasn't cold, then realized why I wasn't. I shut up.

"I knew you'd be up here. When you didn't come home, Papa and I come up after you. It's late, honey, and long ago dark. C'mon, let's get you home. Here, I brought you a Thermos of hot chocolate." Mama busied herself pouring out a steaming cup, thoughtfully giving me time to come to grips with reality. The beam of the flashlight Papa held reflected back from the iridescent droplets of fog, beading eyelashes and hair with diamonds. I got to my feet, holding the blanket around my shoulders.

"You know, I wasn't cold, Mama. I really wasn't." I stooped down, and felt the warm earth next to where I had lain, then looked off into the swirling waves of mist. Nothing. No sound, no movement. But I knew we weren't alone. I knew she must be there, just beyond the feeble reach of the flashlight — well. Time to be going home. She didn't frighten me, although I didn't quite understand. Her musky, warm smell felt like home inside my nose. Papa put his arms around Mama and me as we set off down the hill, and it made me jump a little.

"Tomorrow, baby, we can come up here with sage and sweetgrass, and do the death ceremony for Barbara Nadine. I've got some real Indian tobacco, too." Mama didn't talk about it, but I knew she'd been training for the White Path before circumstances had made her leave Cherokee country in Oklahoma. She kept certain supplies she gathered from around home, or got in trade or as gifts from Indians traveling through who often stayed at our house on their way to someplace else. She doctored minor ills and colds, and had a window box of sweet-smelling herbs growing in the kitchen window. She'd learned things from some of the old hill women, too, who'd learned from their healers back South, before they'd all been torn out of their home earth and thrown on the ant heap of Marin City. A lot of them were dead now, died of being worn out and lost, Mama said. The neighbor women had been coming to Mama for years for soothing teas for their time of the month, and Barbara Nadine and I had grown up preferring Mama's doctoring to the nasty stuff handed out at the clinic. When Barbara Nadine first, then me, had our first woman-time, Mama had made cupcakes and Koolaid, and we had had little parties to celebrate our first steps into womanhood. Mama knew a lot of things, did Mama. And Papa respected it, fallen-away Catholic Cajun though he was. Not that his family hadn't practiced a decidedly strange form of Catholicism, laced with African and Latin stuff from long before Christ. Some of it was really scary.

Anyway, I was much comforted knowing we'd see Barbara Nadine to the Darkening Lands safely and properly, no matter what the Johnsons did.

Surprisingly, once home, I fell into a deep sleep immediately. I slept until late afternoon the next day.

Up on the ridge, small creatures rustled through the grass, seeking fallen seeds and tiny plants. Night-roaming insects preyed upon smaller insects, and those winged ones cursed by genetic imperative to fly by night in the muffled dark were often swept into the cupped wings of the little bats swooping silently through space. Transferred deftly to little bat mouths, they were gone. The fog made it difficult for them to locate the source of the high-pitched sonar calls in time to escape, although many made frantic attempts. A warm, fur-lined nursery amongst the roots of a clump of grass welcomed the birth of 15 naked pink mouselings, keeping them safe from the all-seeing eyes of the great horned owl drifting just overhead. The peeping squeaks of the newborns reached the hearing of the Great One, but the round, yellow eyes in the relentlessly sweeping head saw nothing. The babies would live for another day, huddled in their squirming, squeaking pile. A flash of white, and a rabbit betrayed itself off to the left. The silent wraith turned, there was a brief scream of terror, then nothing again. The She Coyote who had been stalking it turned and put her nose to the ground again, looking for life in the thousands of mouse-runs. The nose picked up the scent of a mole tunneling to the surface, busy paws opened the trench behind it, away from the clump of grass with the new mouselings under it. The mouse mother nursed her kits.

"Mama, I gotta' go back to the base soon. Gotta' go back to work. We have an ADMAT inspection coming up, and they need me." I went to the refrigerator and took out bacon, lettuce and mayonnaise, then snatched one of Mama's ripening tomatoes off the window sill before she could protest. She opened her mouth to yell, then didn't. She just got up, and separated the thick bacon slices, and put them into the heavy cast iron skillet she'd used as long as I could remember. I sliced the tomato and a sweet onion, and toasted the bread, knowing what was coming.

"I think I'd better have one 'a these. See if it's good for you." Uh huh. I knew the urgent messages Mama's nose and ears were sending her as the bacon snapped and sizzled. "Don't want you eatin' anything that might be bad." Uh huh.

"Huh! That's damn white 'a you." I made us each two, to be sure. As it happened, those BLTs were fine, jus' fine, thank you very much.

I swallowed my last bite, licked the juice from my plate just to hear Mama say in an outraged tone, "Tondelayo! Where's yo' manners, Girl? I didn' teach you to do like that!" after which she picked up her own plate and demolished the last reluctant tomato seed, luxuriating in its gelid green jacket and mayonnaisy bed.

Well. Gotta' do it. It be somethin' can't be put off no more. Oh, Mama, help me.

"I gotta' call Napa Bob..."

"You better call Napa Bob..."

We looked at each other in misery, tears welling up again. "I'll go do it. Ruby Anne, too. She in New York, goin' to that school." Mama hugged me, and sat in her chair as I walked out to the living room to the telephone. I sat in Papa's chair, to comfort me some. Before I could make the call, Mama came out, talking fast, like if she could talk long enough, and fast enough, I wouldn't have to call, and maybe, just maybe, it wouldn't be true.

"Of course, Napa should be there, and Ruby Anne. We can all do the ceremony, and Papa can say something; we all can. Then, after, we can have us a picnic, up there. Yeah, right up there by the throne maybe. Baby, what you think we ought to have? Chicken? You always did like my chicken. Tell you what, why don't you run on down to the sto' and buy some lemons? We could have us some lemonade. Or, maybe, we could..."

"Mama. Mama, I got to call."

Mama just stopped suddenly, then turned and ran into the our bedroom and shut the door. I heard her opening the toy box Papa had made for us so long ago. The hinges squeaked. I squoze my eyes shut real tight, and did it.

"Mean Motor Scooters and Bad Go Getters." Smitty always said it, the whole damn thing. It was his kind of humor. Napa

Bob had actually confined the name to the last phrase, but Smitty couldn't help adding the rest. It made some sort of closure for him, completed some circuit in his pitted brain.

"Hi, Smitty. This is Tondelayo Dubois. Is Napa Bob there?"

"Hey, Tawny. Wha's happenin'? Hang on. He's got his head stuck in Joey D'Angelo's Bultaco. Be here inna minute." The phone banged against the wall as Smitty dropped it, already forgetting. I could hear him curse at a ratchet while I waited. Then ...

"Hey, Tondelayo, where you at? Work?"

"No, no I'm home."

"Home? Is somethin' wrong? You sound funny. Tawny? Tondelayo, what the fuck?"

How could I say it? I should have rehearsed something. I could feel the scream gathering in my chest. No! Push it down! Release the throat. Speak.

"Shit, Tawny, what is it? Do you need me there? I'm comin' right over. Are you at your folks? Did somethin' happen to the folks? I'll be there as soon as I can..."

"Barbara Nadine's dead." There. I said it. Silence.

"Barbara Nadine was found dead yesterday morning. She was in the locked duty room, and they broke in when she didn't show up all day for work. Nobody knows what happened. Nobody knows why. But she's dead, Bobby, she's dead." I could hear myself shrieking this, a deep, ragged wail I didn't know lived inside me.

"I'll be right there, baby. Jus' hang on. I'm comin'. Smitty!" I heard him yelling for the shop foreman before he hung up the phone. I carefully replaced the receiver, and sat there. I didn't move.

Within the hour, we heard the full-throated roar of high-powered bikes coming down the road, police cruiser right behind. The fuzz knew about Barbara Nadine, and wouldn't interfere. Long ago, Jack had promised the cops that his boys would never create so much as a single disturbance within the confines of Marin City, and that word had been scrupulously observed. In return, they got an escort in and out, but weren't hassled. Now, the cop stopped his cruiser while the bikers parked in three neat rows, and sat, straddling their bikes, waiting. Apparently, Napa had brought all the muscle he could find on short notice, not knowing what to expect. He told them to just wait, removing his gloves and walking over to the cruiser to speak to the fuzz. Words were exchanged, and they shook hands. Then, Napa came to the house, bikers ranked quietly and respectfully outside.

"Bob! Oh, Bob! I'm so glad you came!" Mama wrapped her arms around this looming man, and he hugged her close. "Hey, Mom. What the hell's goin' on?" He grabbed at me, and enveloped me, too. "What do you mean, Barbara Nadine's dead?"

He was in full regalia. Copperheads' colors, and his kidney-belted leathers skimmed over sinew and muscle. A silver skull hung from his left ear, a diamond stud in his right ear lobe, and he wore a braided elephant-hair bracelet on his left wrist. His right wrist boasted a heavy gold ID bracelet, and an expensive watch. I knew the chains draping his tailored leather jacket were sterling silver, although the "taking care of business" chains hanging from his inlaid-silver belt were heavy-grade tempered steel with razor blades soldered in. Napa Bob was gorgeous, and dressed up to it, but business was business, and he never confused the two. He was beautiful, and utterly deadly. Mama had never seen him in full splendor, as he made an effort to de-emphasize that part of his life when he was at our house, and she was startled. But, she quickly chose to overlook the obvious, and welcomed her second son.

He had been Jack's closest friend, and the two of them had joined the military together. Jack was accepted into the Navy, but Bob found himself in the Army, which coveted his size and strength badly enough to overlook the one or two little contretemps with the law, as well as the "vacations" in Napa. They did not necessarily consider these incidents bad things, considering what they had in mind for him. Jack went to sea, to his death in an "unwar", and Bob went to Indochina. In the late 1950's, John Q. Public had never heard of Laos, or Cambodia, or Vietnam. But Nixon had, and he and his little friends had been busy sending covert troops there since 1954. Johnson and Eisenhower too. Special, secret kinds of troops. Troops like Napa Bob, with all kinds of special training. Not the kind of training proudly watching parents saw demonstrated on graduation day at boot camps. Different training.

When Napa Bob returned, he said nothing about where he'd been, or what he'd done. But he became the War Captain for the Copperheads shortly after, and he was feared by all the other biker gangs, even the notorious Hell's Angels. Copperheads showed him absolute and unquestioning obedience and respect. Mama didn't know about all this, just me and Barbara Nadine, and what we knew we mostly guessed. I didn't see him much, but I knew he would always be there for me.

Anyway, I told him everything I knew; about the autopsy that would be necessary before the funeral could be held, about the trouble with the Johnsons, and we discussed the fact that we needed to finalize arrangements for the funeral with them. By now, Papa had come home, greeted the still patiently waiting bikers, and embraced Napa Bob when he got in the house. Napa went out and told the boys the sad news, and dismissed them, then returned to the house. In honor of Napa Bob, Papa made some of his beloved chicory coffee, as we discussed dealing with the Johnsons. I'm pretty sure Papa had a better idea than Mama did about what his boy was now, and what he had done in the service. He often looked so sad when he thought no one was watching him when Bob was around. Napa had come back so strange, and so silent. We didn't see him much. But now, he was here, and he offered to go with us to finalize things, as Harry Lee tended to be far, far more cooperative within the immediate range of Copperhead colors.

The rest of the Copperheads rode slowly out of Marin City, in formation, and throttled 'way down, in respect for the dead. Most of them had known us since we were kids, and I think there may even have been a tear or two. We had been treated with a rather avuncular tolerance, and even the biker girls knew better than to bad mouth us. Their old men would slap them upside the head faster 'n fast, did they get in our faces. When we grew up and entered the military, we assumed a peculiar status with them. Not that we pushed our luck by hanging out with them, or going to biker bars. I do know they all admired Jack and Napa for being able to complete their service, most of they themselves having quickly been ushered out for myriad infractions or "unsuitability" if they even managed to get in. Jack had been raised to near cult status, dying during war as he had. The bikers tended to be deeply patriotic, even maudlin in their cups, and were perfectly willing to wage war for their country whenever and wherever needed. The fact that the government was not equally fervent in accepting them was a source of much pain and frustration. At one point, the Hell's Angels even began caching monumental amounts of arms of all kinds in preparation to go over and liberate Vietnam, since the government seemed unable to do so on its own.

The Johnsons proved quite cooperative. The funeral would take place on Monday.

Ruby Anne flew in Saturday, and I picked her up at the airport. At first, I felt awkward, she was so tall and beautiful! Heads turned as she sort of swiveled down the ramp, walking that New York model's walk like she'd been born to it. No longer that short, even squat little figure in overalls! She was smooth and velvety, with huge doe eyes, and she smelled very, very expensive when she crushed me in those thin, wiry arms. She'd been daunting enough, staring out at the world from the cover of Ebony and other magazines, and in person, she fairly riveted attention from every eye.

"Tondelayo, Girl, I've missed you! Look at you, Girl, all dressed up in that uniform! Man, if you don't look boss!"

Then, we were both crying, and everything was like it always was. Except Barbara Nadine wasn't here. Would never be here again.

But even with mascara running all over those fabulous cheekbones Ruby Anne had kept hidden all those years, she was
stunningly beautiful. I was glad I had Yellow Bird to ride her in
style.

We held the death ceremony and the feast up in the hills,
and I packed a bag to go back to T. I. I kept some sage and
cedar for my medicine bag and locker. As I kissed Mama, Papa,
and Ruby Anne good-bye, I could smell the sage smoke clinging to us all, cleansing and blessing us.

Napa Bob followed Yellow Bird all the way to the T.I. Main
Gate before his big Harley peeled off and headed for Oakland.
I watched him as long as I could see him in the traffic then
went on through the gate. It was time to face the room again.
The room Barbara Nadine and I had shared since we had been
promoted out of the cubicles in the old barracks. I opened the
door and walked in to the pristine neatness demanded of us;
squared corners, not a speck of dust, teddy bears squared on
their pillows, supposed to be sitting at attention. Barbara Nadine's
had fallen over, as if it knew, and had lost its will to sit upright.
I went over and straightened it up, then picked it up and hugged
it to my chest as the sobs forced their way up my throat again.

Later I would have to deal with her locker and dresser. Take
down the neat, newly cleaned blues still in their plastic shrouds,
her stiffly starched summer uniforms, her sparkling white shirts,
and her PT gear, all facing the same way, all equally spaced.
Her spit shined boondockers were missing; Oh, yes, she'd had
duty the night … mustn't think about it. Her spit shined pumps
sat primly, just missing touching one another, next to her pol-
ished white tennie runners. Hats and hat covers stowed on the
overhead shelf. Dresser with its meticulously folded cotton underpants, side over, side over, crotch over, turn backside up,
stacked with edges even, bras folded, cup inside cup, back folded
into cup. A life. A life comprised of attention to detail carried
to an obsession, as if to ward off all untidiness, all disaster, all
evil. Only it hadn't worked.

Cedar, sage, tobacco and sweetgrass. The smoke from the small ceremonial fire clung to the blades of grass and the rocks, tantalizing the finely tuned and delicate nostrils of the She Coyote. It was pleasing, and she rolled in the ashes, so that bits of unburned sacred plants adhered to her thick fur. It reminded her of long-ago ceremonies of the two-legged ones; the ones who used to leave her offerings, too. She lowered her tail and head sadly, then quietly walked away. She would not hunt tonight.

Chapter 10

THE FUNERAL

Up in the hills, after the ceremony and feast, Napa Bob and I had talked, alone after everyone ate, and Mama and Papa had wandered off, hand in hand, talking softly about their lost son, and now, their lost daughter. Ruby Anne had gone off alone, saying she needed some time to make a solo pilgrimage to a hidden copse she and Barbara Nadine had discovered one day.

"Shit, Tawny, Barbara Nadine was twenty-two years old. She was in the Navy, gettin' reg'lar physicals, and the best medical care. Couldn't have had nothin' wrong with her. She too young. Didn't do no shit, didn't hardly drink, didn't do nothin' to kill her." Napa sounded like he was crying, deep inside. He wanted answers, dammit, and I didn't have any. "You'd a tol' me, did she have anythin' wrong, wouldn't you?"

I looked him in the eye, and said, "No. There was nothing wrong. She was fine! When I got back from "C" School in

Great Lakes, she told me she had duty that night, then we'd go celebrate my graduation in the City Monday. We were going to go to that $1.99 steak place off Market. She wouldn't not say anything if something was wrong. She wrote me she'd had the flu or something while I was gone, nausea and some vomiting but no temperature. She said she figured she had some passing bug or something, and didn't even go to sick call. We both had promotion physicals just a few months ago, and there was nothing then."

"Well, girls her age don't just curl up and die one day. I got a bad feeling about this, Tondelayo. Real bad. And I think you do, too."

"Yeah, I do. I'm a Hospital Corpsman, and I lived with her f'crissakes. I'd know if something had just gone wrong. Shit, she wasn't ever even sick, hardly, just that one time; and that turned out to be nothing, I guess."

"What one time?" I could hear him seizing on the chance of an answer, any answer.

"Oh, we were at the Twelfth Naval District Command Picnic. You know, they have it once a year, and everybody goes, and it's this big deal. There's always big barbecues, and we have hot dogs, and hamburgers, and potato salad and Navy beans. The officers play baseball against the enlisted and stuff. They're a lot of fun, actually. There's kegs of beer, and it's pretty loose. This time, some of the Admiral's Filipino stewards made Filipino food, too, and it was really cool. I liked it. Kinda' like Chinese, but different. Anyway, Barbara Nadine was having a great time, laughing and carrying on, when all of a sudden she choked, or something. She started breathing funny, and then she really began to have respiratory problems. The Command Duty Officer happened to be there, and he said he'd take her to Sick Bay in his duty car faster than an ambulance could get there, so he did. The Corpsman gave her a shot of antihistamine, said it looked like asthma or something, and put her on the binnacle list. The CDO took her back to the barracks, and put her to bed. He had to carry her in, she was so pole-axed from the shot, the Officer of the Day told me. I left and went back to the barracks as soon as I could get a ride, since I didn't have Yellow Bird; all that beer, you know, and when I got there, she was all covered up and sleeping like a baby, breathing fine. She looked OK, and I just stayed there with her to make sure I could get help if she woke up sick or anything. Next day, she said she was fine, and had just had a bad attack of hay fever or something, and she was still a little loopy from the shot, but OK. She didn't want to go back to Sick Bay and see the Doc, because she was fine, she said.

"We never did figure out what hit her like that. But that was it. I left the next day for school in Great Lakes, and was gone for the rest of the four months, but she never wrote nothin' about feelin' poorly again. She just talked about work, and stuff, and gossip, like always. She had a real hard on for her XO, and she used to make up funny stories about terrible things happening to him. She had a really weird imagination, that girl.

"Then, when I got back, she was dead. I can't fuckin' believe it. I wish I hadn't had to go off to fuckin' school like that. Maybe I would have seen something, noticed something..." I felt myself brimming over again.

"No, no, honey. You couldna' done nothin'. You can't let yourself fall into that trap. We got work to do." Napa Bob handed me a tissue out of my purse, and said again, "We got work to do."

"Yeah, somethin' ain't right here. Somethin's jus' not right. My Mama din' raise no fool, and I'm gonna' fin' out what happen. It wadn't no accidental death."

"Yes, I'm modeling now, and it was thrilling being on the cover of *Ebony*. But I know I won't be young forever, and I'm taking courses for a B. A. in Fashion Design. I'm very excited about it!" Ruby Anne had swept in, expensive little black dress adorned only with pearls, and the latest in sumptuous black net swirls perched on her severely straightened and French-twisted hair. A cloud of Joy enveloped her svelte figure as she moved into the crowd, greeting people she hadn't seen for so long.

It was quite a crowd. In fact, most of Marin City was there, filling the Community Center and spilling out onto the sidewalk. The Baptist minister was sweating as he shook countless hands, continually having to wipe his own hands on his snowy handkerchiefs, of which he seemed to have an endless supply. I stood with my family, receiving loving embraces and teary condolences, while the Johnson brood stood sullenly across the big room, reluctantly grasping proffered hands and dropping them as soon as was decently possible. We had asked them to stand with us, but they had refused. Harry Lee disappeared at frequent intervals to the Men's room, and was redder and more unstable in his gait every time he reappeared. Pearlie Mae just stood there, snot-nosed baby on hip, grubby paw of another one hanging on the hem of her dragging housedress, grossly pregnant again. Two older ones darted through the crowd, gleefully grabbing handfuls of food off the tables set out for the mourners and stuffing their faces. The oldest, grown ones weren't in evidence. Her eyes looked dull, dead. Mama went over to her and gave her a quick hug. She didn't even move, but a single tear slid down her face. I thought about going over and trying to say or do something that might help, but I couldn't think of anything. I had nothing left to help anybody myself.

Even the entire clan of our Waitingsnake cousins were there in force, having made the long trek up from Bakersfield. Terry Waitingsnake, the oldest girl, surprised me with her beauty and blossoming maturity. She was going to be absolutely breathtaking. I remembered her as a wild, big-eyed little demon who continually dogged my footsteps, aping my every move. Even then, I hadn't really minded, although I complained heartily to Mama, but she had been so intense, so dedicated to doing it, I couldn't help admiring her singlemindedness. Now, here she was, preparing to become a cop, of all things. Terry wanted to be the first woman on the tribal police force of one of the nearby Indian tribes. So far, she hadn't succeeded, but I knew eventually she would. Terry Waitingsnake never gave up.

Copperheads in their full leathers and club colors mingled in the crowd, long hair and bandanna headbands standing out in stark contrast to all the flowered hats and heavily pomaded hair of Marin City society. It made some of the more staid members of that society nervous to suddenly find their white-gloved hands engulfed in the black studded leather mitts of the outlaw bikers. However, they had nothing to fear. The Copperhead President himself was there, along with Napa Bob, and they had given orders that there would be no disturbances, no rowdiness, no booze, and no drugs. Period.

The Copperheads had not attended the earlier services held in the Chapel on the Navy base, as they would not have been permitted through the Main Gate. However, they had been waiting in formation, just outside, with their bikes draped in blankets of yellow roses. These had been Barbara Nadine's favorite. Small American flags flew from each handlebar, and the bikers all wore black armbands. The funeral hearse, and the casket itself, bore white roses, with a single blood-red rose in the center, just above the draped American flag.

The funeral procession had proceeded to the San Bruno National Cemetery with a full honor guard of solemnly throttled-down Harley Davidsons, leather-clad warriors astride their powerful machines in perfect formation fore and aft of the big, black automobile Mama and Papa and I were in. We rode in the Commandant, Twelfth Naval District Admiral James B. Smythe's car. He rode beside Master Chief Manns, Barbara Nadine's immediate boss, who was driving. Since the Admiral himself was aboard, the fenders of the car flew his personal flags. The Copperhead President and Napa Bob preceded the Navy car in royal splendor. While the limousine provided by the funeral home carried the Johnsons, no honor guard attended it. The hearse was flanked by eight more bikes, with two each of the riders wearing the colors of the attending clubs. A truce had been called for the funeral, and the Copperheads were joined by the Mo-Fo's, the Rattlers, and the Hell's Angels. Their bikes were all draped in white roses, with a single red one over the headlight. The cortege stretched for blocks, and civilian motorcycle police were assisted by the Shore Patrol in clearing traffic along the route. I doubt if any military funeral ever equaled the final rites for Petty Officer Second Class Barbara Nadine Johnson. Virtually the entire staff of the 12th Naval District was there, as well as a hefty representation from Oak Knoll and other local commands.

Now, after the burial, Marin City was gathering us to its bosom in the time-honored traditions of the Deep South. The military contingent had mostly returned to the base after the last, sadly lingering notes of *Taps* had been blown, and the guns of the military honor guard had sounded their final salute to a fallen comrade. The admiral, Master Chief Manns, and Barbara Nadine's Women's Representative, Lieutenant Monroe, and mine, Lieutenant Madden, had come back to Marin City with us to pay final respects. Here, in the Community Center, long tables groaned with food of all descriptions, and the services of every large coffee pot in Marin City were called upon to supply the mourners. Ice tea and Koolaid supplemented the coffee, and there were enough pies and cakes to supply an army for three weeks.

People kept getting up on the stage and playing the old, old blues of the Mississippi Delta and Chicago, and voices often rose in plaintive answer. In the crowded heat and mingled smells of food, cigarette smoke, perfume, pomade, and sweat, I grew a little dizzy, and the music kept tearing at my soul, trying to pull it away to follow some dark and sorrowful road. To follow after my friend.

"Tawny. Tondelayo!" I started. Napa Bob was leaning over me, whispering urgently.

"Oh! Sorry. Just wool-gathering, I guess. What?"

"You know that officer that sat next to the Admiral? That blonde one?"

"You mean the XO? Strang?"

"Strang. Yeah, that's the mutha'. Strang. He was Barbara Nadine's XO?"

"Yes. You know him? How? She didn't like him. Said he was really strange. I met him a few times. He's got those not-quite blue eyes with no color, look like he's dead or somethin'. I don't like him either. He gives me the creeps. How do you know him?"

"Oh, I seen him around, I guess. Never mind." Napa Bob looked thoughtful. Or as thoughtful as he could, considering he seldom changed his expression in public, and he was wearing mirrored shades like he always did. I found myself intensely curious about his interest in Commander Strang. Strang was the kind of man who made the hair stand up on the back of my neck and along my arms, even when he just happened to be in my line of sight. I had no idea why, as I'd never even spoken more than a word or two to him, strictly along the lines of business. I felt a strong revulsion toward him; he was so pale or something. I don't know. I could never put my finger on it. Now, Napa Bob had singled him out, too. Why? Before I could say anything else or ask him to say more about Strang, he looked around and said, "Better move the boys on out. No use tempting fate. I'm glad the other clubs didn't come here."

I agreed. Expecting too much circumspection was unrealistic. It had been several hours since the solemnity of the funeral cortege, and there were signs of restiveness. Napa caught the almost imperceptible nod of the President, and began quietly rounding up the Copperheads. When they were all alerted, they made their formal good-byes to us, trooped outside and mounted their bikes. The Marin City police escorted them out to the Waldo Grade overpass, and waited until their column of paired bikes roared on up toward the Golden Gate, and the loving watch of the San Francisco and Oakland police. There had been no incidents of any kind, which pleased the Chief.

It was very late by the time most of the mourners had left, and we were exhausted. Lt. Monroe told me I didn't need to report the next day to start my leave, and I staggered home and into my bed hardly knowing what I was doing.

It was over. Barbara Nadine lay at rest with the hundreds of other fallen comrades in the neat, exact rows of the sleeping military dead, and we would never run through the Marin Hills again. Hot, salty tears were running into the corner of my mouth as my head hit the pillow.

Chapter 11

DREAMTIME

Since I was on leave, I didn't have to get up, get dressed, go to work, do anything, really. I slept a lot, I think, and didn't sleep at all. It was a strange, vague time, marked only by flashes of events and memories, or the necessity of going to the bathroom. We all walked around like zombies. Mama and Papa went to work, leaving the house to me, but we all lived in a fog. I somehow went through Barbara Nadine's things, keeping, giving away, discarding. It's funny how little a life comes down to; a pair of Levi's, some uniforms, pictures of two maniacally grinning ragamuffins in droopy drawered, stretched out bathing suits playing in a sprinkler, a fake silver turtle ring with a beautiful blue glass stone I'd given her for Christmas once. I cooked supper so Mama and Papa would have dinner when they got home. I just never remembered what it was. A lot of time, I just stayed in our room, playing *Death of an Angel* over and over and over. Crying for real now.

The hardest time to sleep was at night. I kept waking up at three o'clock, or four in the morning. I'd lie there, hearing myself breathe, nose stuffed up with old crying, waiting for a new onslaught of tears. Then I ran out of tears for awhile. So, I just lay there, open eyes staring into darkness, waiting for morning to happen. When it did, I spent the day waiting for night to happen.

One night, I lay staring into the blackness, the featureless space around me. I turned my head, eyes swollen and dry, and saw two green-gold eyes staring back, glowing at once commanding and compassionate. Gradually, I became aware of a faint phosphorescent light tipping individual golden and black guard hairs. A magnificent creature stood before me, summoning me without word or sign. I knew her immediately. The She Coyote was large for her sex, and fully coated in her winter pelt. As she moved, powerful muscles slid barely perceptible under the shining coat, and she made no sound as she turned and padded away, up the road toward the Tarzan swing.

I was not surprised; I'd always known her, I think. Nor was I surprised to look down and see that I, too, had paws, and I could see every leaf and twig along the route up the hillside past the last houses clinging to the edge before the woods. Starlight shown dimly through fog, but it was enough. Mostly, though, I was acutely aware of smells; damp salt air, iceplants pungent from above us, myrtle blooming beneath the oaks. A quick, warm musk fleeted by in the ditch along the road, and I knew a mouse was out, gathering seeds and grass. A momentary tensing of muscles, an involuntary, instantaneous impulse to search out and pounce, but I didn't break stride, loping after the big shape in front of me.

As we left the woods, bright sunlight and the intoxicating scent of heated grass erupted. I could hear the excited yells of children just around the bend, and we melted into the tall grass and sparse shrubs on the up side of the slope. Darting from tussock to scotch broom clump, we were invisible. Soon, we looked down on Marin City, and the lower slope of Waldo

Grade. The sound of R & B drums on several hundred radios all tuned to KWBR in Oakland provided a background of rhythm that reminded me of the dance drums at the pow wows I'd been to with my folks. It made a massive heartbeat I found myself entering and becoming a part of.

Although it was quite distant, I had no difficulty seeing the sturdy, overalled little figure heading toward Barbara Nadine's house. Ruby Anne was on her way to Johnson's, wrestling a big piece of cardboard behind her, dust and gravel spewing in her wake. Just then, another little girl came outside of the neighboring house, tossing her long, glossy black braids behind her as she caught up with Ruby Anne.

"Hey, Tondelayo. Grab 'holt. This thang's heavy!"

"Hey, Ruby Anne. I got us some fried bologna samiches and lemonade!" brandishing the paper sack. The girls stood on the sidewalk waiting, as Barbara Nadine clambered through the open window at the side of the house.

"What you doin', girl? Yo' daddy gone' skin you alive!" Giggles, as tennis-shoed feet hit the ground, slightly mashing a geranium rash enough to grow alongside the wall.

"Yeah, well, he's passed out drunk from last night still, and Ma's feeding the baby. She don' care nohow. C'mon." She set off, dragging a corner of the cardboard. Her uncombed tow head and mossy teeth demonstrated parental neglect, and it was highly likely she was unfed as well.

When they got to the grassy ridge on the hill, they joined the other children whooping and hollering joyously as they tobogganed down the hill, bottoms bouncing on cardboard, hands clinging desperately to the sides. The runs of flattened grass were slick as glass, and the makeshift sleds hurtled down at great speed. Tirelessly, the children struggled back up the steep hill, only to mount their cardboards and do it again, sweat glistening on glowing faces and trickling down backs.

Finally, the sun high and beating down, the three little girls carefully stowed their cardboard pieces under a concealing shrub, and started trudging around the bend and farther up the hill. We padded silently along above and somewhat behind them.

"C'mon. Let's go up to the throne and eat. I'm hongry."

"Yeah. Me, too. Who's gonna' be queen today?"

"Me! You were yesterday!"

"Nuh uh, girl, you lie! It's Barbara Nadine's turn. She wa'nt here yestiddy. Her daddy ... oof!" The childishly whining voice abruptly stopped as an elbow met ribs. Hard. Ruby Anne glared at Tondelayo, but remained silent. Barbara Nadine just kept her head down and continued walking, saying nothing.

"OK. Let's eat. Barbara Nadine, you queen. It your turn to sit on the throne." The girls stopped before the solitary granite boulder perched overlooking the sweeping hillsides and folds of surrounding terrain. The boulder had hollows filled with sharply scented iceplants, vivid magenta flowers adorning the thick stalks above the crowded hen'n'chickens utilizing every stray speck of dirt in the cracks and pockets along the sides. The top was slightly concave, making a royal throne, indeed. Barbara Nadine clambered up and sat, master of all she surveyed. As Tondelayo handed out sandwiches and passed the bottle of lemonade around, Barbara Nadine dug a nail-chewed mitt into her jeans pocket and produced some mints. Again, they were the kind that are kept by the cash register in the tonier saloons her father favored when the Welfare check arrived.

"I got dessert," she said proudly. It was so seldom she was able to provide anything at all to the frequent picnic lunches, I realized sadly, watching. And candy was the treat of all treats.

"Hey! Cool!" Enthusiastic grins split little faces as grubby paws reached toward the coveted hoard. Barbara Nadine must have felt like a queen, indeed, gratified by the reception of her generous offering. She could have kept them to herself, and pigged them all in secret, but she chose to share them with her girlfriends. That was true friendship! And no little sacrifice for a child who seldom had enough to eat.

"Race ya to the water tower!" They were off and running, tearing back down to the cross-ridge road, intent on exploring the forbidden world fenced off as the exclusive property of the white hunters' club and enforced as a private killing ground by frequent signs with dire warnings of what would happen to those foolish enough to venture onto the sacrosanct lands across the barbed wire.

To the kids of Marin City, it was an utterly compelling goal to brave the signs and the hateful barbed wire to discover whatever hidden mysteries lurked unknown in the copses and draws of the forbidden empire. All the kids were convinced the land crawled with heavily armed, rich white men who would be maddened into a frenzied blood lust at the sight of a Marin City brat trespassing on their privileged territory.

This added a fillip of adrenaline-laden excitement no child could have resisted. So far, tentative forays had progressed only a few daring feet beyond the fence, which displayed a view of terrain seemingly identical to that on their side of the fence, but everybody knew that untold mysteries were to be found over there, just on the other side of the ridge. Otherwise, why would the white hunters be so intent on keeping them out?

So, Marin City kids continued to defy death and gunfire by wriggling under the deadly strands and sidling just a little further before turning and bolting back to safety and a place where they were more welcome.

She Coyote play-bowed at me, and I found myself responding with a feint and lightening turn to dash off in an unexpected direction, tongue lolling happily as I was immediately chased by my companion. We romped wildly in the hot sun, chasing and being chased in a mad game of catch-me.

After, we flung ourselves down and slept, exhausted from all the riotous play.

A tiny, twitching nose sniffed anxiously at the tail sprawled out in the grass, and the owner of the nose, a gray and white field mouse hurriedly changed her itinerary of seed-seeking in that particular area, departing at top speed. A green-gold eye lazily watched her go, then lidded over again to sleep undisturbed.

Next morning, I woke up feeling more rested than I had in the days since Barbara Nadine's death. I swung my legs over the edge of the bed and padded barefoot out to the kitchen. It was Saturday, and Mama sat at the yellow Formica and chrome table, beading a pair of moccasins with a pattern of brilliantly colored autumn leaves and green vines. The orange, yellow, red and gold of the leaves contrasted against the deep green leaves were a musical harmony on the soft golden brown elk hide. The finished pair would bring good money at a pow wow.

"Well! Hi, sugar! You slept good. It's almost noon." She got up as I came in, and kissed me. "You want somethin' to eat? I can fix you some ham and grits, and red-eye gravy, too. Or would you eat some griddle cakes? Maybe you'd rather have some oatmeal ..."

"Mama, Mama. I ain't no starvin' chile' in China! I could fancy some ham and grits, though, now you mention it. And maybe an egg? Do we have any chocolate milk?" Suddenly, I realized I could pass for a starving child in China. I hadn't been eating too well, either.

"Mama ... last night ..." I couldn't say it. It sounded so weird. I knew it was real, though, not a dream. I'd known that She Coyote; seen her, all my life. I could still feel the hot, penetrating sun on fur, taste the tang of tarweed in nasal passages a thousand times more acutely than normal, see Marin City far below in images so sharp they seemed surreal. But it wasn't to be talked about.

Mama turned and looked at me, her eyes black and deep. She smiled slightly, almost secretively, and turned back to the stove. She didn't say anything.

To say something, I picked up the unfinished moccasin and said, "These are just beautiful, Mama. Gorgeous. I do believe you do the best beadwork of anybody. Everybody says so, too."

"Oh, now. You go on. I've just been doing it a long time, honey. You do it as long as I have, and you'll be as good as me. That bracelet you made was somethin'." She lowered her head modestly, suddenly busy with the pan of water for the grits. It wouldn't do to be listening to praise, even from me. A person just used the gifts given by the Creator to try and return a small gift of beauty. It wasn't any credit to her that she could bead well. She'd been doing it since she was a tiny little girl, under the tutelage of her mother, aunties and grandmother. She'd started me with a loom and bigger beads when I was about four, and Barbara Nadine began her learning when she and Ruby Anne used to spend rainy days at our house. By the time Barbara Nadine had come to live with us, she was a skilled beadworker already. She loved the peyote stitch, and Papa used to joke that he dasn't leave his cigars around where she could find them, or he'd come to find them all covered in beads.

The next day being Sunday, I suggested to Mama that we take Yellow Bird into the City and go to the zoo. I had to go off leave Monday, and all I'd done was mope. Mama was overjoyed at the prospect.

"Why, what a wonderful idea! Papa's goin' fishin' with Ray, and us two can jus' have us a time! My, I haven't been to the zoo in so long! I don't think we better go in Yellow Bird, though. I don't like the idea of parking her there on Sloat. She's too tempting a target. Let's just take ole' Betsy." Betsy being the Buick Papa refused to give up, lovingly fixing her every mutter and grumble as she grew ever more creaky. I knew the concern was well-grounded, but I also realized she was just ever so slightly nervous about my driving. Now, I was a perfectly safe, well-trained defensive driver, but Mama had a hard time believing it. Lord, I hadn't had a speeding ticket in years! But, why spoil the mood. OK. We'd go in the Buick. I felt kind of excited myself for the first time in a long time. I even found myself humming as I moved around getting dressed the next morning.

The sun sparkled on the waves as we sped over the Golden Gate, exhilarated at the prospect of our big adventure. Mama even forbore to change the station from KWBR, and I could swear I heard her humming along at times. When *Dance With Me Henry* came on, she couldn't help herself, testifying and putting' down the lines like a pro, demanding Henry rock and roll with her. She looked to be not much older than me right then.

When we got to the City, things got a little hairy. There was the usual construction, and traffic congestion, and one way streets, and at some point we realized we had been past the same motorcycle cop several times, sitting astraddle his bike, mirrored shades scanning passersby for anyone foolish enough to defy the law and commit an infraction.

Finally, Mama pulled into an open space at the curb, and said, "Excuse me? Could you help me?" She swung her long hair back in a glossy black wave, smiling into the impassive reflection of the shades. The cop looked at her, beautiful and golden, and dismounted to approach the Buick more closely. He was a massively muscled man, high black motorcycle boots curving around strong calves, powerful sleek haunches blocking out taut navy gabardine. His manhood was tenderly cupped against his massive thigh by the hand-tailored uniform which contained his body like a second skin. A flat stomach was outlined by the tailored shirt, which swelled up and over the impossibly broad shoulders. The name tag on his gorgeous chest read " Tony Troche." Moving with predatory grace, exuding palpable maleness, he came to the side of the car. He bent his handsome visage down to look into the car at us, his black curls falling over his forehead in a silky wave. Removing his sunglasses, he smiled appreciatively at us, his eyes so black they appeared to lack pupils. I mentally licked him from below his shiny brass belt buckle up his flat stomach to his bulging pectorals, and had to consciously jerk my wayward thoughts back to the business at hand. He was The Man, and undoubtedly crushed and ate outlaw bikers for breakfast. I gave him the ole' come hither look from under my lashes, just for drill. The Man, yes. But a rare and truly boss specimen just the same.

"Yes, Mam'n, I'd be glad to help you any way I can." His voice was faintly lilted with Spanish, and maybe that accounted for what I heard as an odd emphasis on the "any way." His black eyes caressed our faces with languid interest. Frankly, we were well worth looking at. Mama was smooth and golden, high cheekbones emphasizing mahogany eyes with black brows eternally quirked in questioning amusement. Her lips were full and dark red, without the artifice of lipstick. Her hair was wavy and thick, with a hint of tight curls wisping out around the temples. I, with a double dose of African influence, was several shades darker, but I had Mama's upward slanting eyes, while my cheeks faithfully recreated the dimples of my Papa. My short hair was a cap of curls, neither wavy nor nappy, but in between. People had told us that together we could make strong men lie down on the ground and bite sticks. And this Tony Troche, motorcycle cop, who had to be at least an eleventh degree black belt Karate expert, and lover extraordinaire was not immune. He, too, was a tasty morsel, and I was positive more than one panting female had crashed herself against his craggy shores.

In the space of a few heartbeats, the flirting game began, was played to its end, and both sides thoroughly enjoyed it. Troche mounted his machine, and paraded his broad, muscled back in front of us, erect and heartbreakingly seductive, as he led us to the long street running past the zoo and to the ocean. Once there, he waved and wheeled his bike away, his powerful legs wrapping the sleek sides of the gas tank caressingly, yet tightly. I was glad I didn't have to try and stand up right away; I didn't think I could.

"Oooh ooh wee! There's an Indian in that woodpile!" I slanted a grin at my mother. Why, Mama, you fox, I bet Papa'd like to have seen that little show!"

"Did you see the way he got on and off that bike? Umm mmm. I wonder if he mounts his women that way." Mama looked pensive.

"Mama!!" I was shocked. Then we were both giggling like fools.

We found a place to park on Sloat, and walked along the low wall to the opening guarded by the great crouched lions, ever vigilant, ever welcoming. Fleischacher smelled distinctive, and just the smell awakened a nostalgic, excited feeling of adventure. It was a mixture of salt, peanuts, pink popcorn, eucalyptus, and elephant and monkey shit. I loved it. We hurried down the slanting walk, past the wonderful Art Deco building housing the gift shop and offices, to the original old wooden carousel. Buying tickets, we flung adulthood behind us, as we scrambled for our favorite mounts. Mine was a coal black stallion, his mane flying in the wind, jeweled harness flashing. Happy yells and splashes sounded from the huge saltwater swimming pools behind the carousel, and we could see the frolicking children trying to sink themselves with futile glee in the heavy water. The tiny steam train chuffed around and around its little track, kids and adults hanging over the edges of the green cars, engineer in his striped overalls and hat sounding the whistle as he rounded curves.

It was a good day, and we wended our way back over the Golden Gate toward home feeling better than we had in a long time. We felt strong and alive, our blood flowing warmly through our bodies. As the Buick came to rest against the accustomed concrete stop alongside the house, the air was redolent with spice and frying fish.

"Papa's cookin' Cajun!" I fairly skipped onto the porch. The door opened and Papa peered out.

"Who dat?"

"Who dat say who dat?"

"Who dat say who dat say who dat?" The worn joke warmed the air as Papa enfolded his wife and his daughter.

"Bout time you'uns got home! Out flitting around, leave a man to starve! Where my two girls been? You look like cats, canary feathers all over yo' moufs!" He laughed and released us to go into the kitchen and turn the food in the old black skillet. "I done brung home the bacon! Or fish. Yessah, I done went out and caught dinner for my fambly like a man got to do."

Mama and I looked at each other and giggled, then went to wash up and set the table. No need to tell Papa everything! Some things mens not meant to know.

"I'll stir up some hushpuppies," Mama offered. "Tawny, you go on and make up that cabbage in the icebox. There's carrots you can grate, too. We'll have us some coleslaw. All we need to do is get us some shrimp, and we'd be back in the bayous."

"Yeah, reg'lar Loosiana Satiddy night, only Sunday!" Papa went over to the records stacked under the old record player, and pulled out the big 33 and 1/3 of Dennis McGee singing and playing the old-time Cajun music he'd grown up on. Sometimes, he really missed being there, tapping his feet to the accordion and fiddle music, watching long streamers of soft Spanish moss dipping and swaying with the warm, velvet breeze playing over the smooth brown water as it went sliding by the ramshackle shacks of his people. He could see Sukey, and Melissa, and lovely Jeannette, and hear all his cousins and aunts and uncles gossiping in their flowing French patois. His heart carried a piece of the bayous with him always. Seeing the melancholy slide over his broad face, Mama went over and tickled his sides.

"C'mon, Old Man, les' have us a Loosiana Satiddy night!" She twitched her hips provocatively to the beat as she went back to dropping spoons of cornmeal mush and minced onions into the bubbling pan of grease. Papa brightened, and began to two-step around the kitchen, dancing with the broom, and crooning to it as he whirled around the floor.

It was very late when I finally tore myself away and headed back to the base. The Marine guard barely sketched me a "navel salute," the somewhat contemptuous salute centered at belt buckle height and reserved for enlisted pukes, as I showed him my ID and drove slowly through to the barracks. It had been quite a time, I thought as I laid out my uniform for the next day and gave my glittering shoes one last swipe with the cotton ball.

Before I went to sleep, I thought about Tony Troche. Of course, he'd turn out to be married, no doubt. But, oh me, he'd be someone to consider giving up my "most precious gift" for. Almost. Not quite. But almost.

Chapter 12

THE MASTER CHIEF

"**G**ood day, Petty Officer Dubois. You're looking very sharp." Master Chief Manns inclined his head slightly, and smiled at me. I stopped myself from saluting; barely, and smiled back. He looked sharp, too. To say the least. As I walked through the glass doors of the Chief's Club and gave him my hat to put on the shelf placed there for the purpose, I looked around. Nice. Very, very nice. The Navy being the Navy, I suspected the Officer's Club wouldn't be as nice. Chiefs, after all, were Chiefs.

"Afternoon, Bill."

"Hi, Bill, how's it going?"

"Chief, it's good to see you." People greeted Master Chief Manns from every side. He was obviously not only well known, but well liked and greatly respected. The other Chiefs made sure to greet him and to acknowledge me with reserved, but friendly smiles. Chief Manns returned the greetings with dignity and grace, and we followed the headwaiter to a table in a prime central location. However, the Chief gave him a soft word, and our course shifted toward a more secluded site, where we could talk uninterruptedly and in privacy. I found myself holding my back even more straight, and my head high with pride as we crossed the dining room. I thought to myself that no one, no other Chief, looked as fine as my escort. He was tough, man. Even the grizzled Senior and Master Chiefs scattered here and there were no match for the squared-away Master Chief Manns. Right there and then, I decided I would strive all my Navy career to be as squared-away as Chief Manns was, to wear my uniform with the obvious pride and respect he wore his. I was glad my pumps gleamed from the last-minute touch-up with the dampened cotton ball, and that I had driven stocking-footed to the club, so as not to mark the heels on the floor mats. And, of course, I was wearing a set of blues fresh from the cleaners, and even clean underwear. No sense taking chances. What if I got in a wreck, and was wearing the same set I'd had on all morning?

He made conversation general and easy as we read the menu, made our selections, and ate. The Chief ordered baked sole, and I did the same. It was groovy, fresh and succulent. Had to be, the Chief's Club and all. His conversation was relaxed and friendly, and I found myself telling him all about the decisions Barbara Nadine and I had made to stay in the Navy, and to seek college educations to further our careers.

"… so, I decided to go ahead and do it, like we'd planned. I'm taking the on-base courses now, and only have a few credits to go. I'll graduate about the same time I'm up for First Class."

"Oh, that's good. I'm glad to hear it. What interests you, particularly? Will you become a Registered Nurse and apply for a commission in the Nurse Corps?"

"No, I don't think so. I'm more drawn to the Line. The challenge of a variety of duties and assignments appeals to me. I'm getting a Bachelor's in Liberal Arts, with a heavy concentration in Languages, and I'm going to apply for the

1100 designator. Perhaps I'll do a tour in Intelligence at some point." I was perfectly capable of expressing myself in Standard English, although I seldom bothered, but the Chief's Club, and Chief Manns, seemed to elicit my most formal speech. It turned out we were both compulsive readers, and the conversation made time pass far more quickly than I realized. Next thing I knew, the club was almost empty, and we still sat there, chatting.

"Don't worry about getting back to work, Tondelayo, (When did it become 'Tondelayo' and 'Bill'? I don't remember, but it just seemed right.) I've squared it away with Senior Chief Benner. The man thought of everything.

Then, we got down to business. Chief Manns proceeded to tell me he was aware of the snooping and questioning; he called it "investigating," I'd been trying to do around Barbara Nadine's death. I was convinced it was murder, but couldn't pin it down. He seemed to know everything I'd done. For a moment, I wondered if he were actually omniscient, and knew all about my manipulation of the duty roster so that a bitch who had called Barbara Nadine "white trash" would be standing duty on every holiday for the rest of her tour, but finally determined that if he did know, he didn't care.

"I am well aware that you're not satisfied with the findings of the JAG investigation that it was death by accident, possibly by an anaphylactic shock from a bee sting. I talked with a friend of mine, a Master Chief in the morgue, and he told me a few things that didn't show up on the JAG report. Several dead bees were discovered behind the locker in the duty room. The autopsy showed symptoms consistent with anaphylactic shock."

I snorted. Almost said, "Shee-ut", changed it to "Surely" just in time. "Surely, that can't be true. When we got stung by bees as children, nothing ever happened to Barbara Nadine but a sore spot, just like me. You want to know, I'm convinced someone killed her. She was murdered, sure as shit." My emotion overcame my manners. My slip was graciously ignored.

"Well, as you know, the door to the duty room was locked, and no one could possibly have entered without passing directly in front of the Watch Officer's desk. The Watch swears the desk was manned by one or the other at all times, and no one approached the duty room. The OOD states Barbara Nadine seemed fine when she was dismissed to go to bed after she performed her usual duties. But, Tondelayo, I have to tell you, there is a whisper; a small suspicion of suicide. It turns out ..." and here, Chief Manns looked distinctly uncomfortable, "... it seems Barbara Nadine was two months pregnant."

"What?! Pregnant! No. No, dammit, ain't no way." All semblance of civilized formality was swept away by my anger. "That's impossible. No way. Ain't no way, Jose. I know Barbara Nadine didn't mess around, Chief. I know that. It's flat out not possible."

"I rather thought that might be the case. But you were gone to school during the time she ... well, do you think ...?"

"No. No, Chief. Barbara Nadine wouldn't ever let nobody touch her. She never even went out on dates unless it was a double with me. Didn't neither one of us want to end up pregnant, to begin with. We wanted to be successful in the Navy. "Sides, Barbara Nadine was scared to death of, uh, sex." There. I said it. After all, this was certainly an adult conversation, and I certainly knew what was what by now. "Her Daddy interfered with her when she was little, and that's how come she lived with us. She didn't want no part of it."

Chief Manns jaws tightened, and his ears went white at the tips, but he didn't say anything for a minute. "So. So. Well, I made sure the Doc knew what he was talking about. Certainly, I would never have expected Barbara Nadine to turn up pregnant. I've seen a lot of WAVES come and go, and she was one of the finest among a lot of fine young women. I've tried and tried to come up with an explanation, and failed. There's no doubt, though. She was two months into a pregnancy. That's why I've decided to talk to you. I know you've never been satisfied with the results of the investigation, and I know you're doing what you can to investigate. I want you to know that I'm behind you one hundred per cent, and I'll do anything I can to help you. I want to know Barbara Nadine can rest quietly, in peace." At this, Chief Manns' voice shook slightly, and he paused to blow his nose on a pressed, snowy white handkerchief. He handed me another, equally pristine, as I was sniveling myself.

"I can get any records you need, and I have friends just about anyplace you can think of, including Washington." I knew from experience a Master Chief Petty Officer of Bill Manns' caliber and service reputation would have far, far more influence and clout in high places than most Captains, even Admirals. The Navy really was run by Chief and Warrant Officers.

"Thanks Chief." I felt an immense sense of relief. It wasn't just me anymore.

"Well, well, well. Aren't we the privileged one, though? Lunch with a Chief! And gone over two and a half hours. My, my." Naturally, they had to bug me about my absence. Any break in the routine was an excuse to skylark and mess around. I didn't mind. I was as bored as they were on slow days. Plus, I had plenty to think about besides the teasing of my office mates. After awhile, they quit when they couldn't get a rise out of me, and I started my routine job of conducting an inventory of the controlled substances in the dispensary pharmacy. That's when I got the idea. I finished typing up the paperwork, and took it into Senior Chief Benner's office to give it to him. He was very busy, as I'd known he would be.

"If you want to just glance at it, and initial it, I'd be glad to run it over to Lt. Monroe to save you the trip. There aren't any discrepancies."

"Thanks, Dubois. That's a big help. Here, let me see it." He read it over, then signed it, handing it back to me. I grinned to myself at my own cleverness, and whipped right on over to Miss Monroe's office. Knocking on her door, I entered and held out the inventory toward her.

"Excuse me, Mam'n. I've brought up the daily inventory on controlled substances from Senior Chief Benner."

"Thank you, Dubois." She took it and placed it on top of the stack of her "in" file. Since I still stood there, she looked up at me with a questioning smile.

"Miss Monroe, I was wondering if I could request a favor?" I was counting on her in order to carry out my plan. She was a rarity; a black officer, from Oakland, at that. There were damn few blacks in the WAVES, and I knew damn good and well she'd gotten as much shit as I had, and more, probably. She also knew all about Marin City kids, and what it had meant for me to be here, and I'd always thought she had a secret soft spot for me. Not that I'd ever take advantage of it, of course! I knew it had been her routing all the notices about college courses on base, and educational programs and stuff to me, especially, and I had no illusions that being black, with or without the gold on the sleeves, was easy. The prejudice and overt discrimination in the Navy were rampant, and she would have had a gut full to get where she was. She couldn't show me any favoritism, of course; quite the opposite, because all the whites were just waiting to scream about how us niggers stuck together, and I got special treatment, or whatever bullshit they'd put down. So, Miss Monroe had been more than circumspect in not paying me any particular attention, but I'd caught her looking proud of me at inspections and stuff more than once. I knew she liked me, and was pleased I was trying to better myself. I was counting on it.

"Mam'n, I was wondering if it would be all right if I used the Medical Library. I'm interested in learning all I can about the illnesses we see, and so on, and I know the hospital has a great library."

"Well, wonderful! I'll see to it that you get an ID pass. Say, did you know that U.C. Berkeley and Stanford have marvelous medical libraries, too? You can get a guest pass to consult there, too. I'll approve your request if you put in a chit. I have a friend over there who can fix it for you. She can help you learn how to research things there. I'm pleased you want to take the extra effort!"

OK. So far, so good. I felt a little guilty about — well, not that I lied, exactly. I did want to research illnesses. But not for the reason she thought. For a minute, I considered telling her the truth; the whole truth. But, then; no. The less she knew the better. Especially if anything hit the fan because of what I was going to do. I was going to prove Barbara Nadine was murdered, find out how, and who did it. The Navy might not like that. They might not like that at all. At the very least, they wouldn't like some uppity Indian girl showing up their JAG investigation and forensics work. And if the murderer happened to be someone who mattered to them, an officer, say, well ... No, better not risk her ass, at least.

So, off I went on my quest, threading through the labyrinth of buildings and corridors and connecting tunnels, descending deeper and deeper into the bowels of the hospital into areas casual visitors never saw; never thought about. But, of course, all hospitals have them. Eventually, I got to the inner sanctum of the forensics staff, whose offices presented bland, closed faces to the quiet corridors. The morgue was down here, and it was not a popular destination for most of the Nurses and Corpsmen assigned to other areas of the hospital. It gave me the creeps, too, and I kept trying to look around corners before I got there, and checking behind me as I walked a whole lot faster than I usually do.

A friend of mine worked here. Billy Ray Jones was god of the Records Section. He was one smart mutha', too. As a Corpsman, I doubted anyone could beat him, and he'd been around since World War II. He just wore a Third Class crow, and that was because he'd been forced to go for rate. Most of his time had been served as an E-3 Corpsman Striker. He said he didn't aspire to chickenshit responsibilities; all he needed was enough money to buy smokes, get drunk once a week, and get laid once a month. The Navy gave him everything else he needed, and E-3's never had to deal with Mickey Mouse shit. He did, however, have a chest full of medals he'd won as a Corpsman with the Marines during three wars; I knew, because he had to surface for inspections from time to time. When they made him go for Third, he simply added Cuban cigars to his lifestyle with his extra income.

Billy Ray knew everybody and everything about Oak Knoll, living down in "Troll Town" or not. He did not suffer fools gladly, and he chose his friends with great care. Importuning or imperious medical staff found themselves enveloped in expensive clouds of cigar smoke and obfuscation if they displeased him with unnecessary rudeness or undue demands for haste, and supplicants in need of his services soon learned to practice the utmost in tact when approaching him. His Chief, even older and saltier than Billy Ray, was wont to tell complainants to "Bugger off. He does a 4.0 job," if they were enlisted, or that "It will be looked into and corrected soonest," if they were officers. After which, nothing more would be heard. The hapless complainer foolish enough to persevere would find himself inexplicably buried under an avalanche of report forms, blanks, and statements to fill out, which would then be lost, and require resubmission, in triplicate, and so on.

These procedures tended to leave the Chief free to spend his time as he would, and Billy Ray continuing to run a ship taut to his own definitions. Billy Ray lived a serene and hassle-free life down in the lower depths. He was, however, far from isolated. Nothing, literally nothing, happened within the entire, heaving, scurrying, massive anthill of the hospital command without Billy Ray's instantaneous knowledge of it. Billy Ray did not like to feel he could be subject to unwanted interruption of his lifestyle due to unforeseen events, and who knew what seemingly petty and irrelevant happenstance could lead to unpleasant reverberations? So, he had established a scuttlebutt system that would have made the combined minions of the CIA and the FBI fall down and cry.

Barbara Nadine and I were, or had been in her case, two of Billy Ray's closest friends. When I talked to him, he told me he didn't feel comfortable with the pathologist's report and conclusions either. Billy Ray Jones would investigate. He would get a copy of the report itself; I would acquire one of the JAG investigation, since I had connections in the place to which all Judge Advocate Investigations flowed. We would look into things.

That night, I allowed myself to think about what Master Chief Manns had told me. I hadn't been assigned a new bunkie yet, so I had the quiet privacy of my room to consider the shocking concept of a pregnant Barbara Nadine. I sat cross-legged on her bed, hugging her soft Teddy, and realized it was just not fuckin' possible. Barbara Nadine was definitely all show and no go. Yeah, she had plenty of sailors after her; she was pretty and lively. We both had the wild child image, of course; it went with the Harley, the outlaw biker thing, the ability to hold our own in a man's world. Frankly, neither of us minded much; we were viewed with awe by some of the more easily impressed girls, and even feared a little. A little fear is a wonderful thing to be able to arouse at times. Face it, we were both just the tiniest bit flamboyant, and we liked to liven up otherwise dull days from time to time. But, by God, we were still both virgins. With me, it was more technical than otherwise, maybe, but with her, it went well beyond technical. She hated even making out, and wouldn't even French kiss if she could get away with it. Mostly she did. And wan't no fuckin' way she'a given in during the short months I was away at school. Shit, she didn't even have anyone steady. Most guys lost interest when they got the picture. She had told me over and over she would never get married and have kids, and she hated even the idea of sex. I didn't, but I wadn't gon' mess up my career with no baby, neither. Nor a husband, neither.

Barbara Nadine was even touchy around us family. She softened up to Mama pretty fast, but it was years before Papa even tried to hug her unless he had us both gathered up in his arms. He was real careful not to spook her, and so was Jack, when he was alive.

No, Barbara Nadine hadn't gotten pregnant voluntarily. She must have been raped.

Chapter 13

SEARCHING

I don't suppose it was much of a secret among the troops; scuttlebutt never misses anything. Even the Chiefs probably knew, although I'm sure Chief Manns never uttered a word out of line. Still, his inquiries among his friends were bound to create some curiosity and speculation, discreet though he may have been. It was highly likely that most of the enlisted people in the area knew I was looking into Barbara Nadine's death. The officers, on the other hand, tended to be fairly oblivious to whatever the troops were doing on their own unless it caused them some personal inconvenience or discomfort. Lt. Monroe and Lt. Madden, their mamas not having raised fools, no doubt figured things out from the git-go, but did not interfere or even mention my investigations. So, I was able to move around and about with no problems. At least at first.

Things appeared on my desk like magic, in brand new guard mail envelopes with no prior addressees listed to trace their journeys. Things like duty rosters, copies of OOD's logs, anonymous speculations and accusations. Much of it was crap, of course, but I kept everything in a locked file at a friend's house on the beach. You never know.

Billy Ray obtained the coroner's report, which was sickening to me, but enlightening. It seems the autopsy had revealed no sign of a bee sting or other point of entry, but simply a generalized rash, particularly prominent in the moister areas of the body, such as the armpits. Since the body showed signs of recent shaving, the rash was attributed to this. Stomach contents revealed she had eaten Sloppy Joes and mashed potatoes, green beans, and tapioca pudding some twelve hours prior to death, and the Chow Hall menu listed all those foods for the evening mess the night before. Since she had eaten all those items countless times before with no ill effect, and no other illnesses were reported among those eating in the Mess Hall that night, the conclusion was that none of the food ingested had acted as a pathogen. Her heart and circulatory system were healthy, and she was described as a "healthy well-nourished female Caucasian of approximately twenty-two years of age." The body was found on the floor, clad in underwear and stockings, and showed no sign of violence other than that consistent with convulsive choking to death. Cause of death was respiratory failure believed to result from anaphylactic shock due to unknown origin, with the possibility of an extreme allergic reaction to bee sting. It was noted that several dead bees were found behind the locker in a more thorough search of the room a week after the death. The report told me little, except that she was, indeed, pregnant with a fetus approximately two months old, and that there were no signs of recent sexual activity.

The Judge Advocate General's report, a procedure routinely done after any death, suspicious or otherwise, was a little less terse. It noted that the room in which the body was found was locked from the inside, and that it contained no other means of entrance. Again, the presence of dead bees was noted, and the fact that the room was not thoroughly searched for a period of one week after Barbara Nadine's death. The JAG investigator toyed with the idea of suicide due to the presence of the pregnancy, but could discover no means of self-inflicted death, and so proclaimed the fatality due to accident.

Barbara Nadine's personal effects were handed over to me. I kept the things from the duty room in my locker, and took everything else home from her side of the room, except for her teddy bear, which joined mine on my bed. I kept taking her ditty bag out and spreading its contents out on my bed, believing that if I just stared at them long enough, they would tell me something. They were the only witnesses to the day she died. What would they have seen?

Certainly, nothing appeared amiss. Barbara Nadine, like most of us, kept a ditty bag ready for her watches, replenishing it with clean underwear and so on immediately after standing the previous watch. So, we had: one ditty bag; one pair of clean white cotton underpants, size 4, one pair of them worn; two white cotton bras, size 34B, one worn; two white cotton full slips, size 34, one worn; two pair panty hose, neutral, one worn; and one "itty bitty ditty bag." (The phrase, from boot camp, was maintained by most of us to refer to our toiletry bags, many of which were, indeed, the original navy blue zippered bags from boot camp.) Barbara Nadine's contained the usual soap in a plastic container, razor and blades, deodorant, hand lotion, talcum powder, tooth paste, tooth brush, comb and hair brush, hair rollers, curler cap, sanitary supplies, and the minimal makeup she wore; a pale pink lipstick and dark brown eyeliner. Nothing out of place there, except what appeared to be spilled deodorant, maybe from a loose cap. It was a roll-on, and all the knocking around may have loosened it so that some spilled. I dabbed it up where it had gotten on the case, and tried to tighten the cap. It wasn't loose, but I suppose it simply tightened up on its own in all the jostling. Nothing out of place anywhere. Just a coming baby.

Two months pregnant. It must have happened just before or just after I left for "C" School. But why wouldn't she have told me? Two months. Maybe, just maybe, she didn't even know she was pregnant! After all, she had always been irregular. The doctor said it was because she'd suffered from malnutrition and neglect for so long as a child, and her body couldn't make up for it. She'd lost several teeth due to calcium deficiency, too, and she never seemed to gain weight, no matter how she pigged out. So, it was just possible that she hadn't noticed the lack of her period.

But that didn't explain why she hadn't told me she'd had sex. Or been raped. And I'd bet my hat and ass, it was rape. But she still would have told me, I'm positive. She still hated Harry Lee for what he had done to her, and at one time had even considered asking Napa Bob to take him out. She didn't though, realizing that might not be a good idea. But anyway, I was pretty sure that she wouldn't let a rapist get away with it without making sure he paid. She was too pissed about what had already been done to her. A lot of girls would be ashamed, and not tell anyone; we knew that happened to the girls in the barracks sometimes. But not Barbara Nadine. Not with me and Napa Bob, and Papa, when it came to that.

A look at the duty roster gave me an idea. Time to talk to everybody else on duty that night, see what they might know, might have seen or heard. This was dangerous. This meant talking to several officers, letting the brass know I was investigating. I had all the statements from the JAG report, of course, but they were pretty cursory. I wanted more detail, more thought about what somebody might have seen or heard. But I had to take a chance. It was complicated, too, since the rotation of the various watches differed. I would have to figure out all the watch bills, which wasn't hard, but I also thought I'd go back a few months of Barbara Nadine's watches to see if anything odd stuck out. I was pretty desperate for something, anything, to strike me. I'd talked with all our friends already, of course; nothing. According to them, she had seemed perfectly normal. Judy told me she had been kind of excited about my return, as she had a line on an old black Cadillac that the elderly aunt of one of the other girls owned and might sell. It was quite old, big as a yacht, and had very low mileage; practically mint. The old lady was in no hurry to sell, and would love to have a friend of her niece buy it. That sure as hell didn't sound like suicide to me. Barbara Nadine would have loved a cherry old Caddie; tail fins and leather, and big enough to run over VW bugs without even noticing.

I thought about the baby. Barbara Nadine would have known we could get her an abortion. We knew how that was done, and where. She also knew she could have kept it, although that was unlikely. A bastard resulting from rape, no more Navy, no more school, and a sure trip to the welfare lines wasn't something I thought she'd choose. Mama, Papa, and I would help, of course, but she'd still have no future. The fucking Navy didn't give a shit about how you got yo'sef pregnant, they'd thow' yo' ass out, Baby, in'na fuckin' street, faster than fast. But she wouldn't kill herself. She wan't a fool. Besides, I was positive she didn't even realize she was pregnant yet.

So, the duty rosters.

Just looking at them, I was able to reconstruct the lists of people on watch for Barbara Nadine's last three months. They told me nothing. The only name I even recognized was Commander Strang, who had stood watch as Command Duty Officer on the same night as Barbara Nadine had the month before her death. The CDO on the night of her fatal watch was a Captain Nickles. The appearance of the COM12 Executive Officer on Barbara Nadine's watch wasn't much; CDO's didn't stay on board the way the Officers Of The Day and others did. They made rounds, checking in from time to time by telephone or in person, then were free to go wherever they wished as long as they were readily available by telephone. If something were happening, they would report to the duty room. The duty logs showed nothing out of the ordinary had occurred, that the CDO had reported all secure on rounds, and had duly put in an appearance once in the early evening, then gone ashore.

I talked to the Petty Officers on the rosters, and was trying to think of a good way to approach the officers of the various OOD watches and the Chiefs of the Watch, but couldn't come up with a good plan. I could hardly sashay into another commands, sit down cross my legs, light up, and say, "So, Mr. Blank, what can you tell me about the night of your watch with the subject?" like some detective novel. Even Chiefs were unlikely to welcome my intrusion into their lives like that. So, down the Yellow Brick Road I finally went, all the way to Master Chief Mann's office.

He was not happy with me.

"Tondelayo, what in hell are you doing over here? You stick out like a sore thumb. And I've heard you've been questioning watchstanders. Are you out of your mind? Don't you realize how dangerous what you're doing could be? Somebody murdered Barbara Nadine, you know! Then, if NISO gets wind of what you're going, your ass is grass, if you'll pardon the expression. I ought to kick your little behind all the way back to the hospital! You could blow everything just when I'm getting somewhere!" Shit, if Bill talked to me like that, he must be really beside himself, and for a moment, I was stunned. Me? I thought I was doing good! I guess my face showed my hurt.

"Look, I know you're trying to find things out, and it's hard, especially when it's not your command. But leave COM12 to me, you concentrate on other aspects. You can't talk to CDO's and OOD's, you can't get records, but you can check out things from your end. What have you been doing besides causing hate and discontent amongst the ranks over here?"

I told him about my studies of forensics in the medical libraries, and my investigations into Barbara Nadine's activities over the last few months of her life. He looked pleased, and questioned me closely about what I had learned about anaphylactic shock.

"It's an extreme allergic reaction, often to a common substance. Bee stings are often a cause, or some food substance. It can cause immediate respiratory failure, with extreme constriction of the respiratory system, a drastic drop in blood pressure, and a rash. It's usually after the first reaction that fatality results unless proper medical care is administered immediately."

"Can you remember her ever having been stung by bees, wasps, hornets, or anything like that?"

"Yeah, lots of times. She just got bumps like the rest of us. We'd pull the stingers out, put spit on the bump, and that was that."

"How about any other possible allergen?"

"Well, you know, I've thought about that a lot. She didn't seem to be allergic to anything, but she would never eat peanut butter. Mama always had to make her tuna or bologna or something, because she couldn't eat peanut butter. She didn't even eat candy bars with peanuts in them, or cookies. She said she got sick from it, but since she never ate it when I knew her, I don't know what happened. But, I do have this idea..."

"Yes?"

"Well, it's kind'a weird. Don't laugh."

"I won't. This is no laughing matter."

"Well, you know how we grew up. Southern. Mama and Papa cook stuff in lard, or in Mazola Oil once in awhile. Lard, mostly. And we don't eat foreign food often. Just Mexican, with Judy, or something. You know, we don't eat different stuff much, and the chow hall always serves sort of American stuff."

"Yes. Go on."

"Well, I got to remembering that day at the command picnic. The Filipino Stewards made some of their food for special, remember? That was the day Barbara Nadine got sick, and couldn't breathe, and the CDO had to take her to Sick Bay."

"Yes! Yes! Filipino food's a lot like Chinese food. Had Barbara Nadine ever had Chinese or Filipino food before?"

"No, neither of us had. We've been to Chinatown, of course, but we always liked to eat shrimp louis on the wharf when we went to the City, so we never got around to eating in Chinatown. You know, we'd look at the stuff in the markets, and it all looked so ... well, we just never did.

"But anyway, that seemed significant, so I did some checking. A lot of Filipino and Chinese cooking is done with peanut oil."

"Yes. It is. That, Tondelayo, is one magnificent piece of work!" Bill positively beamed. "OK. So what do we know about the rest of the incident? She was probably allergic to peanut oil, and that was an anaphylactic reaction that day."

"Yeah. The first serious one. She may have lived through that one because of the antihistamine, but if she somehow was exposed to it again, that morning ..." I shut my eyes for a moment, swallowing hard. But I had to finish the story.

"Since it was a Saturday, there was only a Corpsman on duty at Sick Bay. He was a new guy, without much experience. He came off a carrier, and they had lots of docs and higher rated Corpsmen, so he mostly did records and injections. I know him; he said when she came in, he figured she just had hay fever or something. He gave her an injection of antihistamine, and when she began to breathe easier, he just put her on the binnacle list and sent her to bed. The CDO took her to the barracks.

"I talked to the girl who had barracks duty that day, and she said the CDO was half carrying Barbara Nadine. She thought she was drunk, until he said she was just sick from the sun or something, and needed to hit the rack. She was going to take over and put her to bed, but the phone started ringing, and the CDO told her never mind, he'd see her to her room. She told him what room, gave him the duty key ring, and answered the phone. It suddenly got busier than hell, and she had to run around delivering messages and stuff, and she never noticed him leave. She just found the keys on the nail on the board later. When she checked Barbara Nadine, she was sleeping, and looked fine. Then, I came in, and stayed with her until she woke up the next morning. She seemed fine, except she was all embarrassed. Apparently, the antihistamine hit her so hard she wet the bed a little. We changed it, and she went back to sleep. She slept all day Sunday, too. I had to sort of carry her to the bathroom, she was so groggy. By Monday, she was fine, though.

"But, Chief, the CDO was Commander Strang."

"Commander Strang. How interesting. Our XO. Did Barbara Nadine ever mention him? I mean, other than the fact that he was our XO, of course."

"No, not really. Well, she did tell me she didn't like him. He was always staring at her, she said, and his eyes scared her. She said she tried to keep out of his way."

"Ummmm. And Barbara Nadine being who she was, she never had to see him for XO's Screening Mast, or anything. You know, I've heard a few things from ..." Bill trailed off, obviously not willing to continue here. "Listen, you go on back to Oak Knoll, and keep up the good work. I'm going to do some checking. We may know what killed her; if so, we still don't know who, why, or how. But I think we're getting somewhere. You just be more careful. You may be playing with the Big Time now. You may not realize just what a sleeping tiger you could awaken. A lot of strange things happen to boat rockers sometimes, and no one ever knows what, where, or why. Civilians have no idea of the kind of power some people can wield from unexpected corners. One of you dead is enough!"

"Yes, Chief. I'm sorry. I'll be careful."

With that, I left. I had a lot to piece together. If peanut oil or something with peanuts in it were involved, how in the name of God did it happen? She had nothing in her stomach to explain it, she never would have touched peanuts on her own, and the whole thing was so far-fetched I had to wonder if I could be losing it myself. Sheeeut, talk about grasping at straws!

Walking over to Yellow Bird, I decided to hit the Exchange before going back to the hospital. I was out of cigarettes. As I stood in the checkout line, Commander Strang came into the Exchange. Since we almost collided going through the door, I got a real close look. He spotted me, too, and one pale eyebrow elevated just the merest bit. I know he recognized me, and for some reason, he wasn't pleased at the sight of my brown ass; I could tell. Still, he gave me a snarl disguised as a grin or a smile. It almost floored me. He had gold teeth, even his front ones lined with gold. His eye teeth were big things, and he had gold dragons implanted in them. Shit, that was weird. It was popular in Marin City to have gold, just to prove you could afford dental care, but I had never seen a white man with it. I hurried out as fast as my legs would go without running. I didn't blame Barbara Nadine for not liking him. His eyes were dead, opaque blue marbles, like ice. Not a man to fuck with. Nossir.

Truer words were never spoken.

Chapter 14

THE NAVAL INVESTIGATIVE SERVICE OFFICE INVESTIGATION

I had a lot to put together. Too many missing pieces. I did my job, went through the motions, kept up with my classes, even taking exams, talked, ate, slept, even met my new bunkie. She was a nice girl, I suppose, but we didn't exactly click. She was religious; religious with a vengeance. And she didn't think much of my ways. She was not cool. She was not righteous. She was not a sister. Most of all, she was not Barbara Nadine. We divided up the room with an invisible line, and went our separate ways. I kept trying to make sense of things that didn't make sense.

One piece fell into place though. A big one. The time between the command picnic and Barbara Nadine's murder (Oh, shit, let us not fuck around. "Death" is just another euphemism for "murder" here.) was two months. And I had changed the sheets after she wet the bed, helped her to the head, helped her sit on the pot, cleaned her up, and remade her bed with fresh linen. As a Corpsman, I had lots of practice, and everything went sort of automatically. But now that I thought back, there had been no smell of pee. The wetness was not yellow, and it was sticky. As a Corpsman, all that practice had included a lot of peed-in beds, and a lot of other beds where young men slept. I don't think Barbara Nadine had peed her bed. No, I don't think she did. Although it didn't sink in at the time, probably because I was too concerned with helping her, but that sheet looked more like something else——. I don't think she knew what the hell had happened to her; she hadn't even remembered me doing all that stuff. She was too far out of it from the antihistamines to remember anything at all. Furthermore, who'd undressed her? When I got there she just had a tee shirt on, and it was rucked up under her arms.

"Petty Officer Dubois, this is Agent Smithers. He's conducting an investigation into certain allegations, and wishes to interrogate you. You have the right to request the presence of your Women's Representative during these proceedings to insure your proper treatment if you wish, but you may decline." Miss Monroe looked angry, but cool. She had the Face For The Man down, that girl. I guessed by now that she was pretty tough, and had learned a whole lot getting that gold on her sleeve. I bet she even knew the toe-shuffle if she ever felt the need to use it. Shit, yes, I wanted her there. She had summoned me to her office to tell me that the agent wanted to interview me, and suggested I might want to get my purse. When I got back, she didn't turn a hair at me wearing my shades. We'd walked down to the conference room just as though I wore shades all day, every day. I'd smiled to myself. Napa Bob would have been proud of me.

"I would like to have Lt. Monroe present, please." Just the slightest bit of toe-shufflin'. I knew all about NISO and their witch hunts.

"All right, Dubois, sit down." He flashed a mouthful of tobacco-stained fangs at me, and gave an outstanding imitation of the sincerity of Governor Wallace talking about how he didn't hate niggers on a personal basis. He gestured toward the hard wooden chair across the table from where he sat in a comfortable leather Captain's chair, surrounded by file folders, stacks of papers, and an overflowing ashtray. He ostentatiously turned on a portable tape recorder, and then just sat there, staring coldly at me. He seemed unaware of Miss Monroe standing there.

Miss Monroe pulled up another chair next to me, and patted my hand under the table as if to say, "It's OK, Babe, it's two against one."

Smithers took me through the usual bullshit stuff; name, rank, service number, etc. As if it were all news to him. Asshole. This is where they make you comfortable, I guess. I'd been through this before, as lesbian witch hunts were the Naval Investigative Service Office's favorite activity. Whenever things got dull, someone at NISO would scratch his balls, spit in the waste basket and say, "Les'us go crucify some lezzies. Ain't got none in awhile, and they'll be gettin' outta' hand." We were making book in the barracks as to whether or not there would be any women left in the services after the war. It was definitely not a requirement that women separated as queers actually be queer, just that they be female. A lot of women even decided to say they were just to escape the harassment, or just to get out because they didn't like it once they got in. It would have been funny, except some young kids killed themselves when the net caught them. The witch hunts did not discriminate by gender, however they did tend to heavily favor women. More than one male sailor was dead too, often because he'd been accused of doing things he couldn't even spell. The methods NISO used were often unsavory, and even criminal, I knew. I was glad to have Lt. Monroe there.

"I wanted to talk to you about some information we have regarding one Barbara Nadine Johnson."

Oh, shit. He could not have said that.

"I beg your pardon? 'One' Barbara Nadine Johnson? Would that be the dead one?" Oh, oh. Watch yo' mouf', girl, this ape-raping, blue balled, mutha-fucking cocksucker is just trying to get at you — make you forget yo'sef.

Smithers just lifted the corners of his thin, chapped lips slightly. "Yes, Dubois, that would be the dead one. You are, or were, acquainted with her, were you not?"

"Yes sir, I was. She was my sister."

An eyebrow raised in disbelief. "Your sister? I assume your parents remarried?"

Shithead. "Not my blood sister, sir. Barbara Nadine had lived with my family since we were kids. We'd known one another since her family moved to Marin City when we were four. We were raised together as sisters." In spite of my determination not to let this shithead fuck with my mind, my stomach was in knots. Barbara Nadine was dead, and couldn't even defend herself. What the fuck was this mutha' talking about? Me and Barbara Nadine, f'crissakes? I knew NISO played dirty, and my innocence, to say nothing of hers, would be of no consequence if NISO wanted it that way. I put on my Face For The Man, too. This look, beloved by enlisted people, persons of color, and general underdogs everywhere, was a blank, non-revelatory facade beyond which the wearer lived his or her own life, out of sight of possible hostile forces. All Marin City kids beyond the age of six were adept at it. Well, eventually, he'd crack, and let me know what he was after. Meanwhile, time to remember the First Law of Life In The Military: Never Volunteer. I'd teach him not to fuck with the Phantom. If only I didn't need to pee so bad.

Smithers stared at me just long enough to relay the message that that had to be the one biggest crock of shit he had ever heard. Then he said, "I'm here to discuss some information I've received from some of your friends about your relationship with the deceased." Now it was "the deceased?" Who wrote his scripts, anyway?

"Marin City? You're from Marin City?" Just a hint of another raised eyebrow and a subtle change in tone let me know I'd been dropped down the social scale at least two notches. He must not have been listening when I'd given my Home of Record earlier. "Isn't it rather unusual for, uh, coloreds and whites to intermix to that degree?" Oh, Alabama, dear Alabama, wither art thou, Alabama?

"I don't know that it's all that unusual. All the kids play together in Marin City. There's quite a variety of people there; Mexican, Black, Indians, whatever. I'm Cherokee on my mother's side, Cajun on my father's. The Johnsons are whites." Shut up, girl, you're babbling. "Yes, we were friends. Is that a problem for you?"

"I'll ask the questions, Dubois. Insolence will not help your case."

I felt Lt. Monroe stiffen at that. "Agent Smithers, I'd like to remind you that this is a routine interrogation in a routine investigation. You are not a member of the military. I will deal with infractions of military protocol and order should it arise. I do not feel Petty Officer Dubois was in any way insolent." Take that, you bastard.

Smither's face twitched slightly. I could see "Another uppity nigger bitch" parading across his acne-pocked forehead like a message tape in a movie theater. He cleared his throat.

"Now, I don't mean to say you couldn't be, or that there's anything exactly wrong about it; it just seemed unusual. Please go on. Tell me about yourself and the Johnson girl."

The Johnson girl. Sort of like, "tell me about the dog," or something. Behind my shades, I felt my eyes narrowing. I bet doin' shit like this makes you hard, don't it, mutha'fucker? Yeah. Power, Man. Power. Us niggers had best watch our step when you on the prowl, huh, Big Man?

Ms. Monroe shifted slightly in her chair, bringing me back to the question at hand.

"I'm not sure what you want to know, sir. We were raised together, and we were friends, and we joined the Navy together. She went to Treasure Island, to COM12, and I went to Hospital Corps school and Oak Knoll."

"Why did you both decide on the Navy?"

"Jobs are hard to come by on the outside, and we wanted to make something of our lives. We were both interested in the schooling we could get, and we wanted to make a contribution."

"I see." Another crock. Patriotism amongst savages? The man was as transparent as glass. I think his contempt clouded his brain. Brain cell. Singular.

"What did you girls do? What did you do together as you were growing up?"

"Do? We did what all kids do. Played in the sprinklers in summer. Rode bikes. Slid down hills on cardboard. Went to school. Played cowboys and Indians, only neither one of us wanted to be the cowboy; we both wanted to be the horses." I felt Ms. Monroe suppress a laugh. "We went on picnics, and when we were old enough, we used to hike up in the hills around Marin City. Sometimes our parents took us to movies. I don't know, whatever! We were kids!"

"This thing of Johnson living with you. Why was that?"

I didn't answer. I tried frantically to think of what to say, but this line of questioning had me rattled.

"What did her parents say about it? They still live in Marin City, don't they? They weren't very happy about their little girl moving in with your family, were they?" I knew, then. I just knew. This fucker had talked to Harry Lee, and he'd fed him some sort of bullshit story. He was still pissed about not getting any of the insurance money, and he wouldn't mind lying just to make trouble. Smither's attitude of sneering disbelief wasn't helping.

"Her parents didn't care. They were drawing Aid for Dependent Children for her, and with her out of the house, they didn't even have to feed and clothe her, just suck up the money."

"You mean they were illegally drawing government money for a child that did not share their home, and your family conspired in this?"

"Conspired? Come on! She needed a safe place to stay, and the only place she could get it was with us!"

"Safe? From what? Her own parents? Why did she want to live with you? Did you share a bedroom?"

Ahhhh, here it was.

"Yes, we did. My father built bunk beds. We only had three bedrooms, and my brother had one, and my parents the other. She was always staying with us anyway, and when she moved in for good, it didn't seem any different." Snake tongue, licking chapped lips. Flicker, flicker.

"Convenient, wasn't it? Two little friends, together all the time now." Flicker, flicker. "Was it convenient, Dubois? Did it — facilitate things?"

"Things? What things?"

"I notice you two have always shared the same living spaces, even in the barracks." Flicker, flicker. "Why?"

"Because, Agent Smithers, we were friends, we got along beautifully, and not everyone in the barracks would have been pleased to have a bunkie who's colored." There. Deal with that, shithead.

"You still haven't answered my question, Dubois. Are you trying to evade the issue?" At this point, I didn't know which question he meant.

"No, sir. Which question is it that you feel I haven't answered"

"Let me spell it out, carefully and slowly. Perhaps your comprehension skills are slightly impaired." Niggers are slow, you know, but, Man, can we dance! We all got that jungle bunny rhythm, you know. "Just exactly why was it that Barbara Nadine Johnson moved in with the Dubois family, sharing the same bedroom as yourself, Tondelayo Dubois?"

"It's kind of hard to talk about. Barbara Nadine — well, she didn't want to stay in her own house. She was pretty shook up, and things had gotten pretty bad. She had a lot of brothers and sisters, and there's no money because her old man is a drunk. A mean drunk. He beat Calvin, one of her brothers, so bad he broke his jaw, his cheekbone, and an arm once. Calvin was only six, and all he'd done was spill some old sour milk they were supposed to be eating for supper. There was never enough food, and Barbara Nadine often didn't get anything to eat at all."

Pause.

"I see. Anything else?"

"Yes. Yes, damn it! Her older brothers and her daddy were interfering with her. Had done since she was a baby! Besides beating her half to death, and starving her, they fucked her! There! Is that what you wanted to know, you..." Miss Monroe clamped her hand on my arm. Hard. I shut up, my heart racing so hard I could feel the blood pounding in my head. I couldn't see anything but white, and if I'd have had a knife or a gun, Smithers would have been history.

"Agent Smithers, I think you'll agree that Petty Officer Dubois needs a moment to compose herself." Miss Monroe gave me a tissue, and just sat there quietly until I could speak again, even though my voice was shaking.

Smithers went on as though nothing had happened. "And you two shared a room from that time on?"

"Yes. I told you. We shared a room. What of it? What are you trying to say?"

"What makes you feel I'm trying to say anything? Is there some reason you're so defensive? You know, telling the truth now can save you a whole lot of trouble later. I'm trying to help you, but you have to help me, too. Why don't you just tell me the truth?" Poor Smithers; I suppose due to government thrift, he had to play "Good Cop, Bad Cop" all by himself.

"I am telling you the truth! Yes, we shared my room. Yes, we had bunkbeds! We didn't have a spare room!"

"Ahhh, no spare room." Flicker, flicker. "It is my understanding that your older brother, Jack, was killed in combat in Korea, is that not so?"

Jack. Oh, God. Jack.

"Yes."

"Is there any particular reason you chose not to utilize his room?"

"Yes, there is. Mama and Papa left it the way he left it for years. They couldn't believe he wouldn't be home. Then, when they tore down the old houses and built the new units, they only got a two bedroom. But while it was his room, neither one of us would have even considered using it. It was his, and had all his stuff in it. Later, Mama put her sewing machine in there, and used to go in and sew, with the door closed. We could hear her singing gospel, and I think it comforted her. Barbara Nadine and I got along fine in one room, and there wasn't nothing wrong with that!" Careful, girl. Grammar, grammar. Don't want to let The Man know how rattled you are.

"Wrong? Did I say there might be something wrong? I'm just asking you about your room; your, uh, sleeping arrangements. Is that a sensitive subject?"

"No! I just know all about you and your witch hunts!" I suddenly knew I was out of control, enraged to the point of making stupid mistakes.

"Well, now you bring it up, maybe we ought to take a look at possibilities. You know, I have statements from several of your friends that say you and Johnson were — very good friends. Very, very good friends, indeed."

"Friends? Who? What friends? Ain't none'a my friends 'ud say shit like that. No fuckin' way. Me 'n' Barbara Nadine wasn't into that scene, Man. Not even. Whoever tol' you that shit needs their fuckin' lips ripped off! Wan't no kinda' foolishness like dat, Man. Nuh uh. Who tol' you dat?"

"Oh, I can't say. You know that. But there are several statements that you and Johnson were, ummm, a little light in the loafers, so to speak." Flicker, flicker. Smithers leaned towards me, breathing kind of hard. His eyes looked shiny, and he had just the merest suggestion of spittle at the corners of his mouth, and he crossed his legs, no doubt to hide the pathetic little bulge in his polyester pants. "Why don't you tell me about it? You'll feel better!"

"That's bullshit, Man. Bullshit. Somebody's lyin', or I'm dyin'. Neither one us like that. No."

"Well, someone must be lying. Only I think it's you, Dubois. You know, you'd do better telling the truth. I'll make it go easier for you; you can save us both a lot of trouble."

"I got nothin' more to say. And I gotta' pee." I sat back, arms folded. I'd had enough.

"Oh, I'm not finished, Dubois. I think you can wait for your call of nature."

"No, Agent Smithers. I don't believe she can. May I remind you that this is supposed to be merely an interview, and that Petty Officer Dubois has rights. Among them is the right to utilize sanitary facilities when she feels the necessity to do so." Ooooh weeeeh! Miss Monroe even had a little English accent when she got up on her high horse! I was allowed to go pee. It gave me a chance to get some circulation back in my ass and legs, too. Ms. Monroe had left too, I saw her on the phone in one of the offices down the passageway. I thought about not going back in until she got back, but Smithers was up, smoking. He came over to the doorway, leaned over me, blowing smoke directly in my face, and said, quietly, "You know, Dubois, you're nothing. Not even spit in the wind. Nobody's gonna' save your black ass when it comes down. I strongly suggest you listen to me, and let me help you. I can make it easy on you. Cooperate with me, and I can grease the skids for you. I can make it so you can take the easy way out; no hassles, no bad paper, no problemo. Fuck with me, and you'll do hard time. Fuck with me, and you'll get a paper so bad it'll follow you for the rest of your miserable fuckin' life, bitch. I, personally, will see to it that you never, ever get away from this. You're gonna' fall, baby, if you don't smarten up. I'm The Man. I'm The Big Man. But I'm willing to step in for you if you smarten up. What's the difference, honey chile', your little girlfriend is dead, nothing can hurt her now, and the others don't give a rat's ass about you. Shit, they're already singing about you like they were canaries. They're white, and you're the only nigger in the woodpile. You don't really think they're going to take a fall for you, do you?

I noticed his cracker accent came and went, and that his breathing was heavy. Sweat ringed his pits in huge circles, he having long ago removed his coat. He stank. Miss Monroe was stuck on the phone for quite some time, and Smithers really hit his stride. Alternately threatening and cajoling, he tried to batter me down. Finally, Miss Monroe hurried back in, apologizing. She looked sharply at me, sitting numbly on my chair, not even trying to answer Smithers, and she told him that she thought that was enough. When he balked, she smiled sweetly and said she'd just call the admiral then, and asked for guidance. He gave in, and let me go. But only after I signed a statement he wrote up, supposedly a synopsis of what I'd said, but actually a slightly twisted, ever-so-slightly altered version that subtly, but definitely, changed the tenor of it. Tiredly, I read it over, noted the differences, but decided it wasn't important enough to protest. I just wanted the hell out of that stinking, airless prison. Besides, there was no doubt about it; he was The Man, and I was the only nigger in this particular woodpile. Of course, I had to deal with the old bullshit, "You must sign this statement. It is not an admission of guilt, it merely attests to the fact that you have read it." Now there was a crock if I ever saw one! But I signed, I signed. My fate, whatever it would be, was sealed with or without my signature on that stupid "Statement."

Chapter 15

MILITARY JUSTICE

Smithers and I became quite an item. I never knew when I'd be summoned, trapped in that horrible, stinking room with him. Miss Monroe tried to be there, but she couldn't always. On those occasions, he excelled himself. I got less and less frightened, and more and more angry. One day, I even presented him with a beautifully wrapped present, a box containing antiperspirant, toothbrush and toothpaste, mouthwash, and little bottles of shampoo and detergent. I told him I was only trying to help him, and wanted to be friends.

He didn't think it was funny. And he still stank. After awhile, I got used to carrying a hankie in my purse, which I would spray with my favorite cologne and hold under my nose. It drove him crazy. Miss Monroe pretended not to see it, just as she never noticed my ever-present shades.

Smithers took to dragging me out of the rack at any hour, and he often interrogated me in different places, deserted and dismal. Places I didn't recognize. He became more and more vicious, and at one point, told me I would "...have to be really, really nice..." to him, "...to prove I liked men..." if I hoped for any mercy from him. I had nothing to say. The whole thing was a sick, perverted sack of sheep shit. After a while, the ugliness was so bizarre, so far from any reasonable facsimile of the friendship Barbara Nadine and I had shared, that I forgot this was supposed to be the basis for the lies. It seemed as those this whole thing was a nightmare involving fictional people and activities I didn't even know or understand. It became almost fascinating to watch Smithers sink further and further into the mire of his own foul imagination. His terrible need for his sick mouthings to be true led to an almost palpably visible specter of perverse sexual acts and shadowy people I couldn't even imagine.

Once, just for the hell of it, I calmly announced I was ready to tell the truth now. Smithers heaved a deep sigh, and prepared himself to hear his dreams come true. Then, calmly and steadily, with my voice soft and even, I told him. I said I know Barbara Nadine had been murdered, and I was pretty sure I knew by whom and how. I told him he should be busy trying to catch her killer, not be engaging in masturbatory activity by interrogating me over and over. He nearly shit a brick.

"Murdered? Are you out of your mind? Murdered? Listen, girlie, don't try that bullshit with me. Just what crazy thing is it that you think you know?"

"I told you. I know she was murdered. I know she was raped. And I think the Navy and NISO should be spending their time and effort trying to find out about that. This lesbian thing is just bullshit, and you know it."

"If you know anything, if you have any proof of such a serious charge, you'd better be able to back it up. What evidence do you have?"

"I ain't tellin' you nothin', honkey. You figure it out."

The interrogations went on. I was called off shift, called in on weekends, hounded to death, nearly. I lost a lot of weight,

not only because I had no appetite, but because I didn't want
to go into the chow hall and sit by myself, assiduously avoided.
I got no sleep. Nobody would talk to me, or spend time with
me in the barracks. It was too dangerous. I knew that, intellec-
tually, but it still hurt. I was all too well aware that once a girl
was fingered by NISO to take a fall as a lesbian, even casual
conversation with her could lead to inclusion as a suspect in
the witch hunt. They kept us off balance and divided that way.

They said lesbians always were to be found in "nests," with
homosexual activity spreading out to infect anyone in the vi-
cinity, as though it were contagious. No one could afford to
befriend a current suspect. No one could be trusted. Your name
could be handed to the agents by someone desperate to escape
the torment. The atmosphere of fear and loathing was so intense that any contact, however innocent, could condemn a
woman to the hell of suspicion and officially sanctioned abu-
sive interrogation.

Girls who entered the Navy with no concept of sexual activity between or among women became "educated" immediately. Many of them found themselves accused of committing
acts they had never even heard of. They left as women old
before their time, many of them smeared with the offal of mind-
less hate they could not even understand. Lives were shattered
and spirits broken, all on mere, often totally groundless suspicion.

And now, it was me. Barbara Nadine was cold and dead,
and couldn't even defend herself. Sometimes I had to concentrate very hard to summon up the real memories of the laughing little girls that had roamed the hills of Marin City with me.
Sometimes, the pictures in my mind faded behind a haze of
smoke and confusion. The pain was indescribable. Gnawing
rats of depression began to assume tangible shape. Maybe this
would never end. Maybe Smithers was right; maybe I was going
to take a fall.

Sometimes, I wondered if it wouldn't be easier to just give
in, agree. Or maybe, just maybe, I ought to join Barbara Nadine,

wherever she was. The only thing that held me together was going home to Mama and Papa, and knowing Miss Monroe and Master Chief Manns didn't believe it. Mama and Papa didn't know, although they knew something was wrong. There was no way in hell I was going to let the filth touch them and hurt them. Once started, I was afraid the slime and stench of Smithers and his rotten mind would never wash off. I found myself showering in scalding water after a session with him; I scrubbed my skin raw with hospital antiseptic and brushes from the operating theaters. Anyway, I told Mama and Papa I was just still trying to get over Barbara Nadine, and that work at the hospital was bad. This was certainly true; the war in Vietnam was going full swing, and casualties were flooding in. Coffins were stacked like cordwood, and body bags flowed into the staging area at Alameda faster than they could be processed. I had the stink of death with me, clinging to the inside of my nostrils, no matter what I did to try and get clean.

I still had my hills, though. I could still go up there and be wrapped in the cool, caressing fog, or warmed by the hot sun on my skin. I could still smell the pungent tarweed and ice plants, and crackle over the dried eucalyptus leaves. The old cemetery welcomed me back, and the only sounds were those of birds, and wind in the trees, and insects. Smithers couldn't find me there.

Then, one day it stopped.

Smithers disappeared as quickly as he'd come, and I let my breath out again. Lt. Monroe called me in.

"Tondelayo, I had lunch with Lt. Madden, over at COM12 the other day. We've been friends for years, you know."

"Oh, Barbara Nadine's WR?"

"Yes. It was a most interesting lunch. We had been talking about this witch — uh, NISO investigation, and discussing some odd things about it."

"Odd, Mam'n?"

"Yes. She's Barracks Officer, you know, as well as WR, and so she knows the entire extent of interviews and interrogations for all the girls living in the barracks, whatever their commands might be. It seems this particular investigation is oddly concentrated. Very little scope. Very few interrogatees."

"Oh?"

"Ummm hummm. We thought that was quite odd. Lt. Madden spoke to the Chief, to find out who authorized the investigation. The Admiral normally signs off on the requests for investigations, you know. It seems this is not only a very narrow investigation, centering primarily on you and a dead woman, but that somehow the paperwork slipped through the cracks. It seems it never got past the Executive Officer. Only his signature is on the request. The request also orders the investigation be confined to investigating unspecified allegations concerning you and Barbara Nadine, with others being added as necessary. This is most assuredly not standard procedure."

Strang. That bastard.

"Since things seemed so peculiar, Miss Madden spoke to Lieutenant Commander Jackson, the Assistant for Women. The investigation has been terminated, and all records, notes, and information ordered and pertaining to it must be turned in to the Admiral's office. Master Chief Manns is personally seeing to it.

"Thank you, Petty Officer Dubois. That will be all." Miss Monroe turned away, but not before I spotted the canary feathers on her lips. I wanted to hug her. I was free!

"Hi, Tondelayo. It's me, Napa Bob."

"Napa! It's cool to hear your voice again! How they hangin'?" I was surprised at the intensity of my joy in hearing his gravely voice again. I missed him. I missed the comfort of his strong, hard body to lean on as we rode his bike along back roads, smelling the dry hot smell of the hills with the sudden, sharp rivers of scrub oak scent cutting across the roads in low places. I missed the amused flicker behind his shades when I got smart and sassy. Most of all, I missed the familiar feeling that he was always there, somewhere, and would appear instantly before I knew I had needed him.

"Where you been, you shit? Haven't seen you since the funeral. I know we decided it was best not to hang together all the time, but, shit, Man, it's been months!" We had talked about my career in the Navy, and his in the Copperheads, and agreed that it was probably prudent if I were to lose my rep as a bad girl and a biker. No Chiefs I knew of rode with outlaw biker clubs. He had seen me and Barbara Nadine to women fully grown, like he'd promised my brother, and we both knew if we didn't quit, we'd give into what we both recognized as a hot, hot longing. He'd told me he was going to stay with the Club, and we both knew things were changing. The Hell's Angels were doing more and more business big time, and business was getting meaner. The Copperheads would have to follow suit or die. Napa had told me then that he was never going to be able to be OK, that what the Army had done to him had killed something inside and left a wild, ugly thing in its place. I knew it was true.

"I want to see you. Got a lot to tell you. But not at the Clubhouse. Don't come here no more. Meet me at China Camp; that's good. Or, no. That's no good. Too many bikers out there. Les' see. Oh, Lagunitas. Yeah. The dam at Lagunitas. Drive Yellow Bird, and wear civvies. I'll be there in a car, not my bike, and I won't be wearing colors." No colors? Shit! This had to be serious. He damn near slept in the damn things.

He sounded strange. Almost choked. "I'm in Novato. How soon can you get here? Or, no. I'll meet you there at 3:00, OK?"

"OK. Hey, is everything cool, Man? You..." He hung up, not hearing me. Shit. Something must really be wrong. We were both supposed to look like citizens? I couldn't believe he wasn't going to ride his bike. I didn't ride mine much anymore, what with my new image and all, but I thought Napa had grown on to the saddle of his.

Thinking hard, I gently placed the receiver on its hook, automatically felt for returned coins, of which there were none, as usual, and walked back to my room. Luckily, it was Stand Down for the pre-inspection Field Day, and I was free after I'd squared away my own section. I'd done that an hour ago, as I kept it ship shape at all times. As a Petty Officer, I no longer had to swab decks or run the buffer.

Standing in front of my locker, I surveyed my wardrobe. Well, he didn't mean a cocktail dress. Levi's and leathers were a no-go. Finally, I selected my dress slacks and a sweater set I'd gotten for Christmas. Conservative, tasteful, nicely fitted. Perfect. I could have passed for middle class. I looked so citizen-like it was scary. Tying the bows on my tennie runners, I began to feel positively buttoned down. If I weren't careful, I'd find myself out shopping for a camel hair coat. Sheeeeut!

Yellow Bird started with a purposeful roar, and settled into a steady purr as we hit the freeway. Lagunitas was way to hell and gone in the interior of Marin County, and the route to the dam was winding and complicated. Good thing it's a nice day. At least the drive will be pretty, and I put the top down. Shit. Why Lagunitas? It was almost as far as Sonoma County, and the roads were circuitous, even torturous. As I crossed the Oakland Bay Bridge, I noted just the slightest chop, barely white-capping the sparkling azure waters. Good. The breeze would keep the mosquitoes down in the heavily wooded Lagunitas Park.

As I rolled on down the road, singing lustily "Hit the road, Jack!" with the Raelettes, I noticed other motorists grinning at me. What the hell. I waved, and they waved back. "Yeah, Man! Tondelayo Dubois is a rockin' and a rollin'!"

After I left Drake Boulevard, there were no other cars. Accelerating around the numerous curves, I reveled in the road-hugging control of my baby Thunderbird, and relished the feeling in the pit of my stomach as I rollercoasted in and out of the dips. I was almost sorry when I drove through the gates of the park. But Napa Bob was waiting, and my defiant heart skipped a little when I saw him. But things did not bode well.

Cigarette butts littered the ground around him, and as my eyes traveled up from the shocking sight of a pair of thick-soled wingtips in place of his accustomed heavy black motorcycle boots with the chains over the insteps, I was relieved to see him still wearing Levi's. But they looked weird without the usual wide studded belt. Instead, a thin strip of brown (!) suede circled his lean hips, and a plaid, short-sleeved shirt, albeit with the sleeves rolled and the collar turned up covered his top half. A shirt buttoned all the way to the next-to-the-top button. Had the cat lost it? Most shocking of all, he was leaning against the door of a 1960 Chevy sedan, of an indeterminate buff color. I nearly vomited. Sober now, I parked Yellow Bird next to the Chevy with a silent apology, got out, and sped over to hug Napa. He hugged me back, hard, then, somehow, our lips were together, feeling very, very nice. But we wrenched apart. Enough of that, Man.

He turned and started up the path toward the dam, me panting after. There was one picnic table up there, set so it commanded a view all around us. No one could come upon us unawares.

"OK, c'mon, man. You got somethin' to tell me. What's happenin?" I braced myself. "No, wait. I have somethin' I wanna' do first. Whatever you say, it won't change this." With this, I dug into my pocket and took out the worn keychain and keys to my Hog. Jack's Hog.

"I want you to have Jack's Hog. She's still primo, and I don't do right by her no mo'. She don' like to jus' set, waiting for me to have time to ride. Jack woulda' liked you to have her, and I'm gonna' give her to you. She's waitin' for you over at Mama and Papa's." A pang struck my heart as I handed over the keys, but I knew I had to do it. I had to really commit to another life, a Navy life, and Navy women didn't go around riding Harleys; she couldn't be part of it. I knew Napa Bob would love her like Jack done.

Napa caressed the keys lightly, taking off his shades and looking into my eyes for a long time. Then he snapped them on his own chain. "Thank you, Tondelayo. I'll take good care of her." We sat there, silent, lost in our own thoughts and memories. Each grieving terrible losses.

Finally, he said, "Well, I got things to tell you. You know, I ax you who that blonde guy at the funeral was?"

"Strang? The XO?" My gut tightened.

"Yeah, Strang. I recognized him. From 'Nam." This shook me. Napa Bob never talked about the time he'd spent in Indochina with the Special Forces. Supposedly, the United States had not sent any troops to Indochina in the late 1950's and early 1960's, although Nixon was rattling sabers and making speeches about the Communist Threat poised throughout Asia, ready to strike against democracy and family values. We didn't have troops there! Well, maybe an "Advisor" or two, later on. But I knew better. I'd guessed from the broken bodies and shattered minds which started to wash through the hospital. John Q. Public may not know, but some of us had a pretty damn good idea that all was not copasetic. Unacknowledged, unheralded, trained to hair-trigger deadlines, the killing forces had been unleashed in Southeast Asia long ago. And Napa Bob had been one of them. The public didn't know. Didn't want to know. They preferred to think people like Napa Bob were products of some hidden, alien thing which had nothing to do with them. A result of Negro instability, perhaps. Or even poverty, if they were too lazy to go out and make something of themselves. But cannon fodder, per se, is only good when it's in use, and it's best to forget what happens to it afterwards. But, I was woolgathering. I think I was afraid to hear what came next.

"He's older now, of course, and all dressed up in dress uniform like that, I wasn't sure for awhile. But then, I knew it was him. He was there for a second or third time in 1960 when I got there. He kep' goin' back. I heard about him before I ever saw him. He was one bad stud, man. Had hisself a big bidness goin', runnin' shit down the Pipeline and on to the States. Once I figured out who he was, I been doin' a little investigatin'. One of the Angels did bidness with him, and it took me awhile to put it all together. I had to find a negotiator, make arrangements. But I got some info for you."

I waited, still.

"You forget all about Hell's Angels, hear? You don' know nothin' 'bout no bidness, hear? You don' wanna' fuck wi'dem Phantoms!" I had no intention whatsoever of worrying myself with whatever business the Hell's Angel might have been conducting in Vietnam. My silence was one of total and complete assent.

"It might have somethin' to do with Barbara Nadine's murder." I jumped.

"This Strang, he one bad dude, man. He was sellin' shit big time, runnin' it out through Laos and 'Nam, usin' body bags and casualties to move the stuff, but he had him a couple side bidnesses, too. He was gettin' kids out of shelled hooches and villages, kids that were still alive, even babies, and sellin' 'em to the pimps. There's a good market for them in Thailand, and some of the whorehouses in Saigon. Mostly little ones, couple years old, and little boys up to eight or so. He'd find 'em wandering around, and grab 'em. He done things to the babies, too, the ones he couldn't sell. He had him another bidness sellin' souvenirs. Pieces of the dead Slopes, women and men — Lissen, Tawny, I don' like tellin' you 'bout this shit, but I think you got to know." I tried to breath through my mouth, and gestured for him to go on. Having seen battlefield casualties before they were divested of their "souvenirs," I was aware of the thriving trade in severed ears, penises, vulvas, breasts, fingers, and other items many of the soldiers collected. John Wayne's movies were closer to Disney's than to the realities of war. I knew that. Still, I was shaken by the picture of Strang. The XO, working with Barbara Nadine; touching her — Jesus.

"There was this other guy, he lived in 'Nam, but he was a white man, French. A doctor. He worked for one of the big drug lords, takin' care of the whores in his houses, and so on. The drug lord was really rich; he got millions of dollars in arms and planes and stuff from the CIA. He was a big shot in the government. Anyway, he had his own planes, his own army. So Strang and this doctor had planes and helos they could use, movin' shit along the Pipeline. They got along real good. He taught Strang all about poisons and shit, and him an' Strang used to get off on tryin' stuff on some of the whores that acted up or somethin'. They'd off them with different shit, and they liked to watch how they died. Strang always had some snake ranch somewheres, and when he got tired of one'a his broads, he'd off her. He liked to watch." Napa Bob was silent a moment. Then he said, "You know, a lot of the guys liked killin'. Hell, I got to thinkin' it had its moments sometimes. The military taught us how to do it fast and quiet, and it was our job. But Strang——Strang was over the edge, man. Nobody ever wanted to work with him. He was a loner, except for this doctor. I mean, he did a lot'a bidness, but nobody ever hung wit' him, you know?"

There was a long silence. I almost didn't hear him at first, but then it sunk in. "Yeah. I usta' feel somethin' about killin' onct. At first, it bothered me, those little bitty people, nothing but grass huts and pajamas, the pretty little girls. They all look for all the world like little children, they're so small and delicate. Then, sometimes, I just hated them for all that mess, and for tryin' to kill me. But the worst is now. Now, I don' feel nothin'. I'm War Captain, and I take care of bidness when I'm told to, and I don't even remember it sometimes. You know, Tawny, you the only feelin' I got lef'." I turned to look at him, but it was dark. I hadn't noticed. Finally, I just took his hand and we started stumbling our way down the hill. On the way, I told him what I had learned, or guessed, about Strang, the rape, the murder, and Strang's attempt to get me through NISO. I told him I supposed Strang had found out I was trying to investigate, and sooner or later I would remember about the picnic.

Just then, a sudden glaring light hit us. Headlights. I saw a flash of green as the lights hit Napa's eyes, and with a feline snarl and sinuous move he got out of the light.

Leopard.

It was only a split second, then we were in the parking lot, and the Sheriff's cruiser was there. The cop turned a spotlight on our two cars, and waited until we got to him.

"Good evening, officer. Beautiful night, isn't it?"

The deputy was eyeing us closely as he got out of his squad car and strolled over, his hand resting lightly on the butt of his gun.

"Bit late for hiking, isn't it? The park closes at dusk."

"Yessir, it is. We got a little lost. It got dark sooner than we expected, and we had a hard time finding the path down. We were quite a ways up there, you know." Napa widened his shit-eating grin, and seemed to shuffle his feet, although he didn't actually move them. He must have just thought real hard about it.

"ID's, please." I pulled out my ID, and he looked at it and said, "Navy? You're in the Navy, young lady?" Then he shone the flashlight on the red sticker on Yellow Bird's bumper.

"Yes, Sir! I am Hospital Corpsman Second Class Tondelayo Dubois, Sir! Pleased to meet you!" I stuck out my hand from my stance of attention, and he slowly reached over and shook it.

"Girls in the Navy! Great! My mother was a nurse in World War II." He retrieved his hand, gave Napa Bob another look, and apparently decided he didn't feel like hassling. "You two get on out of here now. I'm going to lock the gate behind you. Not safe to be here at night, you know. Never know who might come on out here, looking for trouble." I smiled internally, knowing Napa Bob was probably one of the terrors mothers and cops warned people about. He got back into his cruiser, started to back around. Rolling down the window, he stuck his head out and said, "I'm going over and lock the other gate, then I'll come back through this one and lock it."

We grinned and waved good-bye as he continued backing around and drove away.

"Well, we must look like citizens, huh?" I laughed and un-locked Yellow Bird's door. Then, I walked over to Napa Bob and held him tight for a long, long moment. I felt tears start-ing, so I quickly let him go, and got in my car.

"See ya."

"Later, Gator."

Napa must have stood and watched my tail lights for a long time. I never saw the glow of lights behind me all the way back.

Chapter 16

DEEP SIX

There had to be an answer right in front of me. Had to be. I know that fucker killed her, and I know why, even sort of how. But I didn't really know how. Shit, he was nowhere near the day she died, the room was locked from the inside, and the last thing she woulda' done was willingly eat anything with peanuts. I couldn't for the life of me put the last piece in. To say nothing of the fact that I couldn't prove jack shit. Well, I was meeting Bill tonight to see what we'd both come up with. Maybe he had the missing piece. I sure as hell had a lot to tell him!

It had been hard, going back to work after what Napa Bob had told me, pretending I didn't know what was going on. Even though I'd known that everything the President was saying, and the news reports on the war were half bullshit, hearing the full story of just how rotten things could be shocked me. Did I want to be a part of it any more? How much more of what I'd always believed was lies, lies, lies?

Thank God I wasn't working the wards anymore. Now I was in Sick Bay, and the people I saw weren't battlefield casualties. Unless you count the bars and whorehouses, that is. And the just plain old malingerers. Once in awhile, somebody really sick showed up, but it was usually flu, or a broken bone, or something. Not that we didn't get cases that turned out to be cancer, or some other form of slow death; but at least it wasn't courtesy of our own government. I could deal with that.

Shit, my thoughts were morbid lately. Barbara Nadine, my best friend and sister, deep sixed like any ole' trash. Thrown overboard, wasted, jettisoned because she might have been inconvenient. The only comfort I had was that he didn't get to watch, I know that. I knew that when I finally had it all put together, nothing would happen, either. No proof.

"Hey, Bill."

"Hey, Tondelayo. I must say, you look down. Missing Barbara Nadine, aren't you? I do, too. She was some promise, that girl."

"Yeah. Well, I got some information, and I mixed in some guesswork, and I'm pretty sure I know who, why, and part of how. To make a long story short; it was the XO, Strang, who raped her and got her pregnant, although I'm sure he didn't know that she ended up pregnant, and some form of peanut substance that killed her most likely. She was allergic to peanuts, as we've already discussed, and had already had at least two exposures, the second one with a serious reaction. Commander Strang took her to Sick Bay that day, and there was no doctor, just a Corpsman. He gave her a powerful dose of antihistamine which pole-axed her, and that's how Strang raped her. He took her back to the barracks right to our room, and did it. There was even evidence on the bed, semen, which didn't sink in until I thought about it later." I then told him what I'd learned from Napa Bob. The Chief just listened attentively, not even responding when I told him about Strang's proclivities and nefarious "businesses" in Southeast Asia. This surprised me, but I finished my story. "Anyway, I think he introduced some form of peanuts into her system, and in such a way that he didn't have to be there. I'm sure I can figure it out if I just keep thinking about what I know. I think I know more than I realize."

When I finally finished, the Master Chief shifted in his chair. He ran his hand over his close-cropped hair, and sighed. That was his only sign of reaction. Then he turned his head slightly, and I saw the glimmer of unshed tears in his eyes. We sat in silence awhile, then he gathered himself together and spoke.

"Well, what I've got corroborates your information. I congratulate you, Tondelayo. You've managed to ferret out some things that few people could ever access. As for what I've got, it's pretty much the same thing, only official. There's a department in the Bureau of Naval Personnel, PERS F, that almost no one knows about. It's sort of the "Dirty Little Secrets File Drawer." They keep all kinds of nasty information there, gathered from all over, on people. Kind of J. Edgar Hoover in a Navy suit. None of the information is checked out, all sorts of wild claims can rest in files, waiting to explode in faces when least expected. Some is true, a lot isn't. Some of the true stuff sits there, waiting until enough is gathered up to do something, or to use when it's convenient. I expect the CIA has whole floors of files like it, but this is the Navy's very own. Most of the stars featured in its files have no idea this stuff has been collected, let alone what it says.

"Anyway, I checked on all the files I could on our esteemed Executive Officer. I have old shipmates scattered here and there. Yes, Strang did serve several tours in Southeast Asia, including some time before any American military forces were supposed to be there. A lot of this information is classified, you realize..."

"Yes. But we aren't interested in the political aspects, nor the classified things. Just Strang."

"Yes. Well, he is one of our boys in blue favored with a PERS F file. It seems that he was suspected of having something to do with the sad loss overboard of a Seaman Apprentice Martinez while at sea on board a destroyer. Martinez turned up missing under very peculiar circumstances. He was assigned to Mr. Strang's Deck Division, and he cast a pall over their otherwise sterling performance record. He was a general screwup, apparently, always on report, sloppy, and so on. The Deck Division was trying for the Navy E, and had a good chance for it, except for Martinez. Then, he somehow was lost overboard on a calm, balmy night. There was suspicion, of course, but nothing was ever proven."

"Was Commander Strang around that night?"

"No. He was playing poker with the Captain. Wonderful alibi. But of course, his men were loyal to their Division, if not to him, and it's easy enough to interpret an off-hand remark as a direct order if it suits everybody. This sort of thing is not unknown in the Navy. A lot of men lost at sea are lost under suspicious circumstances. The Navy, of course, prefers not to have that sort of thing publicized. One seldom hears of it outside the immediate crew. In fact, there are cases where people disappear without trace, even their records, as though they never existed. Just like the CIA. Even fewer people know about these cases."

"But how could they? Aren't there records in the Bureau? I mean, besides the one at the command ..."

"Oh, yes. Of course. To deep six someone that well requires either immense power, or an immensely intricate set of connections. The service, pay, dental, medical, and other records have to disappear, both from all departments in the Bureau and the local command. Adjustments have to be made to the pay system. Homes and belongings have to be accounted for. It's quite complicated. But nothing for you to concern yourself about, Tondelayo. I'm sure you will never have occasion to worry about it."

"No, no, of course not." I laughed, albeit rather falsely. "It all sounds like some kind of bad novel. Still, I'll bet the CIA has its own file on our Commander Strang."

The Chief spoke sharply then, startling me with his intensity. "Never mind about the CIA, or PERS F for that matter! These people don't play games. They're dangerous. Your experience with NISO was bad enough, and they're choir boys compared to what we've been talking about."

"Was that you? Whatever got NISO off my back?" I knew I shouldn't ask; it wasn't fair. All the records, logs, and so on that had been so helpful could have come from anywhere. For all I know, Chief Manns hadn't had anything to do with them. Quite a few people knew what I was doing, and they all wanted Barbara Nadine's killer caught. Nobody believed the bee sting story. To ask him a direct question about something as touchy as interfering with a NISO investigation was definitely above and beyond. "I'm sorry, Bill. I shouldn't ask. I had no right. I'm just glad, and however it happened, all I can say, is thank God."

"You're right. Don't ask a question where neither one of us wants the answer exposed. But, as it happens, I can't take any credit for that particular piece of work. The Admiral himself did it. Which reminds me, I haven't told you everything yet. Anyway, your WR, Lt. Monroe, and Barbara Nadine's, Lt. Madden, got together and discovered that something was rotten in Denmark about that investigation. Miss Madden talked to the Women's Advisor, and when she was finished, she asked for an appointment to see the Admiral. I won't say I didn't start typing up paperwork when she went in; I know he cared a lot for Barbara Nadine, and was devastated when she died. He runs a taut ship, and finding out a subordinate ordered a vicious NISO investigation without his knowledge; he would be furious."

"So, what were you typing up? Courts Martial papers?"

"No, my dear. I'm afraid Officers are seldom treated to such procedures. Anyway, a Courts Martial would have simply spread the muck around even worse, impacting the innocent still harder, as the false allegations were aired. People are always more fond of smut and lies; they titillate. The truth is a poor competitor. No. However, Commander Strang has decided to resign his commission, and retire. He will no longer be among us."

"Resign? Retire? You mean that sonnuva' bitch gets to ride off into the sunset, drawing retirement pay for the rest of his life? That's it?"

"Well, not the best end, I know. But at least he'll be gone. He will disappear from the Navy."

Right. He'll disappear from the Navy.

I still had that one piece of the puzzle. Something kept nagging at me, some small detail unaccounted for. What? It just would not come.

I went back to my room at the barracks and got out Barbara Nadine's ditty bag again. I'd had the stuff out so much I was beginning to get the clean clothes dirty. Dirty. Barbara Nadine never let anything dirty or messy go. She never left caps off toothpaste, or screwed bottle tops on crooked. She was, if anything, a fanatic for neatness. I guess because it made her feel more secure or something. Yet, her deodorant had leaked. It was still evident, its smell permeating the other contents of the bag.

Why had it leaked? Then I remembered. When I tried to tighten it after discovering the leakage, I found it tightly screwed on. It wasn't loose. So, how did it leak? Examining the bag more closely, I found that even more of the liquid had seeped out, and that the bottle itself was nearly empty. It had been nearly full when I first acquired it. I took the plastic bottle out, and looked; really looked, at it.

It was a popular brand, plastic container, roll-on, roll ball permanently installed. Antiperspirant, perfumed. And there it was. Almost invisible, in the last fold of the threading for the cap. A tiny hole, no bigger than a syringe. A syringe that was almost certainly used to inject something into the bottle, underneath the roller ball. What? What would somebody want to inject into Barbara Nadine's deodorant bottle badly enough to go to all that trouble? Peanut oil?

Strang could have guessed what caused Barbara Nadine's illness at the picnic; he knew a great deal about medicine from his fun and games with the doctor in 'Nam. In all likelihood, he had killed some of his other victims with various poisons and allergens. He may have been able to guess about peanuts being the culprit, as he would have realized how common an allergen they were. Certainly, he would realize that the exotic Filipino food would almost certainly be cooked in peanut oil, and that that was what made Barbara Nadine react so strongly. And even if peanut oil weren't the culprit, nothing would happen to give him away if he tried it, and he could think of another way to dispose of her, now that she was superfluous.

She posed a danger to him as long as she was alive, and might somehow remember something about her rape.

Commander Strang had duty as CDO the month before Barbara Nadine died. So did she. She would have put her bag in the room, ready for the night, as the watchstanders always did. All he had to do was go in the room during the day under some pretext, inject the oil into her deodorant, and leave it; a ticking time bomb. It didn't matter when she had watch next, eventually she would; eventually she would use the bottle of deodorant. And, if all went well, die.

All had gone well.

Now I knew it all. And I knew I couldn't prove any of it. Even the deodorant bottle was almost empty, and probably no longer had a trace of what had been injected into it. Even if it did, there was no way to prove who put it there, or how anyone could have known she was allergic to it. There was no way to prove he raped her; I'd unknowingly cleaned up the evidence she was even raped myself, if my eagerness to clean her up and make her comfortable. The whole thing was impossible.

I had to be content with Strang's removal from the Navy.

On 30 June, 1964, Commander Oscar Harry Strang retired from the United States Navy. As he had no friends, he opted not to have the traditional retirement party. He signed his paperwork, and drove out the gate with no fanfare. We never saw him on base again.

Chapter 17

SHE COYOTE

Warm, sweet, dry smell, now only sporadically green around the edges. Thin, golden grass stalks bending and swaying their full heads to the teasing breeze, wanton husks opening themselves to thrust seeds into passing fur. She lopes up the hill, plops herself into the shadow cast by the lichen-bedecked boulder, still baking in the late afternoon sun. A circular sweep of nose, ears, eyes. Tarweed, pungent, confuses smell, then mellows and fades into the obscurity of normalcy, noted, dismissed. Zzzzzzzznnng and minute whines of tiny insects foraging dust motes, flash of brilliant green of a fly testing lichen for luscious bits and specks of the lately dead.

She sleeps.

Drowse interrupted: a click of metal scraping ancient concrete. Ear twitches, swivels, listens, registers. Colors splinter, form shards, dissipate almost instantaneously. Head up, tongue alert under the sharply questing nose. The She Coyote is gone, blended imperceptibly into the golden hide — disappeared. She leaves only a few ambiguous broken stems to mark her having been there.

*Below, the rank, fetid odor swirls and eddies, sweetish and cop-
pery, sullying the peace, not quite covered in the cleansing medicinal
background of bay and eucalyptus.*

*Near now. Dangerously close, curiosity firing overdrive synapses.
She watches, fur become dappled shade, wet sniffing nose a beetle in
the dark beneath the thicket. She grins an anxious coyote grin at the
slick red smell, heavy and thick, seeping slowly from under the sharp,
plastic fumes from the tarp behind and to the side of the grunting
men.*

"Fuck, Man. This fuckin' see-ment! It din' look so fuckin' heavy."

"Jus' shut the fuck up, Man, and get that hole opened up. One'a
them nigger kids could come up here, and it's gonna be dark soon. I
wanna' get oudda' here. Les' get this fucker gone!"

*The two men bent their sweating backs again, pickax and shovel
clinking and banging as the old concrete pad was broken and thrown
aside. Once cleared, the sunken hole gaped hungrily open, deep with
leaf mold and twining, snaking rootlets. A few rotted pieces of wood
stuck here and there in the sloping, inwardly collapsing sides, but
nothing else remained to show what had once lain there. But some
lingering, old whisper of death made the She Coyote lower her ears
and start to wriggle backward, belly low, before the siren call of the
rich, coppery promise under the tarp called her back again. She
crouched again, and watched, heart pounding, pupils wide in the
gold.*

"Shit, Man. Almost dark. Hurry up!" *The bigger one leaned on
his shovel as the other went on heaving loose, damp matter out of the
deep trench. Then, finished at last, the sweating, reeking men wiped
off their faces with the filthy rags they wore around their heads, and
walked over toward the big, lumpy parcel from which the maddening
aroma emanated. She sat partially up, tongue dripping, alert in every
sense.*

"Fucker's heavy", *the smaller one grunted, half dragging the
bundle. The two thudded the burden down at the edge of the hole,
then tipped it in to fall leadenly to the bottom obscurity, shadows now
reaching up and out. No sounds but heavy breathings and scrape of
shovel hastily filling dirt in again. Even the birds were still, as the day*

birds made way for the night shift. Concrete pieces flung on top, branches and debris heaped over. The men grabbed their colors from the branches where they'd placed them when they began their work, and thrust their arms through the sleeve holes as they crashed their way out, heavy motorcycle boots tripping over the grabbing bay trunks and roots, stumbling across broken graves looming up suddenly in the murk. A last stab of daylight shafted across the grinning winged death's head with the writhing snake gliding through the eye socket on the colors worn by the now-running smaller man. The patch looked disembodied, floating in the gathering dark. She paid no attention, still riveted by the enticing smell she could discern even now. She waited, chin on paws. Slept.

It was fully night when she awakened, and thick fog muffled everything in gray wetness. Leaves dripped their gathered burden of water onto her fur, joining droplets already collected and coalescing. On her feet, stretch and yawn, then a hearty shake. Diamonds of water catapulted off her body, flying through the air all around her. Some reached the piled brush, where they joined with others until they ran down the branches and twigs, becoming nascent rivulets. Eventually, some reached the softened dirt underneath, running off the broken concrete and under it. Pocks developed into tiny craters. One day the rains would come, adding their strength, changing the soil as it had been changed since time began, forming, shifting, moving — always downward, down the slope of the hill. It had begun anew, the interruption meaningless to the general purposefulness.

She Coyote ambled over, scratched desultorily at the pile, squatted and urinated on it, then turned and melted into the bush. Dinner was out and about, scurrying around through the grasses, and she was hungry. Let time do its work.

Back in the Clubhouse in Oakland, the boys were shooting pool and drinking beer. Smoke hung leaden and thick, part of the familiar, homey miasma of grease, motorcycle exhaust, sweat and leather. When the roar of powerful engines became audible, one of the hard-ridden girls watching the men got up when a thumb peremptorily jerked toward the splotchy painted truck door. Belying its ramshackle appearance, the door moved quietly and with remarkable speed when she pressed the button. Open, it was obviously solid steel, running on well-oiled tracks. What appeared to be an old warehouse on the docks from the outside was surprisingly solid and strong when the door was open and the true thickness of the walls revealed. Concrete blocks behind the ordinary corrugated steel were mute evidence of a fortress. Surveillance slits were handily placed to permit an all-encompassing view of the doors and trash-strewn alley in front.

Larry and Mike drove in, Hogs throttled down, and wheeled over to the ranks of bikes parked in back, all facing front toward the door, lest a hasty departure be necessary. The door was wide enough for them to exit four abreast, which was the preferred road formation. It impressed any citizens who happened to be watching.

Momentarily, the dull *chink!* of balls ceased, and everyone looked up as though startled out of sleep. Almost instantly, activity resumed. Leroy said nothing, merely tensed his neck muscles as though about to look around at his men. Suddenly, they were all deeply occupied, not looking at Larry and Mike at all. Leroy's expressionless face registered the slightest upward slant of an eyebrow, and Larry grunted a reply.

"Everything's copasetic, Man." He swept two beers into his paw, then tossed one to Mike. "Fuckin' thick out there, Man. Din't see nobody for miles."

"Where's Frenchy at?" Leroy asked about the third man who had been with Larry and Mike, a young hopeful trying to earn his colors. He'd been along as the driver of the truck, then lookout, where he would have created a diversion and driven off at top speed, luring any cops or watchman away from the others, whose bikes were parked in the trees up the road toward Tennessee Beach. "He's comin'. I tol' him to go around through 'Frisco when we got to the bridge — tell Sonny we'll be at the meet."

"Uh huh. Alvin!" Leroy summoned the Road Captain, and they began to plan the run for the coming Saturday. The

Copperheads would be riding South to Lodi with the Hell's Angels and the MoFo's for the races, and the cavalcade of outlaw bikers would be impressively staged. Give the citizens a thrill, and draw every cop from miles around. The boys loved playing the role. At times like these, racial tensions were in abeyance, a formal truce scrupulously observed, and the various clubs formed a formidable alliance while they put on a show.

It was 1966, and KWBR had been KDIA for so long, hardly anyone remembered when KWBR had been the call sign denoting an oasis of cool sounds and sanity amongst the clamor of the white stations playing endless rip-off takes of rhythm and blues tunes stolen and mutated into sorry imitations of soul by stiffly yowling white boys. Pat Boone — sheeuht! No way could he hope to mimic Fats Domino. Him and all them shiny teeth 'a his. His Cherokee blood may have given him those slick good looks, but soul he didn't have. Not even. KDIA still wailed and rocked with the sounds of the real thing, as it always had. Real people still measured class by the success of the platters, tapes now, sold at Wolf Records and dutifully reported on KDIA. Tondelayo and Napa Bob were swaying, plastered together, in the smoke-filled, funky bar in the duskier environs of Oakland, barely moving their feet, with most of the action in the hips as they had always done to slow-dancin' music. "For your precious love ..." warbled Jerry Butler, reaching deep into interiors and wrenching out a longing, a need for love. It was almost possible for Tondelayo to believe she loved Napa, just for the duration of the song. Fortunately, Ray Charles and the Raelettes admonished Jack to hit the road with a beat that demanded separation and a marked increase in physical activity. Their bodies were unglued, and their feet moved. Cupid watched in frustration as the gyrations of the Dirty Bop replaced sentiment and propinquity.

Finally, sweat pouring down their backs, arms gleaming with a satin sheath of moisture, they sat down to address their drinks gratefully. Napa fished out the forlorn piece of ice rapidly assuming full liquidity in the bottom of his glass. He looked with futility for more, then signaled the harried waitress trying to move through the crowded little tables with full tray raised above the elbows and heads.

"Jack Daniels and Coke, white port and lemon juice." He looked at Tondelayo. "Girl, you drink that shit, you gonna' rot your stomach."

She laughed. "I don't usually. Not any more. Mostly, I drink scotch. But I don't think they have Cluny here. 'Sides, it's kinda' like ol' times. I learned how to drink on black label Daniel's and Coke. Remember?"

"Yeah. Sheee-it, I remember! Now it's scotch. It's those damn sailors. Buncha' dirty old men. Teachin' an innocent chile' like you to drink shit like that. Somethin' on their minds! Oooowee. Nasty!" His face split into a big grin.

"I remember one time, in the Chief's club; we was sayin' a fond farewell to this guy, he got killed in a car wreck. Anyway, everyone'd been to the cemetery for the burial, and we all went to the Chief's Club after to kind of debrief. I had thirteen Harvey Wallbangers, and was dancin' on the tables with this horny old Chief submariner. Sheee-it. He had gold hash marks all the way up his sleeve. We were all in dress whites, of course, for the funeral. All these other Chiefs were standin' aroun', panting. My Chief was a submariner, though, and nobody messes with them. Them others wan't about to move on me. Damn. Sometime, I wonder how I lived through my misspent youth."

"You dig this Navy thing, don't you? You really are gonna' be a damn lifer." A flash of something crossed his face, so fast Tondelayo almost missed it in the murky dark. But not quite. For just a split second, sadness had transformed Napa Bob's face. It was so fleeting, she wasn't sure she had seen it. Without answering, she grabbed his hand, and pulled him up.

"C'mon. I love this song." Bo Diddley's "Great Grandfather" was pounding its sensual beat through the thick air, the words incongruous for the heavy back beat that evoked runways and turgid, secretive longings in strip clubs back through the ages. As Bo Diddley gave way to Mickey and Sylvia, and the lines of the Stroll formed, Tondelayo mulled over what she would say in her mind. She had orders, but she hadn't told him yet. Orders for Japan, and the big hospital there, staggering under the overwhelming, never ending stream of casualties being med-evacced out of the increasingly bottomless pit of Vietnam. Casualties more mutilated, hideously wounded, closer to imminent death than in any war in history. The air-evacs and helicopters, aided by state-of-the-art battlefield corpsmen made it possible to almost instantaneously bring out the wounded grunts who would have died before they could reach hospitals in any previous war. Tondelayo had met some of the nurses and corpsmen rotating back to the states after serving their tours in MASH units, hospitals in Japan and the Philippines, and hospital ships and air-evac planes. Their eyes were glazed somehow, and their faces far, far older than their years. Tondelayo knew the war wasn't confined to in-country Dodge City. She knew what lay ahead would age and wound her, and she knew she'd wish fervently for the comforting bulk of Napa Bob, and familiar sanctuary of home, parents and old friends.

"You're leaven', aren't you? And you don' want to tell me. C'mon, Tawny. It ain't gonna' get no easier. I know you got somethin' on yo' mind." They were slow dancing again, plastered together, swaying to the music. Ivory Joe Hunter this time, with his longing, reaching voice wrapping them in nameless sorrow.

"Yes. Yes, I've got orders for Japan. I've got to leave next month. Oh, God, I'm gonna' miss you! I never thought it'd be so hard to leave here. I knew I would one day, of course, but they left me here so long, I guess I just sort of didn't think about it. And, of course, I always thought it'd be me and Barbara Nadine goin' off to sail the seven seas and see the world. Not jus' me." Tondelayo felt a lone tear slide down her nose and hang, poised, on the tip. She wiped her hand across her face, laughing shamefacedly. "I'm used to you, you fucker."

Napa Bob just held her closer, and said, "I figured it'd be somethin' like that. Well, at least it ain't across the Pond to

Dodge City. It ain't gonna' be no picnic as it is. They sent me to Japan outta' the 'Nam after I got hit. Ain't a pretty sight, Babe. Most them guys they lift out's fucked up bad, Man. Arms, legs, guts hangin' open, faces blowed away. And a lotta' them's doin' bad shit, man. Bad shit! All kinda' shit goin' down there — it's cheap and easy to get. Little Angel Dust, a little hard time in the field — shit, they come in with knives, heavy weapons. They go into the wards still carryin'. They don' take the time to clean 'em up first, or remove they weapons. You gonna' be doin' some hard, hard time, Tondelayo. I don' like that A-tall! But I know, Baby, I know. You gotta' go where they tell you. I know. Jus' watch yo' back, and al'us assume they carryin' and crazy. It's OK, Tawny. I be there, you need me. Jus' call my name. I be there." And Tondelayo knew, somehow, he would be. Napa Bob still had friends in odd places. She knew he would turn out to have a convenient friend wherever she found herself, or close by, in any case. It was extremely comforting to know that sometimes, although it made her feel like she was living in a fish bowl sometimes, too.

"Papa and Mama's gon' move back to Oklahoma, too. Mama's got allotment land on the rez, and family. Papa can't fine' no work here, and one a' Mama's cousin's got a shop he want Papa to run for him. He do a lotta' business, and he's gettin' on. So, they goin' go on East. Marin City's all different now, since they torn all the houses down, put up them high-rise apartments.

With Jack dead, and me goin' to Japan, they said they ought to be gettin' on back home. Seems funny; Oklahoma don' seem like home to me. Marin City does. I know I'll be comin' back some day, and it'll be weird with Mama and Papa gone."

"Well, shit. Ain't even gone' be the same!" Napa Bob looked sad again, and Tondelayo felt like crying. Feeling much the same emotion, Napa pulled her even closer, and nuzzled his lips against her neck. Tondelayo lifted her chin, and leaned her forehead in the hollow between his shoulder and his neck. She felt a small lump, cold and smooth, and leaned back to look.

At first, it was impossible to recognize what he wore on the heavy gold chain around his neck. Some sort of white and gold things, tastefully spaced around the span of the chain, heavily gleaming through the murk of the atmosphere. Then, she saw them. Teeth. Teeth with gold inlay and crowns still intact. Two pointed teeth with dragons intricately worked in gold on the front surface. Yeah. Trophy teeth. Napa Bob said nothing, just held his arms slightly looser so she could see. Tondelayo smiled at him, eyes gleaming up with a gold-green flare as someone lit another cigarette behind Jack's shoulder. He smiled back, his black eyes fathomless, and held her close again. She sank back against him, boneless, moving her body with his as though they were one. As the jukebox began the pounding open strains of a John Lee Hooker oldie, they moved apart and began the age-old dance of sexual enticement and rhythmic teasing the guitar evoked. "Boom boom, boom boom, gonna' shoot you right down," Tondelayo sang, slanting her eyes provocatively at Napa Bob. "Boom boom, boom boom," he replied, jerking his hips forward in an unmistakable challenge, dancing with serious purpose now. They both quirked the corners of their mouths, eyes wild and excited as the music pounded. No one else existed for them right now, just them and John Lee Hooker, and the moment, filled with a wild, exultant power older than time.

After awhile they left for Napa Bob's houseboat.

In the dark hours before dawn, Marin City slept quietly in its respective beds. From the hidden valleys and hills behind them came a triumphant, inexpressibly wild howling that caused many a sleeping form to shift uneasily. She Coyote was hunting, her young cub beside her. The first rays of sun struck blood and copper highlights of the cub's coat, making it gleam like white red gold.

About the Author

Donna Dean is one of those rare people with both an irrepressible wit and sense of creativity. When we asked her for her biography, she sent that which follows. Rather than keep it an in-house secret we wanted to share it with you. Her "real" biography follows. Ed.

Donna Dean

Winter gripped the land in brutal cold, and wind howled mournfully through the skeletal trees, cracking the protective ice sheathing the bare branches. Deep in the mountains, the wolves roamed restlessly, waiting. In Ireland, long dead Druid kings groaned and turned over, and in Tahlequah an old Cherokee medicine woman smiled as she lay dying. The world waited, breath caught, eyes alert. The time was near.

None of this had anything to do with me, of course, as my sister and I were hauled unceremoniously from our mother's womb and slapped into incubators. No, as was to be our fate, neither one of us was destined to greatness, nor would portents attend our birth. I never did find out what all the omens portended.

Time passed, and I grew into a lithe and lovely sex symbol, making strong men fall down on the ground and bite sticks. This led, inevitably, to trouble, and early in my youth I found myself kidnapped by an evil slave trader, who sold me to an overly ambitious Bedouin sheik whose one tiny oil well had given him delusions of undeserved grandeur. I did, however, fetch a rather awe-inspiring price, which has remained a source of comfort to me in my declining years.

At any rate, I was shipped to the dark continent with little consideration for my plans to attend the prom, and slung rudely over the back of a camel with a pronounced case of attitude. This did not bode well, and when I was fitted for a belly button jewel, I decided that this simply would NOT do. We rode through sweltering heat, flies droning meaningfully after us. Watching, waiting for the exact escape route to offer itself, I carefully observed my captors' habits. I soon realized they stopped twice a day, without fail, dismounted their camels, knelt on little rugs such as once sold by Daddy Isaac for a mere $10.00 donation, and faced East, toward Mecca. They were good for at least 15 minutes, I realized, as they performed their devotions to their demanding gods. Too simple, really. I just belted my camel hard with my ankle bracelets and galloped madly West.

Seasick and dusty, I finally crept into a grungy little seaside port, into a babble of harsh tongues and clashing donkey carts, and no one of the teeming hordes paid attention to one more tattered beggar assiduously collecting Coke bottles to redeem for passage home. Except …

Who was to know that the world was enveloped in war? Japan's bid to rule the world wasn't something I could have anticipated, and the submarine moored so propitiously amongst the small native craft seemed like a haven to me. Being naturally silent, no one noticed when I reported aboard like all the other sailors coming back from liberty. I knew not one word of Japanese, but bowing was something I'd learned well on my way to my erstwhile harem. Certainly, the diet left something to be desired, but rice was better than an interminable array of curries to which I had reluctantly become accustomed. As I could understand not a word of my shipmates' conversations, I remained in innocent ignorance of our purpose. All I knew was I recognized the map of Hawaii, and Pearl Harbor seemed as good a destination as any. I was a bit nonplussed when the Commander crossed out that little portion of the map with a triumphant grin, but having no context within which to place the action, merely went on bowing and scrubbing the decks.

You can imagine my surprise when one night I was catapulted out of my bunk by frantic scurryings to and fro, and the most unseemly yelling! Suddenly, the world ended with a monstrous clang, and water poured into the breach in the hull which hadn't been there seconds ago. Torpedoed! Sinking! The screams of the dying shattered my nerves. Without thinking, I dove through the next open torpedo bay I came to, hoping I could hold my breath long enough to make the surface! Fortunately, years of training for grand opera had prepared me for this moment, and I burst through the water into the blessed air just as my tortured lungs could stand no more! I was safe! Of course, the circling sharks were a bit of a bother, but I had my diamond dust nail file upon my person, and was able to not only stave them off, but inflict no end of damage while I was about it.

In due time, I was picked up by the stalwart men of the American Navy, and my journey home was without further ado, as the American Navy man has the strength of ten as his heart is pure.

Which all goes to show, sailors and Indians have a lot in common.

The "Real" Donna Dean

Donna Dean has had a variety of careers throughout her life, and lived in a variety of places, including Marin City for most of her childhood. Wherever she lived, she reveled in the open spaces, forests and woods, feeling a deep connection to them. Her Cherokee ancestry as well as that from her Irish father has given her strong affinity for Mother Earth and all the creatures that share it, and this inevitably becomes evident in her work.

Her education has spanned many years; in the last two years of her eighteen years of Navy service she earned a master's degree at the age of forty-one, and a doctorate at fifty-four. She believes education should serve as far more than mere acquisition of learning targeted to some profession: rather, she views education, formal and informal, as an on-going exploration of the greater world. She began writing professionally in 1996, and this is her first novel. She is also the author of "Warriors Without Weapons: the Victimization of Military Women," a searing expose of the treatment of some women in the military and the subsequent neglect and disregard demonstrated by an uncaring Veteran's Administration until very recently. In addition, Dean has had many short stories, poems, essays and non-fiction pieces published.

Dean lives with her husband, Marvin, cat, The Princess Moonbeam, and Doberman Pinscher, Tesoro del Corazon (Tessie to her friends) on the coast of Northwest Washington, where she enjoys the forests and beaches through the rain.